Louisiana
BLACK

Also by Samuel Charters

Poetry
The Children
The Landscape at Bolinas
Heroes of the Prize Ring
Days
To This Place
From a London Notebook
From a Swedish Notebook
In Lagos
Of Those Who Died

Fiction
Mr Jabi and Mr Smythe
Jelly Roll Morton's Last Night at the Jungle Inn

Criticism
Some Poems/Poets

Biography, with Ann Charters
I Love (The Story of Vladimir Mayakovsky and Lili Brik)

Translations
Baltics (from the Swedish of Tomas Tranströmer)
We Women (from the Swedish of Edith Södergran)
The Courtyard (from the Swedish of Bo Carpelan)

Music
Jazz: New Orleans
The Country Blues
Jazz: The New York Scene
The Poetry of the Blues
The Bluesmen
Robert Johnson
The Legacy of the Blues
Sweet as the Showers of Rain
The Swedish Fiddlers
The Roots of the Blues: An African Search

Louisiana
BLACK

a novel by
Samuel
Charters

Marion Boyars New York · London

Published in the United States and Great Britain
in 1986 by Marion Boyars Publishers
262 West 22nd Street, New York, NY 10011
24 Lacy Road, London SW15 1NL

Distributed in the United States and Canada by
Kampmann & Co, Inc., New York, N. Y.

Distributed in Australia by
Wild and Woolley

Library of Congress Cataloging in Publication Data

Charters, Samuel Barclay.
    Louisiana Black.
    I. Title.
PS3553.H327L6   1986   813'.54   85-31399

ISBN 0-7145-2855-2 Cloth

British Library Cataloguing in Publication Data

Charters, Samuel
    Louisiana black: a novel.
    I. Title
813'.54[F]   PS3553.H/

Printed and bound in Great Britain by
Biddles Ltd, Guildford and King's Lynn

For Sam V

I

1

There was nothing out of the way about the package. There was nothing unusual about it, nothing different. It was only a cardboard box, oblong, about two inches thick, sealed with tape. It was an ordinary cardboard box color, and it had been sent with the usual stamps and battered in an ordinary way by the Post Office. He held it up to read the name on the label. The lobby of the apartment house where he lived was elegantly spare and modern, but it was also dimly lit, and he always had trouble reading the addresses on the mail. Frank Lewis. It was addressed to him. Without thinking anything about it he put it under his arm, still holding on to his briefcase, and with his free hand he looked through the rest of the mail to see if there was anything else for him. The usual bills and circulars. He thought as little about them as he did about the box. He took everything along to sort through when he got upstairs.

Even though the building had elevators he always walked upstairs. It was three flights up to his apartment, and he told himself that walking up the stairs would help keep him in shape. He usually tried not to glance at the mirror on the first landing so he wouldn't notice that he was getting soft, but there was more of a stomach than he ever thought he would have when he was young. Now that he was older it was something that annoyed him, and he was uneasily conscious that he'd have to do more about it than walk up and down the stairs to his apartment. He didn't live far from downtown Bridgeport where he worked, and sometimes he thought of walking home from his office, but every time he started off he found that it was later than he thought and the blocks were longer than he remembered, and he wound up taking the bus. With his letters in his hand and the package under his arm, he started up the stairs, humming to himself so he wouldn't notice when he started to get out of breath.

Inside his living room he dropped the letters on the pile that had accumulated on the coffee table. Still breathing strenuously, but pleased with himself for walking up the three flights of stairs, he made a place for the package in the clutter on the dinner table, hung his coat up on one of the already crowded hooks in the closet, and went out to the kitchen to make himself a drink. He'd lived in the apartment almost two years, but he still didn't feel at ease in it. Somehow it hadn't become his. He'd moved into it right after his wife had divorced him. He was sure that he wasn't irresponsible or thoughtless or cruel, or any of the other things she had said about him before she'd taken their son and moved to Philadelphia, but he had to admit she'd been right when she said that he was messy. He told himself every day that he would have to do something about the apartment, but after a troubled glance around at the piles of newspapers on the couch, at the dirty glasses and cups on the table, the soiled shirts hanging from the door handles, he usually decided to make himself a drink and look for something on television.

With his tie loosened he sat down on the couch and desultorily glanced through the assortment of advertising circulars and form letters that had accumulated. Most of the time he let them pile up until the mess was too much even for him, and then he threw them out. They were advertisements for rugs and carpets he would never buy, for household gadgets he would never think of using, for insect repellants that would kill insects he was certain he'd never seen, for house repairs he didn't need, or for trips he would never take.

When he did open a few of them he was always surprised again at how little they had to do with him. For the first few months after he had moved in, the faces smiling at him out of their slick displays were all white and he wondered why no one had told the people sending everything to him that he wasn't white — that the person named Frank Lewis on their mailing list was black. Or did they even care? He wondered if it made any more difference to him than it did to them. Sometimes, when he received junk mail intended for black men like him who might buy something, he noticed that the men in the advertisements were twenty years younger than he was, considerably thinner, and most of them had extravagant mustaches. He never had bought anything the letters were advertising, but he tried growing a mustache. When he looked at himself in the mirror he looked as ordinary and as self-conscious as ever, but he still had his mustache, for whatever effect it might have. He decided finally that all the mail must have come with the lease to the apartment, and the name simply had been changed on the address when he moved in — and none of it mattered.

He tried watching television, but he was going out in a half hour, and he couldn't get interested in anything on any of the channels. He watched a news program long enough to see Jesse Jackson make a new effort to explain what the other men running for the presidential nomination were saying, but he didn't have any conviction that the country was any more ready for a black president now than it had been when he was still in school. When Jackson finished talking he turned off the set, stood up, stretched, and began working his way around the room, his drink in one hand, trying to make some inroads into the mess. He started with the table, since it wasn't as bad as the rest of the room. He didn't use the table often, since he ate breakfast in the kitchen, and he usually had dinner somewhere close to his office, but the table had gotten so

11

cluttered it made him uncomfortable every time he looked at it. Set out on top of the newspapers and the laundry wrappings from his shirts were dirty coffee cups that gave the table the look of something left over after a party, but there hadn't been any party. Usually when he was on his way out of the apartment in the morning he found he still had a cup of coffee in his hand, and he put it down wherever he could find room. He began stacking them up, to take them out to the kitchen, then noticed the package and remembered that he hadn't opened it. He put the cups under water in the sink and came back with his drink to see what was inside.

When he sat down on the couch and tore the tape off the box he recognized the name of the company that had sent it. It was a publishing company in Cleveland. A friend of his — the man he was going to meet in half an hour — had persuaded him to send away for it.

"Now I know you don't want me to get serious about these things, but a book like that has everything you need to know about what has happened to us in America."

Whenever Jimmy said something like that to him he always thought of an exchange from a play he'd seen years before, when black drama first managed to reach Broadway. One of the characters had shouted, in exasperation, that the woman he was arguing with didn't have race pride. The woman — who made a living washing dishes — protested that she did have race pride, but she didn't need it much on a job like hers. Frank Lewis was a bookkeeper at a small company in Bridgeport where all the other office workers were white, and he had some of the same feelings as the woman in the play.

"I can learn from that, since I don't know what's been happening to you and me?" He tried not to sound ironic, but he and Jimmy had known each other since school, and they had been arguing over the same things for so many years that it was hard for him to take it seriously. But this time they were discussing a present he was going to give to the son who had gone to live with his ex-wife after the divorce, and Jimmy wouldn't let go of the question.

"You got to be serious about this one time in your life. If it was just you we're talking about I wouldn't bother myself —

but this is for somebody young who needs to know. This is one time you got to be serious about what I'm telling you." Jimmy's tone was decided, and he was nodding his head as he spoke.

They were sitting in a little bar not far from his apartment. Perhaps because he burned off so much energy with his intense manner Jimmy seemed smaller than he was, a slight, edgy man with sudden movements. Frank always felt slow and clumsy beside him, and to emphasize the differences between them he usually kept on one of his office suits when he went out, while Jimmy always wore whatever the latest style was for single men who were trying to be in touch with what was going on. He had made the mistake of asking Jimmy what he should get for his son Lester, who was in his first year of college and was about to have a birthday. Jimmy had immediately decided for him.

"Lester must have something that will tell him what he needs to know about who he is while he still is young — while it still will get through to him. Without you there to tell him these things he won't ever know about them. That's what you have to do when you're a black man and you have a son."

"You don't have a son," Frank said mildly.

Jimmy waved the objection aside. "That doesn't mean I don't know what I'm saying. That doesn't mean it at all. What I'm talking about is race and what I'm talking about is history, and that's serious. I mean that now. That's serious." Jimmy was leaning across the table, tapping on an ashtray to emphasize what he was saying. "I got this book myself and it told me things I didn't know. It told me things I didn't even want to know," he continued defensively, "and Lester's got to know these things. Even if you don't tell him, you hear?"

Frank had sent a check off for the book a week later. He had looked vaguely for something else to send his son, but he already felt so confused by their new relationship that he decided Jimmy's idea was as good as anything else. As he mailed the check the thought struck him that this must be how people feel when they send messages off into space — messages that probably will never reach anyone, and if they do no one will understand what they mean.

13

He tore the carton open and dropped it on the carpet. He glanced at his watch. If he spent a minute with the book now he could tell Jimmy what he thought about it, and then he could mail it off to Lester. It had not occurred to him that there was anything in its pages that could affect his life, any more than the person starting off in a car has any idea that this is the day the car doesn't finish its trip to the office. It was a big book, solidly bound, smelling of ink and glue. He put it down on the coffee table in front of him and slowly leafed through the pages. He'd seen histories of black life in America before. He could remember using them to write term papers when he was in college, though they hadn't been as big or as expensively illustrated. This one seemed to be using the same material he remembered from before — the same engravings of slave markets and newspaper headlines — the same nineteenth century photographs of dark men in even darker suits. Women, in dresses as shapeless as the plants they were tending, bent over unending cotton rows, dragging behind them sacks that clung like swollen cocoons. Every few pages there were the usual glimpses of children in ragged clothes standing beside weathered country shacks. They were usually smiling, and he always had wondered what they found to smile about.

It was a photograph that was waiting for him in the book's last pages. He noticed it just as he was about to close the book and push it back on the coffee table. He shifted a little on the couch to hold the page up closer to the light beside him. It was a photograph of a lynching. The caption said it was from Louisiana. It had been taken at night, but the photographer had used a strong flash attachment, and there were torches and lanterns held up against the darkness. He could see the shining perspiration and excitement on the white faces in the mob. They had let the photographer come close enough so that he could read the nervous pleasure in their eyes. The details were so clear he could almost smell the perspiration and the blood. The man they had lynched hung from a tree over their heads, his face contorted in a grotesque mask. In their anger the mob had slashed his throat after they hung him, and rivulets of blood had spilled down his chest, splotching his worn overalls

14

with dark, spreading stains. The stream down his body glistened in the light from the torches. A few feet from the body a grinning, thin boy in overalls who looked about fifteen years old was kneeling on the ground with a baseball bat in his hands.

Frank closed the book and pushed it away. God knows he had seen pictures like it before, and he'd read enough descriptions of lynchings in the books he'd used in school, but there was something else in the picture — what was it? He slumped back against the couch, holding his drink, trying to lose his thoughts in the pattern of shadows on the wall across the room from him.

Sounds from the street finally broke into his thoughts. The distant shush of automobiles, an insistent clacking of high heels coming up the concrete walk to the apartment. He looked at his watch. He was already late, but Jimmy was used to it. Without glancing at the book again he stood up and stretched. He fumbled in the closet for his jacket and went out into the silence of the hallway

2

He was meeting Jimmy in a neighborhood bar at the bottom of the long slope that took Main Street up from Bridgeport's low-lying business section to the ridge of houses and small apartment buildings where he lived. The bar was in a squat, one-storey brick building with a cramped door that looked like it had been jimmied into the middle of its facade as an afterthought. Inside, the space had been roughly divided into two rooms. One was filled with imitation antique maple tables and chairs, even in the dimness obviously a little scuffed, and against the wall was a raised platform for a band to stand on — empty of everything except an abandoned bass drum. The other room had pool tables at either end, and the rest of it was filled with the long u-shaped bar that kept the two rooms separate. The television set was on a shelf close to the ceiling at the back end of the bar.

He stood inside the door, waiting for his eyes to get used to the gloom so he could see where Jimmy was sitting. Usually Jimmy got there first. He noticed the girl at the table before he saw Jimmy, conscious, as he went toward them, that it was because she was white. Jimmy's skin, like his, blended with the shadows. He bent down and kissed her cheek. He had forgotten that she might come.

"I didn't think you were going to pick up Inez," he said to Jimmy as he pulled up a chair beside her.

"Don't you two keep track of each other's comings and goings?" Jimmy was surprised.

Inez laughed. "He doesn't tell me anything. Does he tell you anything?"

"No." Jimmy pushed his chair back, waited for them to decide what they wanted to drink, and then went off to the bar. There was a waitress somewhere, but he was never willing to wait for her. "You never know if she's going to look over our way or not," he had explained once, and it didn't matter to him that she usually was there to bring whatever they wanted for the rest of the evening. Frank was sure that Jimmy didn't expect her to wait on them because they were black, but he and Jimmy had argued over all these things so often that he didn't bother to mention them any more.

Inez took his hand. "Didn't you remember I said I was going to try to get away tonight?"

"I didn't think of it. You left before I did." They worked together in his office, and they usually managed to make some sort of plans for the weekend, but she — like Frank — was also divorced, and there were complicated arrangements for her two children. If their father wasn't coming for them then she had to leave them with her mother, and neither her former husband or her mother wanted to be reminded she was involved with another man.

"You haven't called for almost a month. I asked Jimmy to pick me up so I'd have a chance to see you."

"I didn't know it had been that long," he answered, as Jimmy came back to the table. "I don't know what's been happening," he continued lamely.

"That's right," Jimmy finished. "He doesn't tell me what he's going to be doing because he doesn't know himself."

The bar was half filled. There was a scattering of couples at a few of the tables around them, but most of the people were sitting at the bar so they could watch the television set. Frank had forgotten there was going to be a basketball play-off game, and what he could hear of the talk was about the two teams, Boston and Los Angeles. Since he'd grown up in Harlem he didn't think of Boston as his team, but the Bridgeport crowd had decided that Boston was close enough to give them a proprietary interest. The bar was shabby and rundown, but it reflected the changing status of the neighborhood. Most of the customers were young professionals, in jeans and jogging shoes, with a few working class people left from the place's more earthy days still hanging on.

"Whatever you want to say about him," Jimmy leaned closer to Inez, "he must stay in this place because he's got you on his mind. No other reason for him to stay around."

"You mean Frank? In this bar?" Inez was surprised.

"Bridgeport. That's what I'm talking about."

Frank slid lower in his chair. Jimmy had also grown up in Harlem, and even though they'd lived in Bridgeport for nearly ten years — Frank had moved during his marriage and Jimmy had followed a year later — Jimmy still complained about living in a small town. He never could believe that Frank didn't care. That Frank couldn't see how his life would be changed if he moved somewhere else. Jimmy had a job selling cars, and he was convinced that if he could get to a bigger city he would make a lot more money and he'd get a chance to sell a much better class of car.

"You know he could get out of here tomorrow if he wanted. You got to be the only thing that's holding him. I could go too. But I keep waiting for Frank here to make a move."

Frank was half listening, letting Jimmy entertain her. The other man was already telling her about something that had happened at the sales agency this week and she began laughing. Frank had listened to them laugh together often before. Usually he was quiet because he didn't want to get in the way of Jimmy's stories, but tonight something else had upset him. He tried to think of what it could be. He repeated

18

all the clichés about dark clouds and shadows over the sun to himself, but still couldn't shake his mood.

Sometimes, when he listened to them laughing together, he thought that Inez should have been black herself, instead of a pale, thin, dark-haired woman with an anxious expression. She was in her thirties, at least ten years younger than Frank, and they had worked together in the office for three or four years before he'd noticed her. Then, in the usual way, they had worked late on something that had to be finished, gone out for a drink afterwards, and found out that each of them was as lonely as the other. Maybe he thought she should be black because of her name. The only women he'd ever heard of who were named Inez were black. There had been several Inezes in the stories his mother had told him when they sat out on the stoops in Harlem. An aunt had been named Inez, there was a cousin Inez, two girls his mother had gone to school with were Inez — but all of them had been black. He was certain he didn't want her to be black. He had wanted only a half-relationship, an involvement that would still leave him a little distance. Someone like Inez, because she was white, would never understand him well enough to interfere with his solitary life.

"Now I know you don't like me to say these kinds of things," Jimmy had leaned toward him and peremptorily taken his arm, "but there's a dude at the bar staring over at us, and I know he doesn't like what he sees. Something's offending him, brother, and it's you and it's me."

Without thinking Frank turned around, despite Jimmy's hold on his arm. "Which one?" Maybe somebody had come in that he hadn't noticed. "Which one you talking about?"

Jimmy pulled him back around. "You want him coming over here? It's that big dude along the bar. Back under the television set. He's all by himself, and he's not even trying to watch the game. He's looking over at us every time he thinks we're not noticing. And you know what's offending him. You not going to sit there and tell me you don't know what it is. It's Inez that's offending him."

Frank was unconvinced. "You mean because she's white? You think he's worried about that?"

Jimmy brushed aside his questions. "You all the time telling me these things are not serious, but this is the most serious thing he knows. We have broken that man's rules. We have challenged everything he knows about the world and the way we supposed to behave in it. He sees a white woman sitting with two black men and something in him begins to work, like there's something in his drink that's making him sick."

Occasionally Jimmy decided that someone was watching them because they were trying a different bar, or they shouldn't have been where they were, or they were talking with the wrong tone in their voices — but Frank never noticed. Sometimes he told himself that Jimmy could be right, but since he hadn't seen what Jimmy was talking about he couldn't tell, and it didn't seem important enough for him to get upset. Other times it was another one of the things they argued about.

"Jimmy." Now Frank found he was annoyed. "Inez and I used to come in here three or four times a week, and nobody said anything at all."

"Look at you," Jimmy countered. "Look at you in a suit and tie and everything just like you some white man with a job like a stockbroker or lawyer. With me, it's different. I wear my race with my clothes."

Frank wasn't sure that Jimmy was entirely serious. This was another argument they had every week. "This is what a bookkeeper wears regardless of race, creed, or sexual preference," he answered. It was a tired joke he hoped would divert Jimmy's attention. He touched Inez's arm. "Do his clothes look black to you?"

Jimmy was wearing a leather vest over a turtle neck sweater and a tight fitting black leather cap pushed back on his head.

"Definitely," Inez said, falling in with their banter. "If I saw those clothes laying over a chair I'd say to myself, 'Black man.' "

"Then you tell him to stop worrying about that fellow at the bar there he says is looking at us."

Inez turned around. "Which one?"

Jimmy bent his head. "The one back under the TV. The big one there."

Inez studied the man's face and then held up her glass. The man smiled and returned the gesture.

Inez turned back to the table. "You always forget I come from here. I'd be disappointed if he wasn't looking over this way. I don't know what he's thinking, but I know he remembers who I am. He took me to the Senior Prom."

This time it was the waitress who brought the drinks. Frank swallowed half of his quickly, hoping for some kind of lift that would bring him back into their conversation. Occasionally he answered a question, but his thoughts were too scattered. He idly looked around at the others in the bar. He sometimes wondered if Jimmy created his consciousness of racial tension to give a little excitement to their evenings. He couldn't see anything happening. It was an ordinary Friday night crowd, a little noisier than usual because of the basketball game, but otherwise the same kind of people he was used to seeing every time he came in. Jimmy leaned over to him again.

"I feel something building up in here. Don't tell me you can't feel it. Emanations. If my own Jimmy, Jimmy Baldwin, was describing the feeling here he'd say 'emanations.' "

"Then why don't we leave?" Frank responded mildly.

"No, no. It isn't we who have to leave. We have to stay."

"You get into this almost every time we come here."

"That's because you don't feel things. You don't think what I'm telling you is real."

"Then let's go," Frank repeated.

"No." Jimmy wasn't interested in leaving. Frank knew he wanted to sit and finish his drink, but he was finding things a little dull.

Jimmy abruptly stood up. "I'm going to the bathroom," and he went toward the back of the room to the men's toilet.

Inez took Frank's hand again. "Where are you? I'm sitting here beside you, but I don't know where you are."

"Hanging on the end of the moon," he answered lightly. He could remember odd lines from some old songs and they had become his source for inconsequential quotations.

She ignored the line. "You didn't want Jimmy to bring me," she said after a silence.

21

"I didn't think anything about it, one way or another," he answered without considering what it would sound like.

"That's even worse."

He couldn't think of anything to say, and they sat silently until Jimmy came back. She let go of his hand and fumbled with her cigarets. "I know how these moods can be," she murmured, trying to cover her own obvious distress.

Jimmy sat back in his chair and began describing the vending machines on the wall of the men's toilet. Usually there was the same row of them week after week, but sometimes a new one was delivered. One machine sold a cream to delay orgasm so the couple involved would have "genuine pleasure." Next to it was one selling spectacularly thin condoms to give "you" more pleasure, and the next machine was offering bizarre looking rubber attachments that went with the condoms that were supposed to give "her" more pleasure. The machines were so grimy that Frank couldn't imagine anyone had ever bought anything from them. Jimmy was telling them about a new rainbow pack of condoms, in different colors to make it all more party-like. "Who's going to look?" Jimmy finished, laughing so loudly he had to shout to be heard over his own voice. There was a protest from the bar.

"Can you keep it down a little?"

Jimmy bristled, his shoulders rising like the bowed back of an angry cat. "You see," he hissed to Frank and Inez, "you see! That's what I was telling you. If the two of us sit here with Inez somebody's going to speak up. Just like I said."

Frank bent his head and moved his glass on the table top. He never could handle Jimmy when they got into a situation like this.

"No, Jimmy, I don't see," he insisted, trying to keep his voice low. The man who had called out from the bar, a worn-faced, middle-aged man in a work shirt and a faded windbreaker, put his fingers to his lips and pointed to the television set, which was making a mumbling effort to break through the thicket of noise that ringed it in. Jimmy squinted toward it, trying to make out the figures on the screen without putting on his glasses.

22

"That the basketball game?" he called out after a moment. The man nodded. "The Celtics ahead, right?"

"Two points."

"Way to go." Jimmy waved a clenched fist and in a moment was reciting some new verses from the men's room wall for them, his outburst forgotten.

The air was muffled and heavy when they left the bar an hour later. It had rained, and there was a stream of water dragging bits of debris with it as it clogged the gutter at the edge of the sidewalk. The sky was a lowering mass of cloud that reflected back the city's night illumination in shifting patterns of reddish-orange and violet. The stores were closed, but there still was a stream of late traffic, the cars suddenly noisier as they accelerated up the long slope of the street. Frank stood across from the door of the bar, staring down into the unsteady stream of water as the other two pulled on light jackets.

"You see what almost happened in there?" Jimmy stopped to gesture with the one arm that was in the jacket sleeve, the rest of the jacket flapping like a surprised bird as he talked.

"Nothing happened," Frank said flatly. "Inez, did you see anything happen?"

She was zipping her jacket, twisting her head with cat-like movements to free her hair from her collar. "I don't know about you two, but I got to see an old boy friend, and that doesn't happen every Friday night. I wonder what he's doing now?"

It was difficult to see her face in the dim light from the bar's neon sign and Frank couldn't tell if she was being serious.

Jimmy refused to be dissuaded. He pulled at his leather cap and drew up his wiry body. "I know what I know. What would you know about this anyway? I'm the one who has to keep his head in there if something does get out of hand."

Inez shook her head. "I can feel you getting yourself all worked up. You just want something to argue about to keep from going to bed and that's all I can think about — getting into bed and getting some sleep. You argue with Frank."

"The brother here," he gestured dismissively toward

Frank, "doesn't let himself know what he's feeling. He knows
— he knows — but he say he doesn't. He breathes things in the
air just like I do."

"He didn't say anything tonight," Inez said mildly. "My
Frank wasn't really there."

"You didn't have much to say for yourself at all," Jimmy
accused.

Frank was looking up into the drifting, fitfully lit masses of
cloud. "You're the one who does the talking for us. You
always did." Frank managed a vague laugh. "You always the
one who talks because you have something I don't have. What
is it, that something, you got? You've got . . ." he prompted.
It was an old joke between them from a class they'd shared.

"The vocabulary." Jimmy finished. "I do, that I do. I have
my vocabulary all lined up and ready to do its deadly business.
I have the answers. Whatever you say to me on the subject of
my black fate in white America I have the vocabulary right in
my pocket, ready to take it out so I can use it to the best
advantage. I can answer anyone's question, I can come back on
anyone's insult, I can repartee any kind of sneer and slight
. . ."

"Real or imagined . . ." Frank interjected.

"Frank, I'm losing you. I can feel you trying to slip away."
Jimmy had begun to laugh himself. "You must be serious
when I'm talking."

There was a lull in the traffic and the street was quieter. A
few lights still were on in the apartments above some of the
small store fronts. With a rush of sound the door of the bar was
pushed open, and three or four men bunched through it and
stood for a moment looking for their cars. One of them,
zipping his jacket, glanced toward the three of them, who had
taken a step out of the way. The man was stocky and
heavy-bodied, his stubby fingers fumbling with the zipper.

"You got a laugh on you." He nodded to Jimmy. "Once
you started nobody else could hear what was going on in
there."

"Come on, come on," one of the men with him
interrupted. It was abruptly turning into one of the situations
Jimmy had been laughing about a moment before. A strained

24

moment on a sidewalk outside a barroom. Jimmy's face was lost in the shadows, but Frank could see his body tensing so he could get out of the way.

"Celtics win it?" Jimmy's voice was tentative.

"Yeh," one of the other men answered. "The last quarter wasn't close."

"Way to go," Jimmy repeated slowly. The stocky man who had accosted him had zipped up his jacket and without saying anything more, turned and followed the others down the street. Frank couldn't think of anything to say. It had all occurred so suddenly he hadn't had time to respond to the situation. It was Inez who finally broke into the silence. She pushed her hands into the pockets of her windbreaker.

"We can all continue this some other time, but I've got to get some sleep before I can do one thing more." She was trying to hurry them past the strained moment.

"Now you saw that . . ." Jimmy began, but she put her hand on his arm to stop him.

"Jimmy. Please. Take me home."

Despite her efforts to sound cheerful a heavy mood clung to them. Jimmy finally straightened his shoulders. "Home it will be." He turned to Frank. "How about you? I can drop you after I leave Inez at her door."

Frank shook his head. "I'm going to walk up the hill. I need to clear my head. Give me some night air and I'll be back to my usual self." He tried to adopt a little of Jimmy's manner.

"Then you take all the night air you need." She leaned forward and quickly kissed his cheek. "Jimmy, take me home."

With last goodbyes they separated in the darkness, the humid spring night closing down behind them like a curtain.

At a street corner, where Main began to rise up the long hillside, a sewer had blocked up and water streaming down the slope had swollen into a wide, spreading pond. The street lights gave its surface a glassy slickness, and traces of the corner's traffic signals and the few still illuminated store windows drew wavering lines across the shine with their own streaks of color. Cars going through the unexpected obstacle

25

had to edge cautiously ahead, leaving a swirling, darkly rainbowed wave behind them.

He had to walk a few yards from the corner before he found a place that was shallow enough for him to cross, then after he'd taken a few steps he had to stop where he was to let a string of cars pass him. As he stood there he thought of Jimmy again. Didn't the other man understand that the way he felt caught in the middle of this street was the way he felt about his life? He was in the middle — with his job, with his involvement with a white woman. He was in the middle between the black society he'd grown up in and the white society he knew so little about. And he was only half way, he could feel part of him changing, but part of him still remained behind, waiting to see what would happen. As he waited for the swell that followed the passage of the cars to subside, he stared down at the wavering line of water-borne rubbish close to his feet and realized that at the point he'd come to he'd lost whatever comfort either society offered him, and at the same time he had no other refuge. Where could he go? What was there at the end of his uncertainty? As he picked his way to the sidewalk, he told himself unhappily that what he seemed to be most concerned with now was keeping his shoes from getting wet.

The phone rang a few moments after he'd gotten back to his apartment.

"Frank?"

It was Inez.

"I thought you were going to sleep."

"I had to say something to get Jimmy to take me home. You know how he gets when he wants to talk. Could I come over there?"

She tried to ask the question casually, but he could hear the awkwardness in her voice.

"I don't know . . . it's late. I'm as tired as you are."

"I'm very small, as you remember. I don't take up much room in your bed."

He tried not to hear the pleading tone that had crept into her voice. "I know you don't."

"Then can I come?"

What could he tell her? "Inez, dear," he was groping for something to say. "When I'm tired like this I can't really appreciate you. And after all this time that would be a shame. Why don't we think of some other time?"

"Tomorrow?" He could almost see her anxious longing. It had the face of a small child just about to cry.

He hesitated, then let himself give in. "Alright. Come tomorrow. But you get yourself some sleep now."

"You too," she answered, her voice pleased and light. "I won't let you sleep like that tomorrow."

He put the phone back, too tired and still too preoccupied to think about what he had promised. Maybe she would know where he fit. Someone would know. Someone knew the seasons of the moon, and the phases of the earth, and they would know the answers to all his questions.

3

He woke to the muted, busy sounds of the rain that had been gathering the night before. Sounds of streaming gutters and spattering drops on his window sill — the sudden, flooding noises of cars splashing through puddles on the street outside. He woke slowly. Something still was bothering him, but he couldn't think of what it was. He lingered for a time between sleep and wakefulness, wondering if that was where he should begin looking. Perhaps it was something in a dream, and he should go back to the dream to find it. Perhaps it was something he had planned to do, and he'd forgotten to write it down. He propped his head up with a pillow and stared across the room toward the faint square of light behind the window shade. For a moment he thought of sleeping again, but he wouldn't return to whatever dream it might have been. Instead, through the coverings of his sleep he heard the noises from the other apartments in the building. Everyone else seemed to be doing something. The sounds woke him again by reminding him that he also had something to do. He remembered now. Inez was coming later. He had to try to straighten up a little. But as he got out of bed and looked for a robe he realized that wasn't what had disturbed him.

Then, when he went into the living room with a cup of coffee, his robe trailing after him as though he were being pursued by the wind, he saw the book where he had left it on the coffee table. It was the book, he realized, that hung over him. He had tried to put the photo out of his thoughts, and he had succeeded at it so well that he hadn't thought of it while he was with Jimmy and Inez. But it had been there in the background, and he hadn't been able to shake it off. Like someone who whispers to you while you're trying to talk on the telephone: you can't hear either voice, and you can't help yourself from thinking that something you're not hearing must be important.

He stood looking at the book, still holding his coffee. He'd get around to it when he'd cleaned the apartment a little. After he'd made himself a piece of toast. After he'd looked at the paper. After he'd finished his coffee. He wandered back to the kitchen, picking up some more dirty glasses on the way. He'd get around to it.

For an hour he made himself clean up some of the clutter that had almost covered the top of every table and chair in the living room. Dirty shirts were thrown onto a pile by the door. He'd take them to a laundry later. The newspapers on the couch went out to the trash chute in the hall. Cereal boxes and stale ends of bread went into the garbage. Dishes had accumulated in the sink, and he piled them in some sort of order so he could rinse them and put them in the dishwasher. He even remembered to make the bed. The only thing he didn't touch was the coffee table. Its pile of junk mail lay undisturbed beside the book. He didn't sit down again until he was ready to stop the other things he had been doing. He flipped over two or three of the form letters, then, with a sardonic smile at his own apprehensions, he put down his coffee cup and slowly pulled the book toward him.

It was even harder for him to look at the picture a second time. In the daylight the blood seemed to have taken on a darker sheen. He could see now that the man had been beaten before he was lynched. His twisted face showed puffed, torn marks around the eyes and nose. His shirt had been torn away and there were livid weals on his chest and shoulders. Abruptly Frank decided he needed to take his cup out to the kitchen. He left the book open on the table and went into the other room.

After he'd put the cup down he lingered for a moment beside the kitchen window, trying to force himself to notice what was happening outside. The rain had stopped, and there was only a thin spray of droplets blowing from the wet trees. The street was so different from the scene in the photograph that for a moment neither of them had any reality. Reluctantly, he went back into the living room. He sat on the couch, staring ahead of him at the blankness of the wall, then he took a heavy breath and pulled the book toward him again.

How could the people in the crowd around the body have let themselves be photographed? He couldn't understand it. It was already disturbing enough that they'd committed the crime — but that they would allow themselves to be photographed with their victim! Their faces were turned toward the camera, grinning in the light of the blazing torches. He could make out one man, at the back of the crowd, who was covering his face, but the others, even the ones closest to the dangling body, were posed without any sign of embarrassment.

What were the women doing there? He could understand their presence even less. He could make out two or three of them in the shadows in the background; thin young women with bobbed hair, one with a fashionable scarf draped over her shoulders. The men in the front of the crowd were dressed more roughly, but most of them were wearing clean shirts. Somehow they had managed to hang their victim without getting too much of his blood on their clothes. A few of the men scattered through the crowd were holding guns and clubs, but there were so many of them they obviously hadn't needed all their weapons to subdue the man they had killed. Faces of boys — teenage boys — showed such pleasure at being part of what had happened that their smiles had become a grimace of excitement. It was their faces that tormented him the most.

Why was he studying the picture, why was he staring at it so intently? He had seen so many pictures like it that he didn't think they would ever affect him again, but there was something about the face of the man hanging from the tree. Did he know that face? He had always kept at such a distance from this kind of violence that he had never been able to think of the people the mobs killed as ordinary men who lived ordinary lives. He had never, on an emotional level, understood that they had worked at a job somewhere, that they got out of bed in the mornings, that they must have lived with a woman sometime, that they could have had children. He sat stiffly with his eyes closed, his fingers rubbing the creased edge of the page. They could have had children. He found himself thinking of that again. They had always been "victims" to him before. This man, somehow, had become something else.

He turned to the back of the book and searched for any kind of identification that would tell him more about the picture, but all he could find was the name of a photo service. The photo itself was captioned only "Lynching Victim, Louisiana, 1937." He tried to make out details, any objects in the picture that would tell him something about it. He stared at it a moment longer, then without thinking about what he was doing he pushed it away from him so roughly that it slipped off the top of the table. It thudded to the floor, the pages spreading awkwardly on the carpet. He slid down in the couch, thrust his hands in his pockets, his eyes searching out the pattern of window curtains.

He stayed where he was for a few moments, then he shook himself and sat up. What he was thinking was so impossible that it couldn't be real, but he couldn't stop thinking it. He had no memory of his father. He only knew the little that he'd overheard his mother telling another woman when he was a child. His father had been working on a farm in Louisiana when his mother met him. When he was still a baby, in 1937, his father had been killed. ". . . out in one of those farm places. I

31

never did know what kind of accident it was." After his father's death his mother had brought him to Harlem and he'd grown up there, thinking of his mother's second husband as his father. He'd never bothered to ask her anything more about it, or if he had questioned her she'd told him so little he'd forgotten it. But he could see something in the face of the man in the picture — some suggestion — some resemblance. Finally he forced himself to say what he was thinking out loud. The man the mob had killed could be his father.

As soon as he had said it he went on in a louder tone, "No, there's no way that could be." He jerked to his feet and began moving around the room. He told himself again, "There's no way that could be." And finally he calmed down a little by telling himself that nothing like that could have happened to him — to anyone he knew — because his life was so ordinary. If people were in news pictures they must have something unusual about them, but his life was as ordinary as the ticking of a clock. At the same time he knew that if the photos had no names, it didn't mean that the people in them hadn't existed. They were real, and the things that happened to them were real — so why couldn't it happen — that someone could look at one of those still images and say, "Yes, I know who that is"? He stood on the other side of the room, looking at the book where it lay on the floor.

"No," he decided, shaking his head over his own suggestibility. "It's no way that could be possible." He was like someone who tries to win an argument by insisting on having the last word. "No," he said again, "it couldn't be." He went toward the kitchen door. "The next time the President comes on TV," he snorted, "you going to say to yourself, that's me." Telling himself to think about something else, he went back to straightening up the apartment.

After another hour of putting away shirts and socks, and stacking the dishes in the dishwasher, he couldn't stay in the apartment any longer. He found a light jacket and walked down the stairs, glancing at himself in the hall mirrors and seeing the same ordinary, anxious figure. He decided to try the bar again, to shake his mood, and he walked slowly down the hill. Since it was a Saturday there wasn't as much traffic. An ordinary May afternoon. It was beginning to get hot, the air clearing after the rain. He could see the outline of the two churches along North Avenue as he walked, the stolid brick tower of the Congregational Church at the corner of North and Main, then two blocks to the west the slim, tan stone steeple of St. Patrick's Catholic Church. He wondered if there was a wedding going on. St. Patrick's usually had Saturday weddings when the weather was warm.

He couldn't escape from his dilemma in the bar. There were only three or four people, but there was a numbing sound of music and advertising. He thought it was coming from the television set, but as he settled onto a bar stool where he could watch it, he realized that somewhere Bridgeport's afternoon television station had found a Cuban film dramatizing the overthrow of the Batista government. While he was listening to the rock and roll radio station the television was depicting a heroic Fidel Castro drawing a plan of attack for his jungle band, while a thoughtful Che Guevara stroked his beard and studied the plan with an admiring expression.

Frank could have stayed through this, but the door opened slowly, and a woman in her forties in a faded cotton dress stumbled in, slumped on a bar stool and began sobbing that her husband had just beaten her. One of the girls behind the bar knew her, and she found a cloth, dampened it in the bar sink, and helped the woman wipe her face. "I don't give a goddam how tough a woman is," the woman insisted incoherently, "she can't take on a man." Frank felt as though he'd interrupted a family quarrel, left some money on the bar to pay for his drink and went back onto the street.

He walked a block down Main Street and crossed to another bar that was in a corner wood-frame building, its doors and windows opening onto the street. He looked inside. It was crowded, but there was an empty place close to the door, under the television set. He squeezed past three or four people to sit down, but as he looked up the same movie was being shown. The action had shifted to Havana, and a mob was running through the city streets. The faces in the mob suddenly brought the photograph back to him. He stared up at

33

the people's expressions as they streamed through the streets, and suddenly he couldn't watch any more. He had to get away from the grimacing faces.

He hesitated outside, then he decided he'd talk to Jimmy. Jimmy could tell him something. He walked back up the hill, shedding his jacket. A new layering of cloud had bleached the blue out of the sky, and there was a thickening, yellowish haze at the horizon. He could feel himself beginning to perspire. He licked the sweat from the edge of his mustache. Jimmy had a small apartment a few blocks off Main. He would pass a grocery store as he walked, and he could pick up some beer. The afternoon was so ordinary it made the photograph seem even more impossible. The streets were lined with modest one- and two-storey houses, all of them with wooden porches and some variation on a design of wooden columns that held up the porch roof. Children passed him on the sidewalk, two four year olds, a boy and a girl, chasing a boy in shorts who was riding a new bicycle to the corner. As the girl passed she grinned up at Frank and called out, "I'm beating you." The grocery store was on the next corner, in a frame building with one wall made of knobbled cement blocks. The man who ran it, gray-haired and indifferent, was reading a newspaper propped up on the counter and didn't look up when Frank came in. Frank opened the cooler against the back wall and took out some beer. He bought a dozen cans so he and Jimmy would have something to start on.

Jimmy was washing his car in the driveway of the house where he lived a half block away. It was a three-storey, green painted clapboard house, with a high front porch, and a small yard behind a cement block wall. A dozen windows looked down on the driveway, but no one seemed to be watching as Jimmy dragged his hose from one side of the car to the other. The only sign that anyone else was home was the sound of a radio broadcasting a baseball game.

"What you doing here?" Jimmy was wearing his usual cap, but he had put on rubber boots and a torn denim shirt. "You can't tell me you walked all the way over here just to help me wash the car. If you want I can find you a sponge."

Frank looked for someplace to sit. There was a wooden stool against the house and he pulled it around so he could watch Jimmy soap the roof of the car. "I'm just going to sit. I worked hard enough getting over here." He opened the paper bag at his feet. "You want a beer?"

"I'll catch it when I don't have my hands full of this soap."

Frank sipped from one of the cans and tried to think of a way to begin. "That book you told me to buy — you know, you told me where to order it — it came in the mail yesterday. I was looking at it."

Jimmy was bent over a back fender, the water from the hose streaming over the driveway's cracked concrete in a wavering flood. "Which book was that?"

"The one you said I should get for Lester."

"I don't remember what book that was."

Frank sat silently for a moment. It was so typical of Jimmy that he would spend an hour talking Frank into something, and then forget what it was.

"It was that history book. You know, black history."

Jimmy finished rinsing the soap off the fender, straightened up and threw his sponge into a bucket. "I know the book you mean. It's the same one I got. You see! You took my advice. You took my word about what is important and what isn't important. Now Lester will know the truth, and once he knows it then nobody can tell him anything different. He will know what the truth is all about."

"Is that book the truth?"

"It's as true as we going to get. I don't know anything that's a hundred percent, but that's as true as they could make it."

"So what's he do then?" Frank drank a little more beer. That was his question. That was what he had come to Jimmy for. Could Jimmy answer it?

"What do you mean, what's he do?"

"I mean, a boy like Lester, he's eighteen, and he sees those things in the book, you know, what happened to people a hundred years ago . . ." Frank wasn't sure he was being very clear. ". . . or what was happening twenty years ago. It didn't all change that much. So Lester sees those things that happened — what's he supposed to do?"

Jimmy picked the sponge out of the bucket and moved to the other fender. "I know you stopped for a drink on your way. You let me get this finished here and we can go upstairs and finish off that beer, and I know I can find something else to drink, and we can talk all this over."

"No," Frank insisted. "What's so hard about the question? What am I supposed to do if I see something terrible in one of those pictures in the book?"

He could see Jimmy becoming more and more uncertain. The other man studied his face as he squeezed the sponge over the fender. "You talking about Lester or you?"

"I'm talking about anybody. You. Lester. Anybody. That's what I mean. What do you want them to do?"

Jimmy shrugged and dropped the sponge back into the bucket. "All I can say is the same thing I say to you every time we talk about this. Fire. That's what I'm saying. That's what Jimmy Baldwin wrote. No more water, fire next time. When the punishment comes down on those people, next time it's not going to be water, it's going to be fire. The cities are going to burn, the people in them are going to burn. You just have to read what Jimmy Baldwin wrote . . ."

Frank held his hand up, interrupting him. "What did your daddy say to you about all this?"

Jimmy shook his head. "Talk about can to can't. That thing they used to say about working from can to can't — from when you can see to when it's so dark you can't see. My daddy was that angry. He got out of bed angry, and he was still feeling the same way when he got back into bed at night. That's the way he brought me up — to know I had something to be angry about."

"What did he do about it?" Frank persisted.

Jimmy went back to the hose, washing the last of the soap off the sides of the car. "You know, he did do things about it. He was always joining some organization. I know he was in the NAACP for a long time. And I think he did get out on the streets there in the 'sixties. He didn't want to say nothing about it. Then the last time I saw him, he's out in California and he doesn't have to work now, and he told me those honkies weren't worth all the energy he'd used up being angry at them.

36

He wasn't going to think about them any more."

"So that's what you do? You don't think about it?"

Jimmy was sitting on the driveway, pulling off his rubber boots. "Did I say that? You know me and you know that isn't what I say at all. When I get up to his age then that's maybe the kind of thing I'll tell myself, but I still feel it now, just what he felt. You can't tell me you don't have some of those feelings inside you, too." He stood up, and began walking toward the front of the house, expecting Frank to follow him. Frank pushed the stool back and picked up his paper bag. "We're going to talk about this, and I'll tell you some more that Jimmy Baldwin wrote because that's something else that's true." He stopped at the steps. "You got anything else to do this afternoon, or can we drink up that beer?"

Frank shrugged. "I'm just going to listen to you talk."

4

And what to do about Inez. He couldn't ask her anything because she didn't know anything. And if she cared about these things it was for reasons he didn't understand. He couldn't tell her anything, because he didn't know himself what he had to tell. When she finally knocked on the door of his apartment, he had been trying to drink his way out of his dilemma, and he had realized, an hour or so before, that this was as useless as listening to Jimmy had been. If he knew, he repeated to himself again and again, if he knew anything, then he would know what he had to do next.

"I worried about you last night. Do you feel better? Have you thought you might be getting a cold? Everybody has colds now. It has something to do with the start of summer." She was standing in the hallway, looking at him anxiously, already starting to unbutton her coat. He stood out of the way so she could come in, and closed the door behind her. He managed to get back to the couch while she was looking for a hanger in the closet.

"No cold." He sat down heavily. "Feeling fine. Just maybe a little drunk."

She laughed from across the room and came slowly toward the couch, running a comb through her hair. "Why'd you get drunk? And if you had to get drunk, why didn't you wait for me?"

He tried to think of something to say, but it was difficult for him to put together the pieces of a sentence. "I was talking to Jimmy," he finally answered with a shrug.

She shook her head and continued to the kitchen. "If you've left the bottle out I'll get a drink for myself."

He slumped back against the couch, giving the room a moment to settle around him. He couldn't talk to her about the reasons for his mood. He realized numbly that he didn't talk to her about anything. It was she who needed to talk, to unburden herself, to explain and examine, and she never seemed to be upset if he didn't respond.

She stood in the kitchen door a moment before she came back into the room. She was swirling her glass to melt some of the ice. She was wearing the same baggy sweater and black trousers, with scuffed black ballerina slippers, that she usually wore when she came to his apartment. He was vaguely conscious that these had been the kind of clothes she had worn in college when she was doing something she thought of as daring. No, he wanted to tell her. He was just ordinary, she didn't need to dress for him. She didn't need to do anything more than be there sometimes. "Do you still have a drink?" she asked from the doorway.

"Somewhere," he answered thickly, groping around on the rug below him, trying to find his glass. He picked it up awkwardly and put it on the coffee table. The room was half in shadow. He had forgotten to turn on the overhead light and there was only the lamp beside the couch to fend off the darkness. Outside in the hall he could hear a woman laughing. There was a concatenation of clanking sounds as someone emptied trash into a metal container over his head. Inez didn't seem to notice any of it. She slipped down on the sofa beside him, perching on the edge of the cushions so she could face him as she talked. She sipped her drink, reaching out to press

39

his leg with her other hand, then she put her glass on the table beside his and lit a cigaret. He was trying to stop smoking, but when she held out the pack he took one. It didn't seem important whether he smoked cigarets or not. She sat silently while he tried to light a match with fingers that had lost all sense of feeling, and finally she had to take the matches out of his hand and light his cigaret for him. She smiled.

"What is it you and Jimmy do together? You don't ever get drunk when you're with me, but when I see you like this you tell me half the time that you've been out with Jimmy. What do you do, find girls you know and have a party?"

"All the time," he mumbled. "What do you do?"

"When?"

"When you're not out with us."

She stopped for a moment. He could see she was considering whether or not to lapse into the kind of easy chaffing she had with the other man. She didn't bother to answer when she spoke again.

"Jimmy's a lot of fun. You're a lot of fun. But you and I used to talk more." Sipping at her drink, thoughtfully smoking her cigaret, she began to talk for both of them.

After a minute he stopped listening to what she was saying. He put his glass down again. He didn't want to drink any more. It hadn't helped. He still could see the photo from the book every time he closed his eyes. He knew it didn't mean anything, he knew the photo had nothing to do with him, but it was still there in the shadows waiting for him. He thought about his mother. The whole idea was ridiculous, but she could tell him if the page from the book had any meaning. Why hadn't he asked her about his father? He'd overheard part of a conversation and he'd been satisfied with that. Why hadn't he wanted to know more? Perhaps, like most children, he didn't want to consider anything that might disturb the net of relationships he felt sustaining and supporting him. He was satisfied with his mother's second husband. He was satisfied with the father that was there.

But his mother could tell him something. She must remember — he thought — she must remember everything. He hadn't forgotten anything and he must have gotten the habit from her. She was still there in Harlem. He could drive there in an hour. The idea didn't appeal to him, but he couldn't shake it off. No sense. No sense. Why couldn't he stop thinking about it? Something brushed against his trousers and he opened his eyes. He had forgotten he was smoking a cigaret and the ash had fallen onto his leg. He could have started a fire, he muttered to himself, and began clumsily brushing himself off.

"I don't get the feeling you're listening to anything I'm saying." Inez's voice beside him was tired and disappointed. Mostly he noticed that she sounded tired, and he felt a weak flush of embarrassment at having forgotten completely that she was there. He tried to remember what she had been talking about.

"It's been a long day," was the only thing he could think of to say.

"If you want me to go home, I'll go," she began, but he could hear the disappointment in her tone. "You know I don't want to go home," she added after a silence.

"No . . . no." He held out his hand and felt her fingers clasp his. "But do we have to talk?"

He listened to the confused noises as he struggled with his clothes in the darkness of the bedroom. Their movements, as they pressed against each other, filled the stillness with an incoherent sound that was like weeping. Usually he liked to touch her as she undressed, to feel the uneven texture of her clothing give way to the lean smoothness of her skin, but he could feel so little through the numbness of the alcohol. He could only sense her impatient twisting as she pulled off her black trousers and her underwear and threw everything onto a chair. He was so unsteady with his own shirt and trousers that she had to help him, and when they fell onto the bed it was her hands that reached first for him. His hands slid helplessly over her body while he tried to remember what she was expecting from him. At one point he heard himself laughing. "Black stud." That was what he was supposed to be. But how would he manage that?

She didn't seem to notice his helplessness. Her own body

was wound tightly against his, and he could feel her trembling. He didn't try to say anything. Finally, almost as though it were someone else he was watching from the other side of the room, he felt his body begin to respond to her excitement. His fingers began to search over the planes of her skin. Without either of them being sure of what was happening she drew him into her with an abrupt, convulsive movement, pressing him against her stomach. He could feel her struggling to enclose him, to draw him into her in a heaving pattern of concentric circles — the circle of her arms around his back, the circle of her thighs winding around his hips, the inmost circle of her body opening to him. As they tossed together he was conscious of their movements drawing them closer, then as the pulling of hands and arms slowed he could feel himself slipping further and further from her.

Inez lay with her eyes closed, still only half awake. She had wound herself into a wreath of sheets. It was morning. She could hear footsteps on the sidewalk, the low murmur of automobiles. Even with her eyes shut she was conscious of the soft inroads of light into the room. She loved to lie stretched out to her full length when she woke up in his bed. She felt that every part of the bed was hers. She slid her arms out, as far as she could reach, claiming the rumpled mattress. Everything she could touch — like everything she could see — was hers. She slowly opened her eyes to look out over her new possessions. She could make out unending mounds of sheet and the creased lines of pillows bunched against her face. The smells also were hers. She slid closer to the middle of the bed to be closer to the smell of their bodies that still clung to the mattress.

She was conscious that Frank wasn't in the bed with her, but she didn't think anything about it. Usually he woke before she did and she found him in the kitchen or the bathroom. Sometimes the apartment was empty when she got out of bed. He didn't wake her if he had to go out to buy cigarets or the newspaper. There had been mornings when he'd come back to the apartment and joined her again in bed and they hadn't gotten up for hours. She stretched her legs, feeling the warmth

42

of the sheets, the smoothness of the light blanket. She finally woke up enough to think of getting up herself. If he did go out he usually made coffee first, and this always helped her start the day. She sat on the edge of the bed running her hands over her body. She gently massaged the muscles of her thighs and her stomach. She could feel a familiar stiffness from their love making. She sat for a moment, listening for any sounds that would tell her if he still was in the apartment. It was silent. She shrugged, gently pressed her hands against her breasts, then finally stretched and slipped off the bed.

Her clothes were scattered over the chair where she'd thrown them. She left them where they were. He usually had an extra robe hanging behind the door of the bathroom. When she'd used the toilet and washed she went into the kitchen, bundled up in one of his long bathrobes. She had to roll up the sleeves and pull it almost double around her before she could tie it. The kitchen, as she always found it on Sunday mornings, was cluttered with glasses and half emptied coffee cups, but there didn't seem to be any coffee left on the stove. She couldn't remember that they had drunk so much coffee. Had they drunk any coffee at all? She put the cups in the sink, wondering if she could have forgotten some of what they'd done together the night before.

Still listening for his key in the door, she went back into the living room. The coffee table had been pushed away from the couch, and there was a pair of scissors and some strips of paper scattered over the carpet. Thoughtfully, wondering what he had been cutting up, she bent down to pick up the scissors. She noticed a book lying open on the floor not far from the paper scraps. As she picked it up and put it on the table she noticed idly that a page had been torn out.

5

He was so tired he wasn't sure he could keep driving all the way to New York. He had slept only an hour and could feel the rough graininess that had settled behind his eyes. He had tried to sleep again, stretched out beside Inez in the darkness, staring up into the shadows of the ceiling, but he was too disturbed to relax. Finally he'd gotten up and made himself some coffee. He should call Inez. He told himself to look for a telephone so he could call her. Then in a moment he forgot about it.

While he had been sitting in the kitchen with a cup of coffee he had finally remembered what it was that had tripped his memory. Once, when he was a boy, his mother had let him see the only photograph she had of herself and his father. He'd gotten only a glimpse of it, and he was so young it hadn't seemed important. It was his faint recollection of that early photograph that had stirred when he had seen the picture in the book. But did he really remember it? Or was it some fantasy that had fixed in his mind? His mother could tell him. She might still have the picture. It was then he had decided to leave Inez sleeping and go to New York. He knew she could find anything she needed in his apartment, and she was used to waking up and finding him gone. He would find a phone to call her. He would find a phone when he got to Harlem.

There was so little traffic on the expressway early Sunday morning that he kept going, despite his exhaustion. He was beginning to doze off when the outline of the uptown Manhattan housing projects broke into his confused thoughts. With a cry of tires he jerked the car off the highway onto the ramp that hung over the empty city blocks leading to 135th Street. The project buildings, as gray and orderly as upended cinder blocks, meant so little to him that he saw them as a kind of false front — a setting for a play that had not been performed. He had never lived in any of the buildings. They had been built after he had moved out of the city, so they had never taken on a physical reality. For him Harlem began after he'd driven two or three blocks further and turned into the half-ruined neighborhood beyond. It had changed, and it was the desolation of the streets that disturbed him the most — the fenced-in spaces where the buildings had been torn down and the ground strewn with crumbled brick and glistening shards of glass and scratched bits of stone. Then it had all been flattened with earth-moving equipment and left behind sagging wire fences.

He had read somewhere of the Roman revenge on the city of Carthage after they had defeated its armies. The city had been laid waste, the ruins plowed under, and the ground strewn with salt. Someone had done the same thing to these hapless plots where the buildings of Harlem had once stood. There was enough empty land now to begin farming it again. As he drove slowly along the pot-holed streets, veering to slide past the ruined cars left to rust along the curbs he could look across still, lifeless acres — space enough for rows of corn, harvests of tomatoes. But he was sure that if he were to climb one of the fences and put his mouth against the tamped debris he would taste the bitter sting of the salt.

He was leaning forward in the seat, forcing himself to

45

concentrate on the driving. He was too tired now to know what he was feeling or thinking. He tried to wake up, rubbing his eyes again as he waited for the street light to change. He looked at his watch. He had left too early. His mother would still be in church. He tried to think about what to do next. He twisted his neck from side to side in an effort to force himself awake. He could park close to the church, pick her up when she left the service and give her a ride back to her apartment. As he turned in the direction of the church he thought for a moment of going to the service, but he hadn't been inside a church since he was a child. The noise and the emotional excitement that meant so much to her only frightened him, and he had cried until he had to be taken outside. His feelings hadn't changed, though he was always pleasant to his mother when she tried to persuade him to go with her. He would smile and put his hand on her arm and say, with a half sigh, "When I come down next time." And she always pursed her lips and went without him, telling herself that he would sometime, at last, be with her in church. It gave her so much pleasure to think about it that she was almost able to reconcile herself to the reality that this wasn't yet the time.

He found a place to park close to the church. A space had been left between two abandoned automobiles on the other side of the street. He backed into the opening, hearing the tires crunch over the debris heaped close to the curb. The day was hazy and lustreless, but it was already warm enough so that he could sit with the motor turned off. There was no need for the heater. In a month it would be too hot and muggy to sit with the windows closed.

He slid down in the seat, trying not to fall asleep. Despite the soiled taste in his mouth he reached in his pocket for another of Inez's cigarets and lit it as he waited. Along the sidewalk was a row of brownstone buildings, three and four stories high. Ornate ramps of stairs rose from the cracked sidewalk in a severe row, the warm tone of the stone looking somehow foreign and exotic against the drabness of the pavements. He had grown up in one of the buildings two or three doors from where he was sitting in the car. He still remembered the warm shadows in the corridors of the building, the small, precise shape of the stoop where he could bounce a ball against the brown stones, and where he and his mother could play together when they were alone and no one else was sitting outside at the same time. In the summers, though, there was always someone else sitting with them, newspapers spread out on the steps so that skirts and trousers wouldn't pick up the city's dirt. Then he had sat beside his mother and tried not to interrupt while everyone else was talking and he would be very still, but she would keep her arm around him and he would slyly throw his ball from one hand to the other, hoping she wasn't noticing. When he was older and was allowed to play on the street itself she would sit outside where she could see him, sometimes sewing or looking at a magazine, but usually there was somebody to talk to. Harlem stoops were crowded then — and when he drove in to see her he could still see some stoops crowded with the men who couldn't find anything to do, or with the families who had to get out of the rooms they couldn't afford to air-condition in the summers.

He didn't look up at his old house. Instead he stared off into the street. The block of houses, like most of the other buildings on both sides of the street, had been stripped and gutted, then the gaping windows and doorways had been filled in with gray cinder block and cemented shut. The window he had looked out of when he sat up in bed had become a wall of brick. To him it was as though the house had been blinded, and the masonry blocking the doorway was a gag that stifled whatever life was still left within it. When he remembered the spaces of the porch, the ornate carving of the door lintels and the window sills — despite the muting of the weather and the years since the house had been built — he remembered voices, sounds of people laughing. With the strangling gag of cinder block and cement the sounds had died.

He found himself falling asleep. He rolled down the window to get some air and heard a familiar shouting. "Lord Jesus . . . be with us now! Lord Jesus! It's your voice we want to hear. No voice but Jesus . . ." A window was open in the church and the preacher's voice rolled out into the street with a hoarse, stentorian presence. He had heard the voice so many times, but always as he sat waiting for his mother. The church was a heavy stone building with narrow windows and small arched openings for doors. It had the look of a small fortress, and the deacons inside the door in their dark suits had always looked, to him, as if they were guarding the building against whatever might come in from the street.

He was staring across at the building, half seeing the knot of women and children on the steps, the waiting ushers, the long strip of the neon sign that distinguished the building from its empty neighbors. Cigaret finished, he ground the butt on the floor of the car. He couldn't wait any more. He was too tired to sit in the car, his skin was too chafed with the weight of his clothes, his eyes beginning to burn. He would let himself into his mother's apartment and sleep a little. He started the car and drove away from the church, moving his head from side to side to try to wake up enough to follow the streets.

He didn't pay any attention to where he was driving. He had seen all of it so often that it didn't matter to him which street he took. Harlem had finally become too much for him, its crowding, its dilapidation, its discomfort, but his mother hung on. He occasionally tried to persuade her to leave, to look for some place to live that was closer to where he had moved, but she only shook her head, her lips pursed shut as though there were no reason even to consider the suggestion. Sometimes she seemed to him to be like a survivor of some incomprehensible war. Building after building where she found her small apartments had been torn down, and she had taken her things and found another building only to have it destroyed in its turn. She had moved from one side of Harlem to another, never sure when she would be forced to move again, and never understanding what it was that was laying waste to building after building, block after block, the destruction as sudden and as complete as if there had been some kind of attack, with weapons so frightening that no one could bring themselves to talk about them.

She had always gone to the same church, even though she had sometimes been forced to move so far away from it that it had taken her most of Sunday morning to walk through the rubble-strewn streets to get to the service. She still wore the same kind of white dress she had been wearing to services as long as he could remember. A white dress that buttoned down the front, white stockings that took on a muted luminescence over her dark legs, white shoes and a veil to cover her head. Even when he saw her walking with her determined, small scurrying steps over the pavements on a winter Sunday, he knew that under the bundle of her coat she would be wearing her white dress and stockings.

It was hard to find someplace to park. He had to walk several blocks to get to the apartment. He was too tired to think of what he was doing. She would wake him, they would talk, she would be able to tell him something.

6

Could it be the light that woke him? What he could see of the afternoon was already a fading, discolored form beyond the dim window. He stirred. What had wakened him? A sound. A sound repeated. His mother's voice.

"Frank — is that you? If you inside there you come down the hallway so I can see you. I'm not going to put a foot inside this door until I know who it is that's in there."

He had left the light burning in the small entranceway of her apartment. If he let himself in and moved something or left a light burning she was afraid to come into the apartment until she was sure who it was. So many things had happened to her in the shabby places where she had lived.

"Frank?"

He managed to sit up. He had thrown himself down on the sofa in the living room and was still half asleep. He could hear fear at the edge of his mother's voice.

"It's me. I'm here."

"You never know if somebody can get through that door so

I always call out if I see a light on." His mother's voice was relieved as she redid the maze of locks that held the door closed against the outside. He could hear her heavy breathing as she came up the hallway. He pulled himself to his feet and gave her a dutiful kiss on the cheek. Now that he was with her the storm of feelings that had driven him to her apartment seemed distant and unreal. He didn't know how to begin talking to her.

"You didn't tell me you was goin' to be here. I never do cook up much on Sunday unless I know you coming. You know how many times I told you that, and here you are, without so much as a word."

He sprawled back on the couch. He was used to her scoldings, and for a moment it was easier just to listen to her talk. She sat down on a wooden chair at the small round table that did for her meals when she was alone. She had taken off her hat and coat, but she still was in the white dress she had worn to church. She had owned the dress for years, and it was too tight for her now. There was a youthfulness to her face, but she had to wear heavy glasses when she was reading and she went up and down stairs slowly. She had worked at physically demanding jobs all her life. Cleaning or scrubbing or moving boxes in poorly-lit warehouses and store rooms. Forty years of it had worn down her body and spirit, forty years of jobs like it had made it harder and harder for her to get down on her knees to clean a floor. At night her body took its own time unraveling all the rubbings and bendings the day had left on it. She would never have thought of herself as someone who had led a hard life, but she was tired of what every day forced her to do — even though she only let herself respond emotionally to the hard monotony of the days through her body, which told her simply that it was tired. She sat heavily in the plain, worn chair, her knees thrust out at an abrupt angle to her body, her hands on her thighs as she leaned toward him, her head nodding with small insistent movements as she talked.

"You didn't have no trouble with a woman?"

"No, nothing like that. I just decided to come down and see you."

"I never did get over all that from the last time. You lying around here and that wife of yours on the telephone."

He had stayed in his mother's apartment for three or four weeks after the breakup of his marriage, having turned up at her door with as little warning, and with as little in the way of clothes or baggage. She still talked about it when she didn't understand what he was doing.

"That was three years ago."

"You never know what the good Lord's going to put across your path. It can come any minute. You got to be ready for it." Her voice took on some of the lilting song-like quality of the service and sermon she'd been listening to for most of the day. She shook her head with even stronger emphasis as she finished.

"You know there won't ever be anything like that again. I've been through all that once." His voice was mildly protesting, but he was hardly conscious of what he was saying. He could feel himself beginning to relax, his emotions temporarily yielding to the familiar accent of her voice, even if he knew it was only a respite, that the storm was there, waiting to be faced.

She made coffee for them, talking through the open kitchen door. There had been the usual troubles in the building. A woman had been hurt when she'd opened a closet and the door had come off its hinges and bruised her arm as it fell on her. A man down the hall had fallen asleep in the bathtub with the water running and the overflow had seeped into the apartment below, ruining the slip covers on a living room couch. A woman on the first floor had caught two boys trying to break into her window. There were always problems with the building or one of the tenants, and he had listened to her stories about the newest difficulties for as long as he could remember. She never spoke with any sense of outrage or indignation. These were simply things that happened. He had asked her once why she didn't get more upset. She had looked away and finally answered that she had been so fortunate herself she didn't have any reason to take these things "serious." They were as they were. He accepted what she said.

52

He realized this was why she remained in her old neighborhood. For her the years there had been happy, and she wanted to stay close to the streets and the neighborhoods where she had felt this happiness.

"I got to put up with a whole mess of squabbling on the job. Now they going to move me to a different floor in the building," she sighed as she came in with the coffee, set it on the small table and went back to her chair. "I just learned how they want me to do everything where I'm at and now they going to move me around again."

She had found a job cleaning offices in a new state office building that had been put up in the center of the Harlem business district.

"Can't you complain?"

"I don't have nobody to complain to. I suppose the union could do something, but they already busy with enough things of their own. I just have to learn what it is they want from me all over again."

He was always surprised that his mother was able to find the little jobs that kept her going. When his stepfather was living there had been a steady, if not very large, income, and she had only worked occasionally, usually when she wanted to get something for the apartment or wanted to help him with school. He had always felt a twinge of embarrassment at the posters that showed a black woman cleaning floors and talking about her needing money for her children to go to college. He had gone to college and his mother had cleaned floors, but he had told himself that she didn't need to do it. She had done it because she wanted to feel that she also had a part in what he was trying to achieve. Now he knew he had been naive.

When she finally managed to get into the union there was less uncertainty about keeping her jobs going, and there was as little rancor in her voice when she talked about the problems other people had in the apartment block. He sensed that at some moment she had gone through her life and made a reckoning of what it had given her, and she had decided that the final sum had been generous, and she had never worried about it again. Her complaints were only a way of commenting on the tiredness that her body felt — a way of soothing the aches that were slower and slower to go away.

"If you going to stay to supper you have to go get something. I don't have but some cheese and leftover potatoes and I was going to take the cheese for lunch tomorrow."

He was staring up at the cracked ceiling, listening to her voice but hardly hearing what she was saying. What he was feeling seemed to lack any kind of reality, and her voice had taken on some of that quality. He tried to follow the lines in the ceiling with his eyes, as if they would lead him somewhere where he finally could shed his uncertainty.

"I can go find us something to eat," he answered after a moment.

"You alright? I know when you have something worrying you."

He sat up, trying to shape some sort of beginning phrase, some word that would make it possible for him to begin — but he was silent, still too confused to talk to her.

"I didn't sleep much," he answered her lamely. He ran his fingers over his head, smoothing his hair down. "I have to walk a little to find something for us. That will get me going again."

"You know where to go?"

"I can find something. There's always someplace open. I'll just keep walking."

"You don't want to get something I can cook up?"

He stood up and stretched. "I'll find something that's all ready to go. You can stretch out on the couch here until I come back."

"Then you'll want to take it over again," his mother said, teasing him.

"I have to get my rest." He tried to match her lightness as he went slowly down the hallway.

His mother's apartment was in an old building overlooking a small park in the south of Harlem. It was more of a square than a park, a fenced-in quadrangle of barren earth and some new brick buildings around the base of a stony rise that had been given the name of Mt. Morris even though the "mountain" was less than three stories high. There had been a delicatessen down in the basement of one of the buildings, but it was closed, and leaves and trash had drifted into the doorway at the foot of the stairs outside. There was an atmosphere of uncertainty to the square. Some of the houses — well built, richly ornamented brownstone buildings from the end of the previous century — were in good repair. Others had already been closed up and were barricaded. One group of buildings had been vacated at the same time and behind a fence was a sign saying that they were going to be renovated by one of the city's agencies. The agency had obviously run out of funds, and the sign itself was almost as weathered as the building fronts. There was a small church in the lower storey of one of the buildings, and on a corner across from the park was a large, heavy stone structure that was also a church, though it had little outside ornament to mark it. A cluster of brightly-dressed adolescents were standing on the steps, as though they were some sort of decoration, waiting to be placed inside.

He walked toward 125th Street, unhurried, still undecided about what to tell her. The two or three hours sleep he'd gotten on her couch had helped him a little, but he still was feeling the effects of his sleepless night. It had been so long since he'd been in Harlem on a Sunday that he had forgotten it was still a church day, and he had forgotten there were so many churches. There seemed to be a church on every corner, and there was usually a basement church or a storefront church in a building in between. New model cars were double-parked outside some of the more flashily decorated buildings, but at the older, shabbier churches most people seemed to have walked. In front of all of them were the women, like his mother, who were the force that sustained them.

125th Street was quiet, full of loitering talking couples or vagrants going through rubbish heaps. When he was a boy the street had been busy with stores and crowds and excitement. The theaters had been open, there had been African bookstores and sidewalk agitators. Now it had become only another shabby New York street, with dispirited shops and graffiti and a smell of disrepair and poverty. Only the occasional West Indian shops still stirred with some restlessness. Two men with Rasta hairstyles glared at him as he went slowly past their small shop. In the window was a defiant, hand-lettered sign reading, "Buy Black and Love Rasta."

At a corner restaurant below Father Divine's church — still ringing with shouts and the rhythmic glories of an amplified sermon despite the lateness of the afternoon — he bought some chicken, fried potatoes, and coleslaw to take back to the apartment. He couldn't think of any other place that might be open. He had the perspiring girl behind the counter wrap it as well as she could to keep it warm, and he started to walk back along 125th Street. He slowed his pace as he passed a dark gap in the row of buildings lining the south side of the street. A store had been torn down, and there was the usual scree of crushed brick and glass, shreds of bottles and window panes strewn over the trampled ground. A small thicket of sumac trees had managed to force their way a few feet above the earth, but their stubby, finger-like stalks were bare of leaves. Someone had patiently gathered beer bottles made out of green glass and slipped them over the ends of the branches, turning the spindly stalks into a grotesque, gleaming kind of vegetation. He stared at them for a moment, taking in their ugly caricature of foliage, wondering why it had stopped him. Then he remembered the body in the picture. Somehow the glass suggested the swaying shape of the body, the hanging flesh. He turned and hurriedly began walking away.

When he was halfway up the first flight of stairs in his mother's building he heard a sharp scratching sound somewhere in the hallway above him. He stopped, standing close to the wall, trying to hear the sound again. He remembered this feeling of fear from his childhood in these buildings — when you heard a sound and you had to wait to find out what it was. He started up the stairs again, each step followed by a pause before he took the next. The building was silent, but when he reached the landing he could hear breathing somewhere near by. He felt a surge of blood to his head, a pounding in his chest. He wasn't sure he could move, but he forced himself to take another step forward.

Halfway down the narrow corridor he could see a thin

56

figure pressed into a doorway. In the light of the bare, hanging bulb he could make out the face turned toward him, the mouth a raw opening in the dark, glowering face. The boy was in a sweatshirt and khaki trousers, a knit cap pulled down over his forehead. Frank could see that he had something in his hand, and he had been using it to try to force the door open. They stared at each other. Finally the boy's lips began to move.

"Motherfucker, you get back. I'm going to go down those stairs, and you get back and I won't cut you. You hear me, motherfucker. If you do one thing I'm going to cut you." He gestured and Frank could see a stubby knife blade protruding from the clump of his fingers. "Get back. You hear me, mother. You get back." He slowly pushed himself away from the doorway, his thin body tensed to jump.

Frank knew he had to do something. He had never been able to fight when he was forced into one of these situations. Could he ever become angry enough to fight one of these people? He knew he couldn't do anything with the boy crouched there. With a sudden jump he sprang to the stairway to the next floor. running up a few steps, then whirling to see if the boy would follow him. Seeing his way clear the boy burst out of the hallway and hurled himself down the stairs, thrusting toward Frank with his knife hand as he crashed out of sight toward the door that would take him back to the street.

Frank leaned against the dirty wall, trying to catch his breath, his heart still thudding. He became conscious of the warmth of the food cartons that he'd pressed against his stomach. He automatically held up the bag to see if anything was leaking. After another moment listening to the silence, he continued up the stairs to his mother's apartment. He wouldn't tell her what had happened. It was something she already knew about — just as he knew about it. There was something else he had to think about.

7

They ate on the wooden table in her bare kitchen. A single bulb, shaded with a dark green-painted metal core, threw an unyielding light over the wrinkled cloth and the cardboard cartons he had brought from the restaurant. The window in the kitchen opened onto an air shaft, revealing a brick wall bent away at an awkward angle. His mother had hung soft yellow-toned curtains over the window, and the faint, dim light that made its way down the air shaft added its muted temperings to the bulb's glare. As in the other rooms, she had filled the flat surfaces in the kitchen with potted plants, and behind everything in the room was an unkempt background of green vegetation. When she had to leave an apartment they spent most of the time moving her plants to the new rooms she'd found. Once when she had gone to Cleveland to visit her sister he had come from Bridgeport three times a week to see that they got watered. Her apartment, then, was on 138th Street, on the sixth floor, in a building without an elevator. Every time he climbed the stairs he was reminded again that he was getting heavy and soft, and every time he went down the stairs he told himself that he would change the way he was living and become as elegantly slim and strong as he had been when he was twenty. Nothing about him, however, was like the person he had been then, and as soon as he was on the way back to Bridgeport he forgot all his good resolves.

He was silent as he ate. He tried to think about the chicken. He made himself concentrate on the soggy paper container filled with coleslaw and on the elongated shadow it cast on the oil cloth table covering. He spent several moments fussing with a can of soft drink he'd bought. But the turmoil he was trying to keep at bay edged closer and closer. It was like a noise outside the window, a noise that was swelling louder and louder and there was no way he could shut it out. He realized that he had dropped the piece of chicken he had been holding in his fingers and he abruptly pushed his plate away. He fumbled in his pocket for a cigaret and turned from the table, staring vacantly around the room.

"I don't know what it is on your mind, but you should eat up what you got on your plate." His mother's voice was mildly disapproving. She had already finished and was carefully wiping her mouth with one of the paper napkins that had been stuffed into the bag. Without answering he pushed his paper plate across the table. She shrugged and finished what he had left, her eyes on his face. He had clasped his hands together and was squeezing them between his thighs. He felt that he couldn't move, but at the same time he was conscious that his shoulders were drawn tightly together. There was a knot of pain at the back of his neck, just at the physical point where he was holding himself in so stiffly.

"Can you tell me about who Frank was, the first man you were married to, the one that was my father?" His voice was so low and choked he had to clear his throat and ask her again. His mother was wiping her mouth a second time and spent some time wiping her fingers with a clean napkin.

"You know all about him," she answered after a pause.

"Who?"

"Lester."

"No."

"What do you mean, saying 'no' to your mother?" Her tone was gruff.

"Lester was somebody else. You married him after my father — you said that and Lester said that. I mean my father. Frank Lewis."

"Lester was the one that raised you. Because of Lester you didn't grow up on no street. I could have done something for you. We would have gotten by somehow. But without Lester we wouldn't have what we do now. Without Lester you never would have had your school." She searched in the bag for another paper napkin and wiped her fingers off again with fussy, jerking movements.

"I'm not saying anything against Lester. You know I loved Lester just like he was my father. I gave his name to my own son. Lester knew I loved him. I didn't have anything against him. He was a good man."

She kept her eyes on the table, not looking at him.

He wouldn't be dissuaded. "But what about Frank?"

"It's the same as I told you before." She looked at him, her expression sharp with annoyance. "We got married and you were born and right after that Frank got killed and I come up north."

"How was Frank killed?" His voice had dropped. He was somewhere conscious that he was holding his breath. He was afraid, now, of whatever she might say. As though he had to make his way through a field set with traps. Lester had told him about traps. From his own boyhood in Tennessee, when they'd set out traps for the animals eating the crops. Frank had become still. He could have been standing stiffly in the middle of the coarse fields Lester had told him about, afraid that if he moved he might stumble into one of the traps so painstakingly set out around him.

"He did farm work. You know how accidents always happen when you do farm work." She was carefully considering what she told him. "But you don't know about any of that. It was all when you were so young. Just a baby. And I come north and then I met Lester and I started over again." Her voice hurried on, as if she wanted to finish with

60

the subject. She stood up. "I'm going to put some water on for coffee."

"You had a picture of Frank."

She was running the water in the sink and clattering a pan lid. He had to repeat what he had said. "You had a picture of Frank. I remember one time I saw it."

"Do you want some coffee?" She was paying no attention to him.

"I'll take some." He was breathing heavily now, the pain in his neck growing stronger. He could feel the turmoil closing in around him. "You showed me a picture one time. You and Frank." He stood up, his legs against the table.

"That's an old picture," she said in a defensive tone. Finally she went to the door. "I suppose you did see it one time."

Since she had moved so often she knew where she had put things in her sparse rooms. She knew what was in the drawers of the dresser in her bedroom and what was in the shoe boxes on the shelf in the closet. She went down the hall and came back with one of the shoe boxes. The photo was stapled to a creased and fingered certificate from a Louisiana Sunday school. "We both started in to church at the same time. That's how I come to know him." She shuffled through her things and found a snapshot. "You still have Frank's look. I won't dispute that. You had Frank's look when you were growing up. Of course, now you put on that weight you don't look so much like him, but it's still there. I can see it."

She handed him a small, discolored portrait taken in a small-town Depression photo studio. They were in their best clothes, obviously newly married, thin and apprehensive, the hard light of the studio making them look as though they were trying to take a step back out of the glare. Their faces shone as though they were perspiring. Two names had been written in a childish scrawl at the bottom. Ada. Frank. His mother's face was so young, but he could make out the same features in the face of the woman she had grown into. He stared at her picture for a moment; then forced himself to look at the even thinner and more nervous young man sitting beside her. The face was the face of the man in the photograph.

61

He couldn't speak. There was such a rush of blood to his head that he could hear only a roaring in his ears. He couldn't turn his eyes from the face in the photograph. He felt himself groping for the edge of the table, his hand steadying him so he wouldn't fall. With an abrupt movement he turned to walk into the other room. He had left his coat there on the back of the chair. His mother followed him, a hand pressed to her chest, her expression worried. She started to say something, but he had found his coat, and he drew the other picture out of the pocket.

He had at first tried to scratch out the worst of the blood, but the pencil hadn't covered it, and he didn't want to use a pen for fear of destroying the picture. He had finally cut out strips of paper and taped them over the background and over the man's body. Only the face was showing. He'd pulled the strips of paper up so high that the cut in the throat was hidden, but the expression was still twisted and the head was pulled up at an awkward angle. He understood now that he had never forgotten the glimpse he'd had of his father in the old snapshot, and when he'd seen the face again he had remembered it, even if it had been only a vague memory, so uncertain that he couldn't be sure if it were only something he'd remembered from a dream — or something someone else had told him. But he knew he would have to show the picture to his mother, so he had clumsily tried to hide the spectacle of the man's mutilated body.

Wordlessly he held out his awkwardly masked picture. She took it and slowly sat down. After a moment, her fingers moving stiffly and deliberately, she pulled away the strips he had taped on to it to hide the blood from her. She sat staring at it, and finally she said in a low voice, "I never was told what they did to him."

He usually left a bottle of whiskey in the apartment, and he went to find it. Neither of them said anything. Without asking he brought her a glass, but she shook her head. She went on staring at the photo, her breath forced and uneven. She put the photo down and pushed herself up from the table. "I left the water on. I'm going to have a cup of coffee."

He could hear the effort of her breathing as she came back along the hallway. He had poured himself a drink and was sprawled back on the couch, his eyes on the ceiling. His face was stiff and expressionless, his dark skin almost lost in the shadows. Behind him the row of plants his mother had put against the window formed an uneven backdrop to the couch and his outstretched body.

"You never told me anything," he said finally.

His mother stirred her coffee, shrugging. "I didn't know that much to tell, and I didn't think it would do you no good to know about it."

"But I should have known."

She went on shaking her head. "It wouldn't have done you no good to know."

"But Lester then? Did he know about it and he never said anything? Nobody would tell me and they knew all about it?"

"What kind of a man you think Lester was?" Her tone was indignant. "If I told him he'd have told you. I didn't tell him no more than what I told you. Frank was killed. That's all I told him."

"But how he was killed." Frank covered his eyes with his hands. "I couldn't think about anything else from the minute I looked at that picture and I thought it might be him."

"Where'd the picture come from? You get it out of some book?"

He nodded.

"It say anything with it? What it was a picture of or anything?"

"It didn't say anything. It was back on one of the pages when they talked about lynchings. It was a history book I sent away for. Negro history. I wanted to give it to my Lester to help him in school."

"Now you tore the page out of it."

"I can get him something else."

They were silent for a moment. She pushed her coffee cup to one side.

"I didn't want to think about it. I didn't want to have nobody asking me again to tell them how it happened. I couldn't just tell you and then turn around and ask you not to say anything. You couldn't keep something like that in. You'd have to tell somebody to get your feelings out and then it would go all over and everybody would come asking me about it."

"You can't tell me to forget it now."

"No." She looked down at her hands. Without thinking she was twisting a ring around and around on her finger.

"What happened?"

"I already told you. I don't know so much about it. I just know it happeneu."

"But you must know something about it. You know what happened before. You know what happened to you." His voice was at once angry and pleading.

She sighed. "I can tell you what I know." He could hear her pouring a small drink into the bottom of the glass he had brought her. He couldn't bring himself to look at her, and he was staring steadily up at the ceiling. As she began to talk her voice was low and uncomfortable.

"You meet all the boys growing up with you around your own place, and you get tired of seeing the same ones all the time, so when Frank come to the church we all started talking about him and teasing him because he just had moved to a place not so far away. He had people there. Some cousins and an aunt, and times was hard so people always was moving in together. He was dark skinned. You could see it in the picture. He was darker skinned than me, but it didn't make no difference. Inside he was as good as he could be. But if he was tired, or you took him by surprise, he'd get hot with you."

She hesitated, then went on, her voice more assured. "That's not being fair with Frank. He wasn't no worse than anybody else when they get surprised over something. I just heard people say that after it happened. Frank never had trouble with anybody.

"My folks had already left when we got married. They had gone to Little Rock and they had all those other kids, my little brothers and sisters, so I didn't follow after them. I stayed there with my daddy's sister and then when Frank and I got married we had our own little cabin. It was just a little place, down at the end of a road. It was called Ardell, or some name like that, but it was so little it didn't need to have no name at all. There wasn't much way to get out of it unless you walked, and the road wasn't nothing but dirt; so sometimes when we had a lot of rain we couldn't even get to the store. That's where you was born. We had just the two rooms, but we had you sleeping in with us in a little basket and we did all our eating in the other room. It wasn't much different from what the other people had out there. No electricity. Nothing like that. Just lanterns, and I did all the cooking on a wood stove.

"There wasn't no land with the cabin, so Frank couldn't make a crop on his own, but he was working on the big farm just back of us through the woods. You could get there if you went back over the creek and walked a little, or if you come around by the road it was only two or three miles. There was some other families lived down at the end of the road there and the men all was working on the farm. They didn't make much money — Frank just got enough to keep us from going hungry — but times was so bad we didn't care.

"Then one day one of the men come running from the farm. I could hear him shouting out something to his wife and she come running and they both come up on the porch and they called to me. He was all out of breath from running so hard. I can still see him standing there — he was a skinny fellow and he had on those old-fashioned kind of overalls and his wife was behind him with her eyes all wide open. He told me Frank was in some kind of fight over on the farm, Frank and the white man that owned the place, and they were holding Frank and the sheriff was coming out for him and I should go away somewhere because the sheriff might come after me too. The Negro people there, we didn't have much chance against the white people, but we helped each other what we could. The man's wife come in the cabin and she helped me get some things together and she ran back to her cabin and she brought a little suitcase and we put all the clothes we could get inside it, then she took that with her and I got you out of your basket — you were about a year old — and I come along after to their place. The man was all afraid, I could see it in the way he was looking at me, but he said I should stay until he could get some word back to me. Then he said he had to go back. If he was gone too long they might think he was running off and they'd come after him too.

"I stayed in the backroom there until after dark, trying to keep you from crying, and the woman kept going out on the porch waiting for her man to come back and everybody in the little place was crying and calling back and forth to each other. We couldn't do nothing when we had any trouble with the white people. It didn't do any good to go for the sheriff. They'd put the man in to be sheriff and he was as bad as they were. But finally the men come back through the woods. They didn't know what was going to happen to Frank, but they said the white man he'd been fighting with was hurt and the sheriff and a deputy had taken Frank into town. I started carrying on, but the man come in and told me if anything happened they usually come out after the wife and took her too and I should go out in the back with the suitcase and be ready to run if I heard anything. He didn't know if they'd go looking too hard in the dark.

"Negro people didn't have anything in those days — at least not around where we were — and about nine o'clock a light from a car come along the road and everybody thought it must be the white people coming out after me and they shut themselves in their cabins. Some of the women was already out back and there was a piece of a moon so you could see your way into the trees for a little, and that's where they was trying to hide. But the car stopped and I could hear somebody calling out my name. 'Ada. Ada.' And one of the men went out on the porch and he says, 'What you want, calling Ada?' and I heard this voice saying, 'She's my cousin, and she better get in this car if she's still here somewhere. I think somebody's going to come out after her.' And it was all quiet. Nobody said nothing, but I knew his voice, so I called out and said I was there. I could hear him opening the car door and then everybody helped me get you and the little suitcase into the car and the woman in the cabin there, she leaned in the window with a handkerchief tied up with food, and then my cousin slammed the car door and started back up the little road.

"But we didn't see nobody. He just kept driving. He was the only one of us who had a car. He took a job for a year in

Memphis and he saved up his money and he come back with a car, and he was in town buying seed when they brought Frank in. He just stayed long enough to hear what people were saying about what they were going to do, then he went to his own house and put his seed away and hid his shotgun under the back seat of the car and started driving. He was trying to get to where the cabin was without letting anybody at the farm see him. There wasn't but the one road to get out there and if we didn't make it to the highway before somebody started to come after me they'd see the car and stop us. I was crying all the time to go back to Frank and you kept on waking up and crying and he just kept driving. He had already called his sister in Shreveport and they knew I was coming. When I got to his sister's she took me in the kitchen and made me take a drink and she said it was going to be hard but I just had to stay there for a little.

"Then the next day he called people he knew and they told him the white people had killed Frank and they'd come out looking for me but everybody told them I had run off in the woods and after they looked around a little they went away. I was crying and carrying on and I wanted to go to Frank, no matter what they'd done to him, but my cousin sat me down and he let me cry and he told me I had to leave it all behind me. I had to get out and go away from there. I didn't have anything that was worth taking with me. I should just leave everything. Leave whatever was still in the cabin to the people who was there and they'd use it up. And I should leave those white people behind. I didn't need to think about those people again as long as I lived. All I should think about was you and starting over. And there you were, lying in a little bed we'd made in the box for you and you were sleeping and he said if I kept on crying I'd wake you up. So they helped me write a letter to my sister in Cleveland and without telling anybody who I was they put me on the bus and I started over."

She stopped talking. He had turned toward her to listen, sitting on the edge of the couch, his hands folded on his knees, staring down at the floor.

"I never told you this," she said finally.

"No." He shook his head. "You never told me."

He was still sitting on the couch when she went to bed an hour later. He was too spent to ask her any more questions, and he didn't know if there was anything more she had to tell him.

"You not going to think about this any more," she said, coming back into the room with a bathrobe over her nightgown, a net over her hair.

He looked away, not sure how to answer her.

"Frank," she said sharply. "You got to stop. You know about it now."

"No."

"I can't tell you nothing more." Her mouth was pursed and disapproving. She had managed to return her own memories to the place where they had lain for so many years.

"But I still want to know one thing."

"I can't tell you any more. I don't know any more."

He stood up, went to the table and leaned over the photograph he'd taken from the book. With his finger he stabbed at the grinning face of the white teenager who was sitting on the ground in front of the dangling body. He could see that the finger covering the face was shaking and he found he was very tired.

"Him." He pointed again at the face. "I want to know what happened to him."

8

The light in the room was gray and featureless. His mother had pulled the shades before she'd gone to work. He felt something over him. She must have covered him with a blanket. He was stretched out on the couch, his shirt bunched around him like a wadded towel, his shoes and the empty bottle on the floor beside him. He moved stiffly, his head throbbing. The light was so diffuse he couldn't tell what time it was. There was a sound of traffic, but it was distant and muffled. He had drunk too much, too much had happened to him. He started to get up, then he flopped back on the couch again. He had lost any sense of where he was. His chest hurt him when he tried to breathe. He felt like he'd been trying to run, as if he'd run until he was out of breath, and then he'd fallen. Now he didn't know where he was lying. There was only this gray, drab light like a mist over him. How had he fallen? He tried to lift his leg, but its weight pulled him down. He let it fall against the sodden shape of the pillows. He must be lying beside a road. The sounds of the cars were a steady, indifferent monotone, and the noisy voices — was there a park somewhere? — hung without weight or substance around him, like the whistling of birds. It was so distant. He pressed his hands against his stomach, grimaced at his headache's persistence, and fell asleep again.

When he woke a second time the light still was without direction or intensity — little more than an indeterminate shade of gray-white that had spread unevenly across the room. He managed to drag himself to a sitting position and looked around for his coat and a cigaret. At least he'd managed to get back to someplace he knew. He wouldn't have chosen this place, he told himself, then he shook his head with an ironic smile. Did he have any place else? This was the only place he could lie and catch his breath. Not only because it was his mother's apartment — when she came back at the end of the day he'd have to decide what he was going to do next — but because it wasn't his own home. He didn't have to confront himself here, he didn't have to confront the new person he was going to become. Not yet — that other person was waiting for him when he went outside. Here, he still was the ordinary person he had turned himself into, the person he'd become comfortable with. He was sheltered here; he could stay resting against these faded cushions until he was ready to leave again.

He went out to the kitchen and put on some water for coffee. His mother had left their dinner things from the night before scattered on the bare table and piled on the stained draining board beside the sink. She never had done that. She always had to think of the rats and roaches who lived with her, silently roaming through the walls and crevices of these crumbling buildings. Without thinking he put the cups in the sink and found himself washing them, as he had done when he was a child. He handled them slowly and with intent care, feeling the shape of each cup's curve with his fingers. He found a plastic sponge under the sink and wiped off the table. Like a child again he looked around the kitchen, wondering where his mother had left his lunch, but he couldn't find anything. Only the refrigerator and the sink and the bare table. He held out his hands and looked down at them. They were a man's hands, dark and marked with the fine tracings of the years, but when they touched things in his mother's kitchen they became a child's.

There was bread in the refrigerator where his mother always kept it. He found margarine and made himself some toast. She kept the instant coffee in the refrigerator as well, and he found a little milk left in a carton. With the toast in one hand and the coffee cup in the other he walked slowly through the silent rooms. The grayness persisted. The light that made its way in through the windows groped dumbly, without any form or substance. He went from window to window, not looking outside, but staring down at the profusion of plants on each window sill, losing himself in the small thickets of the leaves.

The earthenware flower pots sat on a collection of plates that his mother had found from time to time in her various moves. Some he remembered from his childhood, a few were newer, one or two he had given her himself. The newer ones were plastic, but the others were in flowered china patterns or made of cheap pressed glass tinted in Depression pinks and greens. He remembered her saying that most of the flowered china had come from nights when the local movie theaters were giving away free dishes. She never got a complete set because she never lived close to one theater long enough. Some of the plants had small, wax-like blossoms, but the rest were a welter of variegated fern-shaped leaves and dark, shining stems. She had never said anything about them, but he had always understood that the plants represented his mother's stubborn refusal to accept the drab limitations of her life, as well as a persistent effort to have living things around her. Without thinking he found himself lifting leaves and putting his fingers on the earth inside the crusted pots, to see if any of the plants needed water.

He was still in the apartment when his mother came back from work. She was later than usual, so he knew she must have gotten them some food. He could hear her tired footsteps on the distant stairs, then down the corridor to the door. There was a rattle of locks being turned and the squeak of the door opening. She wouldn't enter the dimly lit little hallway until she had assured herself either that the apartment was empty or that her son was in. "Frank?"

"I didn't go nowhere," he called, consciously using the way of speaking he had learned from her, which school laboriously had taught him not to use.

"Don't you talk that way," she answered as she went through the routine of the door and its locks. Her voice was drawn and tired. "You don't have to. They give you enough practise in school so you wouldn't have to talk the way I do."

He couldn't think of anything to say, and only shrugged when she came into the room with a lumpy paper bag in her arms. She shook her head and put the bag down on the table. "You know what you look like?"

"No. I didn't have a chance to shave."

"I don't mean that. You look like some old flour sack that somebody threw down in a corner. You didn't get up and get out of your clothes."

He shrugged. He was in his shirt sleeves. He'd made an effort to roll up the cuffs, but the shirt showed the effects of his night on the couch. He didn't have a brush with him and his hair was standing up in unruly knots. He had tried to smooth it down, but his head hurt too much for him to turn on the light in the bathroom. He picked up the bag for her while she took off the light sweater she was wearing over her dress.

"You put the things in the kitchen. Anywhere you can find a place. I got us something for supper and I'm going in to cook it up." He went down the dusk-filled hallway to the kitchen, hearing a light metallic rattling of hangers as she hung up her sweater.

"You tired?" she asked sharply, as she cut up the fish she'd bought.

"I don't know what I am. Tired — not tired. I honestly don't know. My head aches."

"You been looking at that picture?" Her tone was uneasy.

"No."

"Just as well. When you've seen it, you've seen it." She rattled abruptly through her pots and pans and put the fish on the stove to fry.

They ate in silence. His mother asked desultory questions.

72

Had he called his office? Did people in Bridgeport know where he was? She rinsed off the dishes when they'd finished, her back to him as she stood at the sink. Outside the walls of the kitchen the apartment house was filled with the sounds of evening. Water was running, radios and television sets were turned on. People in the hallway were talking, children laughed shrilly as they rushed up and down the stairs. His mother seemed to be listening to the sounds, her head back, letting her hands work without looking down at them. Finally she turned to look at him over her shoulder. He had lit another cigaret and was turning the box of matches over and over in his fingers. His shirt looked even more rumpled in the kitchen's glaring light, his face puffy with lack of sleep and the whiskey he'd drunk.

"You thinking about that picture now?" His mother's voice was flat and tired.

He shrugged.

"It won't do you no kind of good to go on about it," she persisted.

He was still too buffeted to answer her immediately. Sometimes when he was with her he could pretend he was a child again, but this time he could feel his years pulling in around him. He ran his hands along the soft band of flesh around his waist, staring down at the faded linoleum at his feet. "You know," he began finally, "When you see something like that it changes you. It's not like you can just put it back on the page that it came from and then forget about it. I can't hold it against you that you didn't tell me. You supposed it was the best thing."

"It was best." Her tone was stubborn.

"I don't know if it was best, or if it wasn't, but I can't pretend I don't know about it. You have to give me that much. I can't pretend what I know or what I don't know. I have to go back now, and I have to start from the beginning with myself. Everybody has a story about himself in his mind. I know you do, the same way I do. If you find out the story isn't what you thought it was then it changes you. Finding out about that picture, you know that's going to make me different from what I was."

"It don't make anything different, you hear, Frank."

"You knew a little about what happened so it isn't different for you. But I didn't have any idea something like that had happened."

She was becoming agitated, shaking her head from side to side and rubbing her hands together. She wiped her fingers on the dish towel and sat heavily in the chair across from him. She folded up the napkin she'd left at her place and sat smoothing it, her hand running back and forth over the small square of folded cloth.

"Frank," she said after an uncomfortable silence, "You know things like that happened in those days. It was all around you. You was supposed to know how to act everyplace and do everything the right way. If you didn't want to be like that you had to leave, and that's what your daddy was fixing to do. But if we had stayed and everything was alright you would have learned all those things the same as we did — the way to talk to white people so they wouldn't get mad with you, how to keep your eyes down, and how to answer back without seeming like you was being smart. Your daddy Frank would have whipped you if you didn't get it right, just like my daddy whipped me, so I wouldn't get in trouble later on. Now you know about what all that means, so don't you go on thinking about that picture."

"I did know all about those things, but I thought it was some long time ago. Now I find out it was something that was right there in my life from the beginning. I have to try to understand what it was, and I have to understand it for myself." He was as stubborn as she was.

"You not listening to me." It was clearly difficult for his mother to try to explain herself, but she couldn't stop. "A Negro person like I am, you don't look back. Oh, I know you look back at your family, you look back at your momma and your daddy and all the things they done for you and all the times you all was happy together by yourselves. You don't look back at those other things, things the white people did, things they made us do — you don't look back at them or else you just stop thinking about anything else. You hear me, now. Someone like me, I won't look back. I take what's

74

around me, and I tell myself you alright and your boy Lester's alright. You do the same way and you won't have no trouble."

Noises from the street had faded. There were fewer children running up and down the stairs. They sat without speaking, momentarily uneasy with each other. He got up to make himself another cup of coffee. She stared ahead of her, her worn, dark hands folding and unfolding the napkin again.

"You not going to do anything about that picture now, are you?"

He sat down at the table again.

"What could I do after all this time? You tell me."

"I don't want to hear about you doing anything foolish."

"I don't do foolish things. I haven't done anything foolish for so long I can't remember when the last time was."

"Then you don't think about it anymore."

"I can't get that boy's face out of my mind. There's my daddy hanging there, with everything they did to him, and there's that boy, grinning." Frank's voice was tired and confused, but there was that stubborn edge to his tone.

"You don't want to get the same as them," his mother began. It was a lecture she had given him so many times. Everyone he had known had grown up hearing the same lecture over and over again. "If we get the same as them then we're no better than they are. You know that. Now, what with everything that's happened, we're the ones those people will have to come to for forgiveness for everything they've done. The time may not come now, and it may not be here on earth, but it's going to come." Her mouth was set in a hard, pursed line again.

"That boy didn't wait for nothing."

"But what good does it do to go on thinking about him?" She stopped, waiting for him to say something. He looked away, thinking of all the arguments they had been through in the past, but also how close he had been to her through all the years. He couldn't answer her. She knew him so well that no matter what he said she would know what he was thinking from the tone of his voice.

After a silence she sighed, her arms crossed across her chest. "I can't think about that. But if I let myself, I suppose I'd be worked up just the same as you are." He understood that she did know what he was thinking. "Frank," she said in a low voice, "I know God punished that boy. I know God did something to him. But if I didn't know that — then I would be like you. Something in me wouldn't let me stop until I found out what happened to him, and I found out what his punishment was for that thing he did to that poor, poor man. You got to believe God knows, and that's what will keep you from feeling just what you feeling now."

II

9

His mother had a fan made out of a piece of cardboard fastened to a stick, and the cardboard had a picture of the grocery store where he went with her sometimes printed on the back, only it was drawn in a funny way and it didn't really look like the grocery store, but the letters across the front were the same. He didn't know what all the letters said, but he could see that the lines went the same way that they did on the window of the store. His mother would sit on the steps fanning herself with little, jerky movements, and sometimes if he sat too close she would accidentally bump him with her elbow and once she did it and he dropped his ball and someone had to go out into the street and pick it up for him. Sometimes it was so hot his skin got all shiny and wet and he couldn't go to sleep up in his room when it got dark. He just sat on his bed and looked out of the window and ran his fingers over his perspiring chest.

Since everybody who lived in the building with them was also from the South they would all sit out on the stoop and talk about how hot it was.

"It's hot," his mother would say to the woman who lived in the apartment across the hall. "When it's hot like this the air gets all so damp and heavy you think you can't breathe. But it's still not so bad as it was down in Louisiana. Some nights there, I tell you, you couldn't keep any kind of clothes on you more than five minutes without getting soaked through. That's how hot it was."

"Mississippi was even worse," a woman would answer in the darkness. "You go down along the Mississippi coast where I come from, round Biloxi there, and that's hot. You don't dare go out on the sand when it's midday or you burn up your feet for sure."

Another woman would join in, keeping herself cool with a fan like his mother's. "It's all different feeling the air up here, but sometimes I get to feeling I'm back working that job I had in the laundry down in South Carolina. It's like you was steaming yourself some of those days, and I gets just as sweaty some nights up here."

Why was he thinking about the heat? He was sitting in an airplane, and the cabin was pulsing with its usual stream of filtered air. It wasn't fresh, but it wasn't hot. He was sitting with his collar open, and he was sweating and uncomfortable as he thought back to his mother and to his own childhood on the Harlem streets. Could he *see* the heat out of the window? Was it the slack haze shredded with the opacity of the sun's glare that made him think he was hot, just as he'd been when he was a boy? The dull gold of the sun scattered off the rivers and lakes below him, and the patches of open earth looked already brown and burnt, despite a thin covering of vegetation. He pulled his tie down and opened his shirt another button, folded up a magazine he found stuffed in a pocket in the seat in front of him, and began to fan himself, as he'd seen his mother do.

The heat was there, hovering over the drab concrete of the airport, as he left his first plane and changed to another in Atlanta. He could feel it forcing its way in through the small gaps between the plane's laboring ventilation system and the more elegant cooling of the air terminal. The airline was

80

obviously determined to deliver him cool, as well as safe, to Louisiana, defying the efforts of the heat to get at him. The air he smelled was heavy and laden with dust — heat was only a part of the difference he could feel. It made him think of handkerchiefs — something he'd given up in Bridgeport, since nobody there mopped their faces in the heat. He'd have to give up his Bridgeport ways and buy himself a handkerchief, something dark blue with an ornate design in thin white stripes and curves, like the men used to wear when he was growing up. Lester, his mother's husband in New York, had a different one for every day of the week. He could remember his mother ironing them, and sometimes it was so hot when she ironed that she had to have a handkerchief tied across her own forehead to catch the perspiration.

He had found the card printed with instructions for dealing with emergencies and he was using it, instead of a magazine, as a fan. He idly watched its movement as it went back and forth slowly in front of his chest. Its slow swaying motion was like the sides of a horse he had seen on his street once when he was a boy. Its ribs had gone in and out as it breathed. Not many horses appeared in his street, but his mother knew about horses and she said, "Looky, what we got here. When I first come here there was horses up and down the street all the time, but not no more. I always had horses around when I was growing up, but now I don't get to see no horses. You can pet it. You just come up to it with me so you won't be scared and you can reach up and touch its sides."

Flanks of a horse close to him. One round side just beyond his fingers, slowly moving in and out, the shape ridged with patterns of ribs beneath the dark brown, smelly skin of horse. But the horse moved away and he couldn't pet it. He was afraid to run after it and his mother said to hurry up, and she lifted him up, but when he put out his hand to touch the horse's side the horse had moved into the middle of the street and the wagon it was pulling was going to push him out of the way if he didn't get back, and his mother said something in a harsh voice to the man who was driving the horse and the man laughed.

Now the horse was walking down another street. It was the

next street over, where the other children from his neighborhood walked to school. Sometimes he only pretended to play and followed them with his eyes when they turned the corner, because some day he would be walking to school and he would go around the corner the way they did. But he would be a big boy about it, and he wouldn't ever cry like he saw some of the boys do when their mommas only walked them as far as the corner and they had to go the rest of the way themselves. He wouldn't ever cry, because he was learning the way to go by watching them so he wouldn't ever be afraid. Was it the same direction the horse was walking?

Should he cross the street by himself? He wasn't allowed to cross the street, but he didn't see anybody else around. The horse wasn't pulling a wagon anymore, and there wasn't a man to make him go. There weren't any cars. The street was all bright with light like it was sometimes in the afternoon after school, but it was empty. Just cars parked along the curb, like they always were, but nobody was in them. He wasn't supposed to cross the street, but since there was nobody here he could do it this once. He took a little step out from between two parked cars and looked in one direction and the street went as far as his eyes could see and there weren't any cars and he looked in the other direction. All he could see was light from the sun. He could feel the skin on his legs prickling because he was afraid to go out in the street, but the horse was standing still and it looked like it knew he was coming to pet it and it was waiting and nothing was moving except its sides going in and out like a fan. It was a summer afternoon and the street was hot and yellow and he felt like he was perspiring, but he was wearing short pants and it was alright and the horse was standing still waiting for him. One foot was lifted a little like he'd seen horses stand in all the books he had beside his bed.

But the horse wouldn't wait for him. When he stepped out from between the cars and reached up to touch its side it moved away. It didn't turn around to look at him or anything, it just began walking down the empty street. He tried to walk with long steps to keep up with it, but the horse kept moving away from him. It seemed like the horse was growing larger as

82

he followed it down the street, and if he tried to reach up and pet its side now he wouldn't be able to stretch that high, and anyway he was still a baby, and when he walked too fast he stumbled and fell down and he didn't want to walk down this street even if it was the street he knew about because the other boys took it when they walked to school in the morning. He wasn't afraid because he'd seen them going along it with their school books.

If he sat down and waited his mother would come. That's what she told him to do when he was lost. His mother would know where he was. He went back between the two cars and sat down, but there wasn't much room and it was hot and he didn't like waiting, but he would sit there until she came. He got tired of sitting, but that was all he could do. If he waited for her where he was it would be alright.

The horse was gone now. He couldn't see its brown horse shape anywhere along the street and he didn't know where it was. Even if he wanted to go after it he didn't know if this was the right street any more. It didn't look like the right street. He didn't know what street it was, but he wasn't afraid because he knew it must be the street the big boys walked along when they went to school. It must be the next street after the one he could see. If he could cross at the corner like they did he would know if this was the right street. Maybe he had found it already.

Something was moving again, but this time it wasn't the heaving sides of the horse. It was a pigeon's wings. A pigeon that came to his window sill when he was waking up in the morning. It was moving its wings just the way it did before it landed. He thought sometime he should ask his mother to give him something to feed the pigeon, but the pigeon always flew away when he made a move to open the window, so he couldn't feed it, but its wings were moving. Then it suddenly flew away and the movements stopped and he woke from his uncomfortable nap in the crowded plane and he saw that he had dropped the card he'd been using as a fan.

In the casual, lusterless late afternoon light he made his way from one plane to another, and began to travel west as well as

83

south. In each plane brightly smiling young women with identical faces and hair styles that they wore over slightly wrinkled uniforms told him their first names over loudspeakers and offered to sell him something to drink. He barely noticed them, thinking of his mother. She had never gone back to Louisiana. She had never spoken of it. He wondered if, sometimes, when he had been playing beside her on their Harlem stoop and she had looked distant, forgetting he was rolling his ball over stones at her feet, she had been thinking of her own childhood there in a place she would never see again. The accents of the southern voices swelled above the suck of the ventilation system. He caught himself staring at the white men and women sitting close to him. He had heard them speak, and he realized they came from small towns like the one his mother remembered, but what did they know about someone like him? He craned his neck to look at the black men and women, sitting as unconcernedly in the stiff plane seats. They must know what he was feeling as the plane traveled further and further south. He tried to make himself think about something else. His emotions were still too close to his skin for him to manage them. He leaned back and turned to the window to watch the flat, dust-colored landscape slip past below him.

A last plane took him as close as it could come to the small town his mother remembered. It was a commuter plane, only a dozen seats, and most of the people on it were as tired as he was. His suit was rumpled and he was perspiring again, and as they drifted over the mat of trees below them the light plane heaved and swayed with the air currents. To add to his other discomforts he could feel himself getting queasy. When they finally landed, two stops after leaving New Orleans, the sun had set, and a purple presence of evening darkness filtered over the flat countryside. He heaved himself to his feet when the plane stopped moving, then as he stepped down the folding steps to the concrete of the runway and looked toward the lights of the modest brick terminal building he felt the heat and at the same moment smelled the raw, coarse odor of the surrounding fields. It was a smell of thick leaves and heavy vegetation in the dank ground and the sweetness of flowers

84

somewhere in the shadows and a drifting scent of the turned-up earth he had seen from the plane's window, newly cultivated for a last spring planting. It was somehow familiar to him, but he shook his head as he walked with the rest of the passengers toward the terminal. How could he recognize the smells of a place he had left when he was too young to remember anything? How could the feel of the heat steaming against his skin be a sensation he already knew?

10

He woke to the emptiness of a motel room. In the half light that filtered around the curtain the room looked like every motel room he had ever stayed in. He sat on the edge of the bed, groping on the bed table for his cigarets. Without looking he knew where to reach for the light switches, where to find the towels. He also knew there wouldn't be enough hangers and that there would be a creased envelope offering him five sheets of motel stationery, with envelopes, in the top drawer of the dresser. He forced himself to get up and shave; then he pulled back the heavy curtain that covered the glass wall opposite his bed. Outside was the usual stretch of grass and the walk leading to the swimming pool. There would be damp motel towels draped over all the poolside chairs and too much chlorine in the water. Occasionally he found it easier when everything was the way he expected it to be. Now he found it irritating. He hadn't come so far to find that everything was what he was used to. He slammed the door behind him and walked to the restaurant, not bothering to look around him at the monotonous rows of rooms on either side of the grass strip.

He hesitated a moment at the door of the restaurant. He still knew so little about the South he wasn't sure he'd be served. Then he saw two black couples sitting over coffee, and when he stepped into the half-empty room he noticed that there was a mixed couple sitting against the wall. As he waited for a waitress he kept thinking of the restaurants his mother had described, the dirty, crowded, rickety food stands that were the only places she could eat when she came into town. It was either there or standing in line at one of the windows at the back of the places where the white people ate, with their humiliating signs, "colored only." Despite the black faces around him he knew she still couldn't be comfortable here.

He sat over a cup of coffee, pushed his cup to one side, trying to decide how to begin. There had been too much emotional confusion and too little time to make coherent plans before he left. He had told his mother that he had to find out what had happened to his father, and she had given in and said it was alright, but only when he said that was all he was going to do. At the same time each of them knew he would be looking for more than that. The structure of his life had given way under him, and he had to find something to build it up again. He had to know who this new person was. He was impelled almost as much by his desperate curiosity as he was by his anger. What was this world he had come from?

Both of them also knew that he couldn't free himself from the faces in the mob, and as he was trying to find some traces of what his life might have been there, he wouldn't stop until he'd found them as well. But where would he go? His mother thought there was a cousin still living in the small city he'd just come to — if he could find the cousin he might find out something. His mother had remembered a few other names. Someone might still be here. The farm where she had been living was outside of a little farm town an hour's drive away. When he had found out what he could here, he would shift his search to the town. It was in the town, in the countryside around it, where he would find the men whose faces had gleamed out at him from the photograph. With an abrupt

87

gesture he dropped some money on the table, pushed his chair back and left.

It took him most of the morning to rent a car and then find a bookstore that could sell him a map of the small towns of the area. He found that everything moved slowly after New York and Bridgeport, but it was so warm that he was moving slowly himself. Sometimes people noticed his accent and stared at him curiously, but he was as curious about them. After a momentary impatience his irritation drained away. Throughout the day he found himself trying to reconcile the stores and the streets with what his mother had told him. Her memories were of a countryside ruined by the Depression, by sharecropping and violence. Instead he found himself in a new small city that looked something like a suburb of Bridgeport. He had been told about the other South so often that he felt he could almost remember it himself. But what he was seeing now — his only experience of the South — was a collection of tract houses and shopping malls squatting on a flat countryside that ended in a vague haze on the horizon. He kept trying to find his way back to that other South, but he didn't know where to begin to look.

He spent the afternoon futilely trying to find the people whose names his mother had remembered. He did manage to locate one of the houses that had a telephone listed for a name he had written down, but the family in it was years younger. The woman who came to the door only looked at him, at his suit, wide-eyed. Most of the people had been living at the address for six months or a year, and they didn't know who might have rented the place before that. He finally took off his jacket and rolled up his sleeves. When he'd started off it had seemed important to look his respectable best, but it was obvious now that it didn't matter what he looked like.

As he worked his way down the handful of names he found that, like everything else his mother remembered, the people themselves had changed. Curious faces looked at him through the screen-doors, but everyone had moved. The new people had all come there from somewhere else. He found himself driving aimlessly, losing himself in the movement of people and cars through the straggle of traffic. He turned because the car in front of him had turned. It was almost as though he were trying to find someone to follow, but he had no idea who the person might be. Slowly he felt his anger returning. The image in the photograph had singed him so deeply that his eyes were fiery. When he stopped for a red light he stared at the faces of the young whites in the cars beside him, looking like the faces of the mob, but the boy whose face still tormented his dreams would be an old man now. He had to keep telling himself that. What he was looking for would be something from the past, and all that he was seeing now was the present.

Sometime in the afternoon, yielding to the heat's relentless presence, he found a store that sold the kind of work handkerchiefs he remembered his stepfather using. At least he could wipe his face. As he came out on the street again he noticed that the store beside him was selling postcards. He picked out two or three to send back and asked the clerk for directions to the post office. The lobby of the post office was so cool that he stood for a moment letting his skin dry, the perspiration evaporate, then he tried to think of something to write to his son. He considered telling him about what he was experiencing, but it seemed like an incongruous message for the back of a color photo of the Mississippi River bridge at Baton Rouge. How could he tell his son about anything that was happening to him now? He finally scratched on the card — feeling impatient with himself for it,

Dear Lester,
    I bet you don't know how hot it is down here. This is where we all come from, but I bet you don't know that either.
                          Your father

He stood for a moment, reading it over, trying to think of something else to say, but he finally shrugged, bought a stamp, and dropped the card in the mail slot.

The next morning he lay for an hour staring up at the ceiling, trying to decide what to do. It seemed futile to go on looking for names his mother remembered from her youth. Too much

89

had changed. He wondered about the small town that was close to the group of cabins where she had lived with his father. It wasn't too far to drive. It would have some kind of motel, and he could begin looking there. Even if he had to take a few days, he would find someone who could tell him something. He drew the curtains back from the window and looked out into a morning already beginning to glow with a yellow ferocity. He put everything back into his suitcase, carried it to the car, paid his bill and started driving.

The countryside outside of the city was flat and variegated — patches of scrub trees, tilled acres of fields already green with new crops of sourgum and sugar cane. A fine haze hung at the horizon like a pale screen. It was the countryside his mother had described, except that the forests didn't seem as dense or as dark as she had remembered. But she had been young then, perhaps they had seemed dense, protecting and shielding from the shrill sunlit rows of the fields. Most of the farm houses were new, and when he did pass a building that looked like the kind of cabin she had described, usually the doors had fallen in, the tar paper was hanging in strips, the roofs were bowed, and there was only a dead stillness on the ramshackle porches.

When he came to the edge of the town he found himself driving slower, looking from one side to the other around him. Had she described that corrugated iron storage building to him — the row of buildings alongside the railroad tracks, the feed store? She must have seen them — he must have seen them when she brought him into the town in her arms. As he bumped over the railroad tracks he glanced down the side of the low embankment and saw a line of cabins. He turned the car onto the dirt ruts of the road that passed the procession of weathered porches, and he could see the old chairs propped up beside the doors, the washtubs and broken children's toys on the bare ground in front of the buildings. He drove slower and slower, but old men were sitting on some of the porches and they stared at the car with obvious uneasiness. The dark faces were drawn and worn, the fringes of hair knotted and gray, and despite the heat a cuff of long underwear was visible under legs of trousers. Their silent attention made him uncomfort-

90

able and he turned back toward the main street. He could feel the car swaying over the holes and troughs of the old road, the wrenching motion reminding him of some of the half-destroyed streets of Harlem.

He stopped at a gas station closer to the center of town to ask about a motel, and as the man told him where to find one — a middle-aged black man in a baggy uniform who moved with a slow fluidity — he was so nonplussed by the man's accent that he had to ask him to repeat what he had said. Again at the desk of the motel and at the restaurant next to the motel where he went for lunch he found himself turning to listen to people around him. He had come to what was a foreign country to him — a country that was as alien as anyplace on the other side of the ocean — but all the people he met spoke to him with his mother's voice.

He found a new motel at the edge of town, an outspread series of stucco buildings separated by oblong patches of coarse grass. His room, facing one of the lawns not far from the pool, smelled faintly of disinfectant, and the television was up on a metal rack screwed to the wall, but everything else about it was the same as the room he'd left. Without thinking he lifted his suitcases onto the shelf that was in the same place, hung some clothes on the rack beside it, and went outside to look around. The motel was next to a shopping center that was marked with elaborate signs and surrounded with the gray wastes of a parking lot, but the stores themselves were unprepossessing, and the asphalt of the parking lot was cracked and lined with tarry repairs that had broken through again. In some places wild vines had grown out of the irregular gaps. It was hot, but he wanted to see more of the town. He went inside, opened his suitcase and found one of his new work handkerchiefs. He put it in his pocket and went back to the car.

As he drove along the main business street he slowed down to look in the doors of the bars, at the window of the automobile supply store and a small drugstore that looked as though it were being pressed down into the ground by the

91

flamboyant orange and green sign that had been built on top of it to advertise soft drinks. The newer buildings were mostly a bland stucco, but older blocks were lined with brick and wood store fronts. The brick buildings had the oldest look, their outlines softened as the sun had bleached the color from the brick.

He parked the car and began walking, sheltering under the balconies of the older buildings to avoid the glare. He had the vague sense that these streets and these buildings should tell him something. He had come to a place that contained some of his past, but all he could see of it were faint suggestions hidden within the ordinariness of the present, like the half-obliterated advertising messages under the weathered paint of a brick wall. He stared in the windows of the jewelry store, stopped at a display of seeds and canned goods in a general store on a corner. He read the signs in the shabby marquee of a run-down movie house. There were no advertisements for movies, but small, amateurishly lettered posters announced it was now being used for concerts by local rock and roll bands. Somehow he had thought that when he came back to the town it would be the way his mother had described it. He expected it to look the way he had imagined it. Now most of it was bare and run down and empty. He didn't even know if there was enough of the older streets left for his mother to recognize them. He wandered slowly from street to street, until the sweat had formed a dark rivulet down the front of his shirt. Finally, he went back to his car, to its closed windows and its stream of cold air conditioning.

He swam for an hour in the motel pool, ate dinner, and tried to look at the local television programs, but he was too restless to stay inside. He wanted to feel the streets and the neighborhoods again. He drove slowly in the darkness, looking at the dark clusters of bushes under the street lights and the dim shapes of the front porches with their sagging screen frames. Dogs barked as he passed and in some of the houses, with the front door left open, he could see the familiar flickering of a television screen. In the shadows the town didn't look much different from the older parts of Bridgeport, but the vegetation had a coarser scent and the leaves had a thicker consistency. But where was the "New South"? What had he come to? He found himself becoming exasperated at the elusiveness of what he was experiencing — it had no shape or form for him. And behind him was the restless impatience of his anger, pushing him to find something as vague as the wavering line of the horizon.

In the center of town, a block from the courthouse square, he found a small restaurant open, its neon sign blurred with the whirring of night insects. Pasted to the stucco wall was a handlettered notice reading "Home Cooking. Hot Boudin. Shrimp and Burgers." Suddenly hungry for something besides the bland meals he was eating in the motel restaurants he pulled in and parked. It was cluttered and greasy inside, a square room with a low counter and behind it a shining dark stove and refrigerator. There were metal tables on the other side of the counter and he sat down at a table close to the wall. Behind the counter was a large, round-faced black woman wearing an apron, with her hair tied up in a red bandana handkerchief. She looked like she could have posed for a cornmeal advertisement in the 1930s, and he found himself sliding back to the past again, half noticing the rest of the room as he stared around at the framed reproductions of river scenes nailed on the walls.

When she came diffidently up to his table and took his order her voice had the same softly molded accent as his mother's. He leaned back in the chair as she returned to the counter. It was clear from the languid casualness of her movements that he was going to be there for a while waiting to get his food. He was letting himself drift, for a moment not thinking about where he was or what he was doing, when he heard a car squeal to a stop, the doors slam, and he saw three figures coming toward the door. When the door opened he saw they were white teenagers. They were in tight tee-shirts and jeans, hair long and slicked back, their faces raw from wind and sunburn. Still in the mood of the past where the atmosphere of the restaurant had taken him, he turned to look anxiously around for a door where he could get out, sliding further down into the chair so they couldn't notice him. He must have come into a white place, and the woman behind the counter had been too afraid to tell him. Three teenage red-necks. It was faces like these he had glimpsed in the photograph. He started to get up, thinking he could get past them to the door, but he was too afraid to move. He sat down again. The three of them had gone to a table in a corner, pulled out chairs all around it so they each had a chair to sit in and a chair for their feet, and were talking loudly, their voices a persistent din that filled the dimly lit room. He slid further down in his chair thinking of a way to get outside.

When they went on talking he decided that they hadn't seen him. Maybe they thought he was white. He kept his head down as he stared balefully across the room at them. They had the kind of noisy, intense presence he had sometimes felt in Harlem, when people just up from the South moved into an apartment in his building. They had the same overpowering physicality. They slapped their hands on the table, they kicked the chairs, they spat on the floor, and they talked continually in their thin, whining voices. He was pushing his chair back from the table to get out of the place when the door suddenly opened again and another teenager came in. He was wearing the same kind of tee-shirt and sagging jeans as the others, a sweat-stained cowboy hat pushed back on his head, but when he crossed under the room's one yellow light Frank saw that he was black.

Frank turned to look for the woman behind the counter, but her back was turned. She hadn't seen anything. He started to slide to the door, his eyes fixed on them, his mouth sour with apprehension. The boys wouldn't bother with him — an out of shape black man waiting for some food to take out — but what would they do about a black boy their own age coming into their place?

As he straightened up, still hoping no one would notice him, he watched the black teenager strut across the room with the same swaggering set to his shoulders. He came to the table where the rest of them were sitting, and with a shrill, squealing sound of metal dragging over the floor he pulled up two chairs, just like they'd done — one to sit on, the other for his feet. He dropped his hat in the middle of the table, and the

four of them began to brag to each other about how they'd run
somebody ragged down the middle of the street with a new
car they were trying out. Feeling himself beginning to breathe
again Frank settled in his chair, staring at their perspiring
faces. He couldn't tell one from another if he didn't know
which one was speaking. His mouth was still open with
surprise. He wasn't in the past, he was in the new South, but it
was a South that somehow was still open to its past. What he
was seeing was familiar, but it was just as suddenly so new to
him that he didn't know how to respond. He still was staring
at them when the woman shuffled out from behind the
counter, put a plate of red beans and rice in front of him and
wearily made her way over to the table where they were
sitting. As he began eating he could hear them calling her by
her first name, and for the first time he heard her laugh.

11

In the morning he began his search as soon as he was up. If only he could find the place where his mother and father had lived together. There could be someone still there. The clerk who was working the motel desk was an anxious white teenager in a wrinkled short-sleeved shirt and a cheap necktie. Making a nervous effort to clear his throat, he tried to be as helpful as he could, but he had never heard of the straggle of cabins that Frank's mother had described. He rubbed his nose and finally nodded in the general direction of the town's business district.

"You all go down to the sporting goods store there alongside the bank. The fellow there hunts all over this part of the country, and he'll know where it is if anybody does."

The streets in town were empty. It was already hot and the few people he saw were in their cars. In the daylight he could see that the trees in the downtown area were smudged and slack. The leaves hung in dusty clusters from drying branches. When he left the car the only shade he could find was under the

96

balconies of the older buildings. He walked uneasily into the dark shadows of the sporting goods store, trying to ignore the rows of guns fastened to the wall. The owner was a short, pudgy man with a red face and an uneven fringe of hair, who was leaning heavily on a counter with one elbow. His hands were folded across his stomach. Frank asked him about the place his mother had called Ardell.

"Wardell, you mean. That's probably the place you all looking for." He didn't move from the counter, but his eyes studied Frank carefully. "It's just a little bit of a place. Don't hardly have a road to it. What you all looking for in Wardell?"

Frank wiped his face with one of the blue handkerchiefs. It was hot where he was standing, despite a fan whirling in a back window. His uneasiness made him as uncomfortable as the heat did. He still didn't know what to expect from the people he encountered in town.

"My mother told me some of my family come from there." He tried to imitate what he remembered of his mother's manner of speaking before she had been so long in Harlem, but he realized his accent wasn't broad enough. He had no memories from his childhood to go back to, and didn't know how to shape his mouth and lips.

"You not from here?"

He started to say that he'd been born in the country around Wardell, but something made him stop. "I'm from New York," he said flatly, lapsing into his usual accent.

The man nodded, his voice more casual. "Nobody 'round here wears a shirt like that," he said amiably. "You looking for somebody special out in Wardell?"

"No."

"People come and go so much out there, I don't think you going to find anybody who knows anything. They's not much to it at all. How'd you come to ask me about it?" His questioning had taken on a more casual tone.

"The fellow at the motel. He said you hunt a lot."

"Out there the first day of the season, standing behind a tree with my gun loaded up right at daybreak. That's how I come to know Wardell. It's in a patch of woods and I can always find me something to take a shot at. Don't know any people from

97

out there. They mostly do farm work, the ones that's working at all. So you want to go out and take a look at it? You understand it isn't so often somebody comes along who wants to look at one of them little old places out in the swamps. I'd take you there myself, but I got to keep the place open. You all got a car?"

Friendly, now that his curiosity was satisfied, the store owner drew him a map on the back of an order pad, his thick fingers working doggedly with the stub of a pencil he found beside the cash register. Concealing his discomfort with the man and the racks of guns behind him, Frank nodded his thanks and backed toward the door. The man lifted his arm in a desultory wave. "If you need any kind of hunting or fishing gear you all come on back and we'll fix you up so you can kill just about anything you can find around here."

Most of the countryside was divided up into large, flat sections of land, the occasional building nestling behind a thin scrim of trees. At the crossroads were feed stores and small groceries and bars, most of them newly painted and festooned with advertising signs. After reading the metal panels nailed to the walls and the railings of the buildings, Frank decided that people in the area mostly needed soft drinks, bread, fertilizer, insecticides and soap. Beside him on the car seat was the map the store owner had given him. The road he was looking for was just past a narrow iron bridge that crossed over a sluggish creek. It was a dirt road, pot-holed and rutted from the farm trucks that used it in the rainy winter months. He drove slowly, looking around him at the emptiness of the fields. He knew now what his mother had meant when she said they had been afraid until they got off this road. His car was obvious for miles, a lumbering, shining blue form swaying across a bare expanse of chopped earth. A baby, he had been with her then on this road, in the back seat of her cousin's car as they fled. He found himself driving more and more slowly, his eyes searching the ruts, the sky, for any sign he had once been there.

Which cabin had they lived in? There were a dozen of them, almost identical, in a coarse thicket of trees and brush. Box-like wooden structures with peaked roofs and sagging porches, unpainted and in poor repair. They were set on both sides of the road, the bare earth around them littered with broken furniture and discarded children's clothing and rotting garbage. Two or three cars were parked between the houses, and behind them he could see the body of an abandoned truck. Most of the porches were screened in against mosquitoes, and on a few of the porches he could see clothes hung out to dry. Faded work pants and cheap shirts. Which one had been his mother's? He was too dismayed by the poverty and the obvious hopelessness and the isolation of the houses to feel any sense of having come "home," but it had been his mother's home, the only place she had ever lived with his father. He pulled off onto a muddy patch beside the road, turned off the ignition and sat without moving, looking around him. Whatever he thought of it, he had been born here. Through the confusion of what he was feeling he still was hungry to know which cabin had been theirs. He got out of the car, realizing at the same time that in the new rented car and in his careful slacks and new shirt he was as out of place as if he'd come from the moon.

He couldn't find out anything from the few people who were at home. The boards on the front porches creaked stiffly as he looked for somebody to talk to. The doors were already half open, since it was obvious everybody had seen him drive up. Which house had he been born in? He was met from behind the sagging screen doors by teenage girls holding babies, looking up at him with nervous eyes. He felt a sudden lurch. Would his mother have looked like this? Had she been a girl just like these in one of these houses? No, they had never heard his father's name. No, they had never heard of anybody called Lewis. He tried to see past them, to look over their shoulders into the dark interiors, seeing only shadowy bedsteads and chairs circling television sets that flickered with a morning program. He backed off, stepping over pans of food left out for the dogs or the children.

  A ragged group of children watched him from one of the porches. Suddenly one of the girls, about ten years old, with a braying laugh, hurried toward him. "What you doin' here?"

99

Her voice was thin and shrill. "What you doin' here? You got any money?" He started to reach into his pocket to find some coins to give her, and the others ran toward him. When he held out his hand a small boy in torn shorts and a filthy shirt seized his arm and tried to force his fingers open. He didn't know what to do. He started to walk away, shaking his hand until the boy let go of him and handed some loose change to the girl who had first approached him. Without a word she snatched the money and sprang off into the bushes, the others shrieking after her. No, he told himself, he couldn't have grown up here, he couldn't have been like these children. But which house had been his — where on this rundown end of dirt road had his mother held him and nursed him?

Behind the cabins was a thickening shadow of trees, and he could see a path going between the straggling bushes. He walked toward it, seeing everything as it must have been that day when the neighbor came back running along that path. Could it have been the cabin there beside it? He turned to look at the unpainted building closest to the path, but a woman had come out on the porch. She was holding a baby and was watching him narrowly. "You all got any business here?" she asked finally, her voice dark with her uneasiness. He started to say something, but he found he didn't want to say anything to her about himself. It would suggest that somehow they could talk to each other, that she would understand what he was saying, but he had left this so far behind him that there wasn't any way they could talk. "Just having a look around," he answered slowly, wiped his face again, and walked back to his car.

For the rest of the day he let the heat keep him inside. He didn't want to absorb any more impressions, he didn't want to force himself further on the path that was opening up in front of him. Stretched out on the unmade bed, his eyes turned toward the wall-length curtain that he'd pulled back to let the sun into the room, he tried to sort out what he felt about the visit to Wardell. He asked himself over and over, who was the man who would have lived in the defeated clutch of shacks that was a community like Wardell?

As he tried to find an answer he felt his confusion growing.

The anger he had felt in Bridgeport, the anger and the frantic need to know who he was now, had brought him to this small town he knew nothing about, and yet was somehow part of him. It was as though the emotions that had driven him here had split into two identities, the self he knew and a new self he felt in the room beside him. This other self was with him as he drove on the streets, when he sat in a restaurant eating, as he stood looking up into a window. It was the person he would have been if he'd stayed, if he'd grown up in this flat, hot land. It was as though he had found a twin, a twin who never was, but still was so close to him, so close that he was sure they would collide if he were to turn too suddenly. He knew that this twin, this other self who could have been, lived within everyone's consciousness, but somehow he had thought he had lost this part of himself within the complex walls of his own personality.

After dinner he tried to watch television in his room, but again he was too restless to stay inside. The ceiling was low and the curtain hung with a slack, limp disinterest that he found more and more depressing. The air conditioner made a low humming noise that added to the sound of the television set's chattering voices, and after an hour the walls seemed to be moving in on him. He changed his shirt and went out to his car. He thought for a moment of asking the clerk at the motel desk if he knew of any place to go, but there wasn't much chance that the night clerk, another awkward white teenager in a badly ironed short-sleeved shirt and neck tie, would know where to find a black bar. He drove into the empty streets and began cruising through the darkened town, looking for a spot of light or a gathering of cars. He found his way to the black section, recognizing it instinctively because the houses were smaller and the streets hadn't been repaired.

Mostly he found grocery stores open — pools of light and barred windows and a half dozen men leaning against the wall close to the door while teenagers swooped in and out of the shadows on bicycles. Finally, at the end of a darkened street, he saw a dimly-lit ramshackle building with a line of new vans parked outside and clusters of young men leaning on the fenders of the cars. Above the lights there was a swirling cloud

101

of insects as if trying to understand what the lights meant to them as they whirled closer, fluttering pale specks against the opaque sky. It was a battered wooden building, not much larger than the houses on either side of it, but he knew what it was. He had grown up with shabby barrooms.

When he stopped the car against the curb he could hear music. A saxophone, a loud clump of drums. Nobody leaning against the cars outside was paying any attention to it, which was just as he remembered from the years when he'd hung out around bars in Harlem. It wasn't cool to listen to the music if you didn't have the means to pay the little extra tab to go inside. Everybody was in good clothes, which was also the way he remembered. Whoever wore shirtsleeves had to have a good shirt, shining and looking like satin, hanging just right. Two or three of the men were in sports jackets, despite the heat, and one of them, important enough to have several others gathered around him, was in a suit, with a white turtle neck jersey under it and a straw cowboy hat on his head.

It wasn't cool for anybody to stop talking, but eyes followed him as he came closer. He was being looked over. He didn't look like anyone else there. He was too old, his clothes were too casual and his hair was all wrong. He shouldn't have let it go gray at the temples, and he noticed that most of the men had their hair straightened. He had stopped these process jobs when he got married. He could see their eyes turning toward him, he could see their watchful expressions, something he had by now almost gotten used to. The rest of the town was a foreign world, but he knew how to walk into a bar in a black neighborhood. He moved slowly and easily, not looking toward anyone, but not looking away, either. If the rules were the same as they'd been when he was their age, nobody would get in his way unless he did something to start trouble. Finally the eyes dropped, the expressions relaxed, the voices stayed steady, and he went up the wooden steps into the low, crammed building.

The noise inside was so shrill it was like a sudden exclamation. After a moment he got used to the dimness and found his way to the bar, wishing he could find someplace to screen himself off from the din. From what he could see, he

102

was at one end of a long, low-ceilinged room with walls made out of rough boards. The dance floor was uneven and scuffed to a dull whiteness and around it was a scattering of worn tables and chairs. Most of the people at the tables were his age, and they left arrays of bottles and glasses behind them when they got up to dance. It was just like the bars where he'd grown up. From the outside the place might look poor and battered, but a night out was a night out and everybody wore their best and talked their best and danced their best, because that was the best there was. The collection of bottles and glasses, the women's satin dresses and the men's suits and ties, were saying just that, even if every now and then there would be squeals from the women when one of the men hunched his shoulders, pulled up one pant leg, and began dancing one of the old country breakdowns.

The noise was coming from the far end of the room, where he could make out a little raised bandstand in the dimness. A band was playing up behind a wooden railing, and the space between them and the tables was filled with loose dancing figures. Women's arms were thrown back over their heads, men circling around them in a sweating crouch. In the corners there were women dancing by themselves, three or four heavy women in bright printed dresses were standing beside their chairs, their shoulders and bosoms heaving with the band's music. When a piece stopped, there was good-natured laughter and shouting. People went back to their tables for a drink, calling over their shoulders to friends, then a new piece started and everyone streamed back to the dance floor. For a minute he tried to shut out the music, but its volume level was like a heavy curtain that had fallen down over everyone in the room.

He'd never heard anything like it. He couldn't remember his mother talking about any different kind of music so it must have come after she had left. It included too many things that wouldn't have been known about in 1937. Only six men were playing, but there were more amplifiers on stage than there were musicians. A saxophone played every chorus, and a short, stocky man with a red electrified accordion labeled "DOPSIE" sang the first two or three choruses of most of the pieces. He must have started off with a suit and tie, but the suit coat had been stripped off and he was wearing a short-sleeved shirt and a vest. He had on his necktie, but it had been pulled to one side to stay out of the way of the accordion. One of the musicians was scraping the handle of a spoon over a kind of ridged metal vest, and he was walking around the dance floor while he was playing. It was the boom of the bass drum that finally drove Frank back to the bar. Its crashing beat rattled the windows along the wooden walls.

"What's that?" he asked the bartender between pieces. He had a drink, and now that he'd gotten a little used to it, the noise didn't seem so bad.

"You mean the music? That's what they call the zydeco."

"Zydeco?"

"That's what they call it."

He didn't intend to do anything more than buy a drink and ask the bartender some questions, but after an hour and two or three drinks he decided to try dancing. He didn't know the steps they were doing, but it didn't look that important to get it right. Anything seemed to go. The first woman he asked, a dark, short woman in a pleated dress who had been left alone at a table near the bar, didn't even wait to see what he was going to do. She went into one of the local steps and left him to follow her as best he could. He had the despairing impression that he'd gotten in the way of an impatient horse, but he'd asked her to dance, so he tried to smile as she circled around him. He stumbled a few times and finally gave up, trying to stay back in a corner so nobody would see him. He went back to the bar, but after two more drinks he decided to try again, this time with a woman who was a little taller. She must have watched him when he'd tried before, and she made an effort to hold herself back, but when the music got louder she finally backed away apologetically and went into a swaying, strutting dance of her own.

The band didn't seem to get tired. When he was close to the bandstand he could see that the accordion player was perspiring so freely that he was leaving wet shoe prints as he walked around the small stage. Frank led the woman to her table and went back to the bar. He leaned back, looking around the room. He would have one more drink, then he'd go back to the motel. He couldn't dance to what they were playing. Then he felt someone take his arm, pulling him through the crowd, and looked up to see a tall, muscular woman with a dark tan shade of skin and loosely waved hair leading him toward the dance floor again.

"You all don't know what you doin' out there."

He followed her through the maze of discarded chairs. "I didn't think anybody was looking."

She turned to him and shook her head. "You don't think every woman in this place isn't looking at you? You the first new nigger that's come in that door in a year."

He'd had enough to drink so that it took a moment before he understood what she'd said. "What'd you call me?"

"Oh Lord," she took his hand, put an arm around his shoulder and began leading him through a twisting version of the local two-step. "That's one of the words we got so used to hearing we just took it over for ourselves. Now I know you don't come from around here."

"No. I don't," he said loudly. His feet were beginning to find their way through some of the jerky steps he was picking up in the pressure of her arms and hands.

"Where you from?" The music was so shrill on the dance floor that she had to lean close to him and speak into his ear for him to hear her.

"New York," he said loudly again.

She shook her head and pushed him into a different step as they made their way across the dance floor. "Don't nobody know how to dance up there?"

"You're the one who asked me," he protested.

"Nobody new ever comes in this place unless it's white boys seeing if they can find a little something. So you're the one — you're Mister New." The band had stopped between numbers, but they hadn't made a move back toward the tables. He stood beside her, wondering what she wanted to do. He couldn't decide if she was beautiful, but there was a strong handsomeness to her face. Her hips were solidly molded, she had a long waist and legs. He was curious about

105

her, but before he could ask her anything the band started into another piece.

He had already noticed that nothing the band played started or ended with any kind of coherence. It was only in the middle, when all the instruments seemed to have agreed on what the rhythm section was doing that the music compelled him to listen. While he was standing beside her on the dance floor trying to work out what the band was doing, another man scuttled up to her and asked her to dance. She didn't look at him. "Get back, trash," she murmured through tight lips and the man backed off; then she took Frank's arm and again the two of them went into a dance that she led him through.

The music had sorted itself out into two different rhythm patterns, and the building seemed to be shaking with the din from the loudspeakers. The piece went on too long and he began to miss steps and tried to catch his breath. She laughed at him, throwing her head back as she slipped from one side of him to the other. "I would have known you all don't come from here. Don't nobody from down here slow down just over two or three little dances. Come on, I'll make a good nigger out of you before I get through."

She turned to go back to her table when the piece finally ended, but as they reached the chairs he heard the band starting to play a blues. This time he took her arm and pulled her back. She looked up at him questioningly, but he only shook his head, put an arm around her and began dancing. When he pulled her toward him she smiled and lifted her head and spoke into his ear. "At least we know now what it is you can do."

They had begun moving easily together, frankly enjoying the rubbings of hips and thighs. After a moment he pulled his head back.

"What's your name, and what do you do around here?"

She reached up and pulled his head down again. "When I'm here at this place I don't do nothing but dance, and right now you all just hold your mouth because I like to get the most I can out of a man doing what he's good at." And as she pressed herself against him he could hear her laughing. At him, at herself, at them both.

106

12

When he woke he was tired and sore, his legs like heavy weights. He lay in the bed in his motel room staring up at the ceiling. What would the people he worked with have said if they had seen him dancing with the girl he'd met at the bar? Most of them only knew him as stolid old Frank, but he used to go out and dance like that. His wife had been one of the girls he'd met when he was out dancing. He hadn't forgotten that part of his life, and a cocktail lounge liquor advertisement with a light inside it still gave him a nostalgic feeling. Now he was so stiff from dancing for an hour to "Dopsie's" zydeco band that he wasn't sure he could walk. The girl had finally given up on him when he tried again to follow the local steps she was doing.

"You all going to have to learn how to do that by yourself," she said to him with a shake of her head, and she left him as abruptly as she had come up to him. His last sight of her was of smooth, strong hips moving in a tight dance with one of the men from the band. They were looking in each other's eyes and she was smiling.

No, he didn't want his room cleaned. The maid, a disheveled black woman with a cigaret drooping from her mouth like an emblem of defeat, knocked at his door every morning, forcing him to wake up. There was such a dogged persistence to her knocking and the air conditioner in the room made such a sibilant humming noise that it did no good to shout across the room at her. He always had to get up, open the door, and tell her to go away. But after her interruption he usually couldn't sleep and he finally made the bed himself and went through the motel until he found her cleaning another room. Around her was her collection of wet rags and a vacuum cleaner and a pale, soundless television set was gesticulating without meaning just beyond her shoulder. He brought her his dirty towels and she gestured toward her cleaning cart outside the door. He shoved the towels into a bag hanging from the end of the cart, took what he wanted from one of the shelves, and left her to her morning fantasies.

As he sat over breakfast — letting the young, white, hurried waitress bring him more coffee — he tried to think of some way to deal with his problem. Someone must know about the people in the photograph, but he still hadn't found out anything. He shook his head impatiently, stubbing out a cigaret. The sheriff or the local police could probably tell him something, but he couldn't make himself go to the sheriff since the sheriff hadn't done anything all those years ago. And even if he did talk to the police and they looked at the picture and he held his finger on the face of the teenage boy, and then went slowly from one grinning face to another — when the police asked, "What you going to do when you find them?" he would have to say, "I don't know."

He could feel his mind beginning to sort through possibilities. He sighed, slapping his palm in an uneven rhythm on the table. If he could find a point to begin, something that would show him the first step leading to the men he was looking for, then he could find the rest of the way himself. His anger was still there within him, directing everything he did, orchestrating his movements, but it was this dogged patience he needed now, like the rub of a blister as he moved through the long, leeched, hot days.

Sometime during the morning he noticed that one of the metal newspaper racks on a corner was selling a local newspaper, the Sun-News. He put some coins in the slot and took one of the copies. Most of the pages were filled with advertisements, but a scattering of local news made up the rest of the columns. He looked at the masthead for a date. If the paper had been in business long enough it might have printed something about what had happened to his father. He turned the pages until he found an address for it.

Early in the afternoon he drove out along the highway to the side road where he'd been told the newspaper had its office. He was expecting to find it in the older section of town — looking something like the offices of small-town southern newspapers he'd seen in the movies. With the image of Hollywood and the Thirties in his mind, he almost drove past the building. He was thinking of high-ceilinged rooms and men wearing green eye shades standing beside a printing press and a wooden railing that kept people away until one of the reporters came up to ask them what they wanted.

What he found instead was a modern one-storey stucco building with a parking lot filled with small modern cars, and he went toward it with some apprehension. Whoever he talked to would want to know why he was looking in the old papers. They would need some information from him so they would know where to begin looking in the files — and he didn't want to say anything to anyone. The office was as disconcerting to him as the outside of the building had been. There were no ink-smudged men with eye shades and columns of copy, no railing, no one looking up from a desk as he came in the door. He entered a bright, large room filled with desks, and along one wall there were tilted drawing boards where girls were pasting up copy. Most of the desks were empty, but three or four of the newspaper's staff had come back to work on articles. Two of them, he saw, were young and black and women.

As he stood undecided at a counter near the door a plump, middle-aged woman in purple slacks and a loose white blouse she hadn't bothered to tuck in got up and asked what he wanted. When he said he wanted to look at the files she asked him only what year, led him to a worn but serviceable microfilm machine against the wall, threaded the reel of film covering the spring of 1937 into the sprockets, smiled, told him to take his time, there wasn't any rush, and went back to her desk and a friend she was talking with.

He sat for a moment looking around him. It was so little like he had anticipated. He found himself staring at one of the black girls working at a typewriter. It was a new word processor that projected what she was writing up on a screen. She typed a few lines, pursed her lips and read over what she'd written. Dissatisfied, she went back to the point where she had begun and started again. Beside her two other people were working, and they were as absorbed as she was. If he had told her what he was doing, would she have understood him? What would she say if he asked her if she'd ever seen one of those places like Wardell? Could she have grown up in one of them herself? Self-conscious that he was staring at her, he turned back to the machine, flicked on the light, and began reeling through the pages.

There — in the pages of the newspaper — was the South his mother had told him about. At first he was as much interested in the novelty of the spring of 1937 in a small southern town as in anything else. Ford cars were advertised for $529, rice cost 23¢ for five pounds, for $6.95 he could buy a summer gabardine suit. He spent a moment reading about the marriage of the Duke and Duchess of Windsor. On one page he found a headline,

Clouded Skies Mark
Funeral Of Jean Harlow

All of this had been happening as he lay in a crude bed in a cabin in Wardell. Could his father have seen this copy of the paper himself?

The first cotton flower of the new growing season was reported at a farm outside of town.

". . . a flower from the Boudreaux plantation was reported on Friday and on Monday the plant carrying the flower was brought to the Sun-News office."

110

It was only a local paper, with a few pages of news and as many filled with advertising, but there wasn't much local news. The columns were filled with syndicated material from the news services and gossip from New York and Hollywood. He read through some of the paragraphs, finding it difficult to believe that anyone in a small town in Louisiana had any interest in what had happened at a small dance given in honor of the year's debutantes at the Biltmore Hotel.

Weddings Now More Luxurious
Real Lace Returns For Gowns

Beside the headline for the change in wedding gowns there was a photo of a girl in bed with a caption, "Mother of Twins at 14."

From the front pages he began to have some awareness of tumult and uncertainty. He had forgotten that this had been a period of violent labor conflict. In nearly every issue there were pictures of strikers being beaten by police or company guards. The newspaper was always on the side of the police. The threat to the police was the threat of anarchy and bolshevism. He wondered if people out in the shacks at Wardell had known it was going on. But they knew the names of the cities in the pictures — Chicago, Detroit, Cleveland, Pittsburgh — all of them knew people who had left the farms for cities like these before the strikes had begun. They must have known something about it, felt the stirrings even in their dusty rows of cabins. Could the outburst of violence that had overtaken his father been part of this turmoil — this wave of fear and confusion he could sense in the shrill editorials and the slanted news stories?

He sat reeling through the pages of the old issues as the room slowly filled up behind him, more of the staff drifting back with notes and loose pages of material to work from. But he hardly glanced at them. He was becoming so disturbed at what he saw now that he wasn't conscious of the faces around him. He had suddenly realized that to the newspaper, half of the people in the town didn't exist. There were no black faces in the pictures of local events. There were no blacks mentioned in the news stories. It was as though the only

111

people living in the town and surrounding countryside were white. His mother had tried to explain things like this when he was a child, but he had forgotten — or he never had understood what she was saying. Seeing it here in front of him was like opening an old sore. He found himself reading social notices like,

"Miss Ira Durso was hostess this week to members of the Monday Night Bridge Club at her home on Raleigh Street. Pink and blue hydrangeas formed the floral decoration. Mrs.R.Snell, having a high score was awarded first prize; Mrs. Earl Monroe, Second; Mrs. O. Durso, Third, and Mrs. H. Sproul cut consolation. Miss Durso served her guests a salad course and iced drinks."

And as he read he couldn't stop thinking that these women's husbands would have known that the mob was gathering — some of them could have been part of it — and the next morning the women of the Monday Night Bridge Club would know about it as well.

He finally found a black face, but it was in an advertisement, a drawing of an old, gray bearded farmer asking "Please, suh" for a sack of flour the drawing was advertising. And finally a small story. A "negro boy" was described leaping onto a runaway wagon in the town square the day before. He had jumped onto the wagon, then scrambled forward and caught the bits of the two horses on the team.

". . . Tugging mightily with both arms, his feet dangled in mid-air as he thus traveled for fully three blocks. To have slipped was death or maiming and only the thin leather harness kept him free of the flying hooves. Many a throat was dry as the unique entourage flew through the business section; many a heart went out to the unnamed youth as a wordless prayer for his life left the owner's lips and, as the thoroughly frightened young negro brought the team to a snorting, frothing halt, an almost audible murmur of relief rose from the crowd."

As he went through more issues, more pages, he did find occasional mentions of "negroes," but only when they were

112

involved in crimes. A woman had been slashed and the sheriff had picked up both the woman and her assailant, but the paper hadn't even bothered to get the name of the victim correctly. "Mable or Myrtle suffered a slashed leg, the wound having resulted from a razor having passed over the injured member." "Negroes" broke into stores or were involved in fights or were seen close to buildings that later caught fire. Otherwise, to the Sun-News, they were invisible.

He began winding the microfilm in the viewing screen back and forth, sharply twisting the lever in his disappointment. He couldn't find out anything about his father — nothing about the police or the sheriff. His mother had told him the date she thought his father had been killed — but there was nothing. A lynch law was being argued in Congress. There were small mentions of it in the back pages. He caught the word lynching again as he looked through the earlier months of the year, thinking his mother could have been mistaken, but this was in Mississippi. On April 14 a mob took two blacks from a jail and beat and hanged them. Somehow the story had gotten to the newspaper, but only in the form of an assurance from the governor of Mississippi that there would be an investigation. Of his father's killing there was nothing. People like his father had never been part of the newspaper's small world — so nothing could have happened to him. Frank sat with his head bowed, his eyes closed. He couldn't bring himself to look any further. He wound the reel off savagely, pushed his way past the counter and hurried to get to the door and to his car.

He had found nothing. He was precisely where he had begun, with nothing but his anger. As he drove away into the dull yellow mid-afternoon sunlight he began hitting the side of his hand against the steering wheel. He would find the people. He was beginning to know them a little now. He'd gotten that much from the newspaper files. His face set in an angry expression he looked along the road for a bar. He needed something to drink, even if it was only a bottle of beer. A run-down building with plywood strips nailed to the sides advertised four different brands of beer and he could see cars

113

parked on the dirt strip in front of it. He pulled off the road, slammed the car door, and went into the bar. He was so involved in what he had seen in the newspaper that he wasn't thinking of what he was doing.

It was dark inside, and he hesitated at the door, waiting for his eyes to adjust. Then, as he stared around him, he realized that it had become quiet in the room. Three or four men at the bar had turned and were looking at him. At one of the tables a couple had stopped drinking and were slowly putting down their glasses. There was a man standing behind the bar, and he was running a wet towel through his hands. Like everyone else in the place he was white.

"You all lookin' for something?" he asked finally in a flat voice that had no intonation, that spoke the phrase in one breath. Frank stopped, his confusion changing to a sudden fear. It was here, the same thing he had seen in those strange pages, a world that was white, that excluded him — and he was expected to know it and accept it. He couldn't do anything — not in this shabby place — not now — and he backed toward the door. "No, nothing at all," he said, and he could hear the tremor in his voice. "No." And he was out again in the wan sunlight, his anger sweeping over him like a flood.

13

"You all lookin' for something?" The question again. It was following him, waiting for him when he opened a door. He had taken a few steps into the room and was hesitating until his eyes got used to the dimness. But this time he was tired and hot, and he felt his stiffness returning. As he settled heavily on a bar stool his flabby weight hung on him like a thick shirt.

"Just a bottle of beer." His response was relaxed. The question this time had been casual and unconcerned. He was back in the bar where he'd been the night before. The man rummaging in the cooler for a beer was black, and he was only trying to be friendly. Frank, in defiance of the heat, drank half the bottle in one gulp and put it down gently in front of him. A juke box was playing in the corner, but there were so few customers it seemed to be singing to itself, the same tune repeating over and over again in a humming monotone that rattled the glass ornaments covering its sides.

The bartender stood against the back of the bar, his foot propped up on a case. He was looking toward the door, his arms folded across his chest. He was a dark, strongly built man, his hair graying a little, but his face was young and optimistic. Frank felt some of his anger draining from him. He held up a finger to catch the bartender's attention.

"One thing. I'm looking for somebody in town, but first you can tell me a little something about a girl I was dancing with in here last night."

The bartender studied his face and began to laugh. "I thought I knew your face. You the New York fellow that tried to give everybody a dancing lesson. I thought you were going to run that band ragged. How you all feel this afternoon?"

"A little bit stiff. I could have used a lesson or two before I walked out on that floor."

"That's the jitterbuggin' they do to that kind of music here. You grow up around here and you know how to do that before you know how to walk."

"That girl who was trying to teach me?" His tone was questioning.

"You not the only one who comes in and asks about her. You want another beer?"

Frank nodded. The bartender came back with a wet bottle he'd fished out of the metal cooler at the end of the bar, set it down in front of Frank and settled back against his shelf again.

"You can tell me a little more than that," Frank said, mildly protesting. He was beginning to come back to himself. The juke box had finally fallen silent, as tired as everyone else in the room of its simple repetitions. It was a late afternoon stillness, before jobs ended and people started coming home. Through the thin slit of a window built over the door he could see the sunlight beginning to turn a deep gold. It was as though the room were drifting through a warm, placid sea: aimlessly, idly.

"You want to know about her, you come back. I can't go 'round telling stories about people here. Next thing somebody'll be asking me about you."

"She come in every night?" Frank persisted.

"I don't say every night, but you come back tonight you liable to catch her. We don't have a band so she comes in later."

116

"What's her name?"

"Her name's Doris. Doris Clark. The truth is, I don't know that much about her myself. Like I said, you just one of the fellows who's asking."

Frank nodded. "That other question. I came down here to try to find somebody who could tell me about a man named Frank Lewis."

The man looked at him questioningly. Someone at the end of the bar called out for a beer and he went off to get it, drying his hands on a bar towel when he came back to Frank. "That fellow come in here?" he asked.

"He's been dead since 1937," Frank explained.

"I moved here just a few years ago, so I don't know so many people going back very far. You all said the name was Lewis?"

"Yes." Frank found that even with someone as unconcerned as a bartender he was too emotionally involved to talk easily. "Frank Lewis."

"I can ask around. You never know who comes in. But you all try tonight if you want to talk to Doris."

The door opened three or four times to a stream of late afternoon light, bringing in new customers. The bartender went off to serve them. Frank stood up and stretched his stiff legs. At least he knew where to begin now. It was in places like this, where people knew each other, that he'd finally find something. He went out to the parking lot to get his car, and as he walked across the worn, bare patch of earth the heat was so strong he had the feeling that someone was walking beside him, and when he unlocked the car door it was like a presence waiting to slide onto the seat beside him.

She wasn't there. He stood looking up and down the bar. It was late. He'd fallen asleep after he'd eaten and two hours had gone by. But he didn't want to go back to the motel room. He wouldn't find out anything sitting there by himself. The room was half empty — only a few couples and a line of young men along the bar. He asked for a drink. Some people drifted away, and he found an empty stool and had another drink. He was going to leave when a man took the seat beside him. He was in jeans and a work shirt, his sleeves rolled up. His face was round and shining, his skin as dark as the bartender's, his expression cheerfully friendly.

"You the fellow from out of town?"

"How do you know?"

"Small place like this everybody know everybody else. I drive a truck — hauling freight — but it's all just in Louisiana. I never been them places like New York or Chicago, but it don't worry me. You ought to look around a little while you all here. We got some pretty country out there if you know the places to look."

Frank didn't feel like talking, but the man seemed friendly. He offered to buy him a drink but the man held up a newly opened bottle of beer.

"You looking for someone. The fellow that works behind the bar was asking some of the people that come in earlier."

"That's right."

"I don't know all the people around here, but there's a man older than me lives out in the country close to my place. Just a little cabin he got out there, but he got a pension so he doin' alright."

The man was speaking with a lilting accent that Frank realized was French. His broad face showed no sign that he was foreign but he had obviously grown up among French-speaking people. Frank's mother had talked about French people around her — he hadn't understood that some of them were black.

"Now that old man, he know everybody. Even the people who moved away. We got a lot of those."

"What's his name?" Frank's question was casual. He was looking around at the handful of couples still leaning against each other, occasionally laughing with easy, loud pleasure. The bartender was standing at the end of the bar picking his teeth with a matchstick, waiting idly for somebody to order something. The music from the jukebox was almost as loud as the band had been the night before.

"His name's Jessie, Jessie Lewis."

Frank straightened up, trying to hear over the noise. "What'd you say?"

"Jessie Lewis."

Frank stared at him. The man's open, shining face darkened with a troubled expression. "You heard people talk about Jessie?"

"No. No, that's not it. It's his name." Frank tried to keep his voice calm and make himself heard over the music. "Did he ever say anything about something happening to anybody in his family?"

"He never did say nothing to me about anything like that. He don't gossip the way some people do. But he had that brother that was hung up by the white people. I know that for a fact, but he don't never say nothing about it."

Frank held his breath. He knew that he had come to the beginning of what he'd been searching for, that one end of the tangled skein was there now in his hands.

"What was his brother's name?" It was difficult for him to form the words.

The other man looked thoughtful, his forehead creased with his effort to remember. "I don't remember nobody saying his name. He wasn't from round here."

Frank waited, stretching his legs to hide his impatience. "What's your name?" he asked the other man finally.

"I'm Doucet. Morris Doucet." They shook hands, and Frank began searching through his pockets. In his effort to seem unaffected he took a moment finding a pencil in his pants and a piece of paper in his shirt pocket. "Could you draw me some kind of map to get me out to the place where this Jessie Lewis lives?" He put the pencil and paper on the bar and without hesitation the other man drew a rough sketch of the back roads leading to the man's cabin.

"You some kind of family to him?" Morris asked with his easy friendliness.

"I'm looking for somebody with the name Lewis," Frank said slowly. He wasn't letting himself anticipate anything. "It might be he's some kind of relation to me, but I'll have to go out and talk to him to find out."

"Jessie don't talk much, but if you some kin to him I know he'll talk to you all you want. It's hard to get him started, but once he gets on to something he don't want to stop."

Frank motioned toward the bartender, pointing to Morris's

119

almost empty bottle. Morris shook his head, smiling broadly. "I got to take a truck out first thing in the morning. If I drink another beer I'll still be feeling it when I go to work, and that's no good."

He slid off the stool and took a step back. "Don't mean to be unfriendly, but I got to get some sleep. You go out and see Jessie Lewis. He got his pension so he don't go nowhere. You go out there and you'll find him. Now, I'll catch you in here again." He held out his hand. "You take care, you hear." Before Frank could say anything he had turned and was half-way across the dance floor. The noise in the room drowned his steps.

For a moment Frank stood without moving, watching his short, stocky figure go through the door, then he picked up the sketch and tried to follow its uneven lines. It was so little, but he had someplace to go now, someplace to begin.

14

The man standing inside the unpainted screen door was a few inches taller than Frank. His body was lean and wiry, his skin a dry, strong shade of brown. When he pushed the door open his movements were abrupt and decided. He obviously had been hard used in his life, but he looked still as solid as the stones protruding from the dirt in front of his porch. He was wearing washed-out bib overalls and a clean white tee-shirt. His thin arms were ridged with muscle and his body looked as taut as it must have looked when he was thirty years younger. He had a way of looking at someone as he spoke to them, his eyes on their face as if he were studying them; then, when he said something, he took a step or two away and turned to look again, as if he wanted to watch the effect of what he had said from a distance.

He was waiting for Frank inside a kitchen that was as spare as his shoulders and looked as if it had been washed as persistently as his overalls. The shack itself was a thin shell built out of strips of boards raised up on cement blocks. It was covered with a tan, brick patterned building paper which had begun to tear away from the corners of the walls. From the outside the small structure had a distinct lean to one side and the sagging boards of the porch were matched by the sag of the roof, but inside the door, the space seemed to take on an air of permanence, of solidity, which Frank realized was only an extension of the old man's physical presence. His hair was gray, but it was cut short and there was only a faint tracing of lines on his forehead and around his eyes. He still had the look and the sudden movements of a young man. "Spry," Frank decided. In his mother's time he would have been called spry.

"Jesus," he said abruptly when Frank stepped into the shadowy room. "It's getting hot already and it don't get no better 'round here 'til the summer's through. You all picked yourself a bad time to come looking around down here. It always stays a little bit warm, but the worst time's coming up now. I been waiting for you. How long you going to be around?"

He took a step away as Frank said tentatively that he didn't know. He came back and held out his hand and his grip was as spare and wiry as his arms and shoulders.

"My name's Lewis," Frank said suddenly, "Frank Lewis."

The old man studied his face. "I'm Jessie Lewis. We both got the same last name, but it don't look like you come from around here. I never saw a shirt like that nowhere in town. I got some coffee on." He hurried to a stove back against a bare wall, pulling a pot away from a low butane flame that was fed by a gleaming aluminum tank Frank could see outside the window.

"How'd you know I was going to come out here?" Frank asked as the other man took his two or three steps in another direction.

"That boy you talked to in the club there, that boy who drives the truck, he come out this morning before he started working and let me know you'd be coming out sometime today." His voice was deep and hard, but the years had honed away its rougher edges until it was a supple as the floor boards of his cabin.

122

"But he must have gotten out on the road at six in the morning to come by your place first." Frank was surprised. The man put two cups down on a table worn thin with repeated scrubbings. Frank had eaten at the motel, but he pulled out an unsteady wooden chair and sat down. Jessie Lewis sat down across from him, pausing a moment and looking at his face again.

"Morris is a good boy. We done been friends a long time. Ever since he was a little boy and his daddy used to bring him by on his way back from town on Saturdays. Now he got kids of his own and he has to be on the road with that truck of his all the time to keep them eating. You got any kids?"

"I . . ." Frank couldn't decide whether he should say 'have' or 'got.' It didn't seem to be wise for him to pretend to be anything he wasn't with this man who was intently watching him from across the table. "I have a son," he said after a pause, "but he's off with his mother, and since we got divorced I don't see him all that much."

"Most of mine live close," Jessie said. "I got a grandson staying with me for a little. He's been working, but there isn't much doing 'round here, so he's staying with me while he tries to find him something. He's out 'round somewhere. We all do things for each other 'round here. Morris didn't think nothing about coming out even if it was so early. What people are saying in town is that some of your people come from this part of the country. You wouldn't know it from the way you talk and the kind of clothes you got on. You rent that car?"

Frank nodded, conscious that the other man was staring at his face again. Jessie abruptly stood up and went over to the stove. He picked up the coffee pot and shook it to see if it had water in it. It was the first sign he had given that he was nervous about their meeting. Frank could see past him to the dry, plowed ridges of the field beside the house as a handful of birds flung themselves down on the uncovered earth — dark, iridescent shapes that as suddenly hurried off in a light breath of wind.

"You say you all come from this part of the country?" the old man repeated as he sat down at the table again.

"I was a year old when my mother had to take me away

123

from here. She was living in those cabins in Wardell with my father Frank.''

"Frank Lewis?" Jessie's tone was carefully without expression.

"That's right."

"What was your mother's name? It's all been so long since I knowed anybody living over in Wardell that I forget people's names."

"She's called Ada."

The old man was silent, looking down into his cup. Frank realized that the simple questions he was asking were the only way he knew to find out if Frank was who he thought he was.

"What's happened to Ada now, she still living?"

"I saw her a week ago. She's living in Harlem, just where she's been all these years."

"Didn't she marry another man?"

"Lester May. He had a job in the war so he could take care of her and me." Frank could hear his own accent taking on the round mellowings of his mother's way of talking. Jessie had stood up again and was asking him questions from different parts of the small kitchen, pretending to look for something in the cupboard, but turning as he spoke to watch Frank's face.

"When did she and Lester get married?"

"It wasn't until the war started. I was still just little. Maybe 1942."

"What about Ada's family? They move up there with her?"

"Her family was mostly all up in Little Rock. She didn't get down to see them until just before her daddy died. She got a letter and she went down. I was in high school, so that would be about 1951. She had a cousin who helped her get out of here. She kept close touch with him and his wife — that was the only one from down here she got letters from. Maybe he got word to the people out here about what she was doing."

"What was that cousin's name?" Jessie was leaning over the back of the chair across the table.

"Willie Thomas. It seems like everybody who was part of her family down here has a different name."

They stared at each other until the old man finally slid down into the creaking, wooden chair. Awkwardly he reached across and put his hand on Frank's arm.

"You Frank's boy. I could see something in your face when you come in the door, even if you got a little weight on you and you got that little mustache, but, Jesus, it's been so long and I don't know who might get something in his mind to come and bother me with. Even with all that new way you got of talking I can hear something there from the way Ada talked. I used to hold you sometimes when I didn't even know which end of a baby to hold onto, and here you are, back again. That makes me your uncle. It takes a little getting used to, having Frank back, even if it's Frank's boy. You going to have to give me a minute to get myself together." They sat at the table without speaking, each of them hoping he was concealing his emotions from the other.

"What you come back here for after all this time?" Jessie finally broke the silence.

"I never knew what happened to my daddy."

"What did Ada say?"

"She just said he was killed by white people."

"When she tell you that?"

"It was only when I saw her last. I had to get it out of her. She never wanted to tell me."

"You never talk about nothing like that." His uncle stood up stiffly and went back to his stove to rattle the coffee pot again. "Nobody wants to get mixed up in things like that. Nobody ever knows nothing. You just hear stories and most of the time that ain't no better than making it up yourself. Everybody wants to tell you something and they get themselves all puffed up like a rooster trying to scare a dog, but they don't have nothing to tell."

"I know what happened to him at the end."

"Nobody ever knows nothing for real. You just hear things," Jessie insisted petulantly.

"I know what happened."

The older man stopped, noticing the change in Frank's tone. With fingers suddenly clumsy, Frank fumbled in his shirt pocket and brought out the picture he'd torn from the book.

125

The bits of paper that had covered the worst of it were torn away and it had been folded and refolded so it would go into his pocket. He dropped it on the table.

"I know what happened," he repeated, his voice leaden now.

Jessie awkwardly bent over the photo. A shadow seemed to have come into the room. "Jesus, Jesus, Jesus, oh Jesus." He pushed the piece of paper back. "What's this got to do with you?" he asked after a silence.

"That's my daddy, isn't it? Isn't that your brother Frank?"

Jessie looked down at the photo again, holding himself tensely at a distance from it. "That's Frank."

"Then you know what I'm doing here. I'm going to find out more."

"You see your mother's cousin, Willie Thomas?"

"I don't know where he is."

"He was up in Shreveport for a while, then he moved to Houston. He got a house in Houston. You tell your mama she can write a letter to Willie, and she can ask him whatever you want to know."

Frank let the moments pass. Jessie moved from one side of the room to another, pretending to look for something on the shelves and counters. His arms and hands moved in quick, practised gestures, but Frank was certain he was only trying to hide from his own confusions. When he'd exhausted the possibilities of each corner of the room he came back to the table and leaned over the photo again.

"Did you know about it?" Frank asked in a low voice.

"I heard something about it, but there wasn't a nigger that come closer than five miles of where they were at, you know that. The white people buried him, like they do, so nobody could see what had went on. They didn't really bury him, they just threw him in a hole. My other brother and me, Virgil, we went out and dug around looking for him, but somebody seen us and we had to get out."

"So my daddy never even got buried."

"We wasn't going to ask for them to do the same thing to us," Jessie answered defensively.

126

"Can you make some new coffee?" Frank asked after a moment.

Frank found himself talking as his uncle moved around, pumping water from a small sink pump beside the stove and washing the old grounds out of the pot.

"I never thought there was anything like this in my life back there. I didn't ever think about my daddy or where my mother came from. I just had my mother and Lester and I was growing up in Harlem and that took care of anything I needed to know. Then I just saw this picture in a book, that's all. Don't ask me how I knew what it was, but I knew."

He realized how out of place he looked, with his neat slacks and his pressed shirt with the button-down collar so unfamiliar to his uncle, even his soft, complacent body so different from his uncle's, with its hard wiriness. Jessie had turned from the stove to look at him; then he came back to the table.

"There's some of Frank in you, that's for sure. I don't know where you got it, but it's there. You must have got it from Ada. You were just a baby when they did that to Frank."

"When they lynched him."

"If you all grow up around here you never use that word. But that's what they did."

"You can't say it?"

"Oh, I can say it. I'm not so beat down that I can't cry out a little bit. Them sons of bitches lynched him."

"Now that I know about it, I don't think I'm going to be the same man I was before." Frank stared out of the window again. "I don't know what's going to happen next."

Jessie spread his hands out on the table. "You got a job up there?"

"I work in an office." Frank's tone was diffident.

"Ada got you some schooling?"

"She made sure I didn't stay home."

"You go to college?" The older man was speaking quietly, but Frank could hear a tone of envy in his voice, envy and resentment he tried to stifle.

127

"Yes."

"Me and Frank never had no schooling. Virgil got a little, but like us he had to go out and chop cotton. Ada had a year more. Ada even could read."

Neither of them said anything. Frank became conscious of a fly whining against the screen door, of the clear, softened whistling of the birds. He wondered what they were called. He looked away, uncomfortable at Jessie's description of the differences between them. The old man in his way was a victim, as his father had been, but for Jessie the wounds didn't show on his body. Frank abruptly began talking again.

"The way I got the picture — I bought a book to send to my boy, the son Lester I told you about. I wanted him to know things I never knew about, so I got him a history of . . ." he hesitated, not sure what term he wanted to use, then he decided on the old magazine phrase of the fifties, ". . . a history of our race. So I looked through it. I wasn't looking for anything in particular, I was just looking. And I came to this page. At first I just saw the blood. You know how you do, you feel yourself getting upset and you look again — and that's when I saw the face. It all came back. My mother has a picture of the two of them just after they got married. I must have seen it when I was still little and it stayed in my mind."

"Ada and Frank together?" Jessie interrupted.

"That's right."

"You didn't bring that one?"

"No, that was my mother's. She kept it all these years."

"She can get a copy made. They do it in the store downtown."

"You want one?"

Jessie was defensive. "I'd like to see Frank without his throat hanging open."

"When I go back I can get it to you."

"I guess you going to go back, now that you know where we all come from, but you don't want to go too soon. You got a lot of cousins around here and you ought to see as many as you can."

"I can't go back until I know something more about what happened." Frank straightened up in the creaking chair. "I

128

don't know what I'm going to do, but I have to do something about what's in that picture."

"Now I know you not from here." Jessie's voice was loud and firm, and he got up to go to the stove. The water was boiling and he started to make more coffee. "You wouldn't think like that if you had come up the same way I did. It's better now, I don't dispute it, but you still don't go around talking about that you going to do this or you going to do that."

"I'm not talking about going to the sheriff."

Jessie shrugged. "We colored put the last sheriff in; so he'd listen to you, but I still don't know what he's going to do about it."

"I don't know what I'm going to do about it."

"If you're like me you don't do a damn thing." Jessie threw himself fiercely into the chair, "But you all don't know nothing. What do you think? Because we could go walking along the roads or we could get a lift into town and get drunk that we could do what we want? You never knowed what it was like to have half the people in town watching you, making sure you never did anything they didn't like. After a while you get so you don't know what you doing yourself. You begin to have doubts. They always saying you just shiftless and no good and when you work and work and you don't get nowhere you begin to wonder in the back of your mind if they're right. You see all them goddamn honkies, the kids you grew up thinking was just little and mean, you see them coming up and getting so far ahead of you you begin to ask yourself if there isn't something the matter. But you don't do nothing except think about it. It's like you fell into some kind of trap, and all the time you got this trap hanging 'round your leg and you can't get it off, and they got you so messed up in your thinking that it got to be something wrong with you and all that's the matter is what they hung on you."

His outburst had upset the old man and he began moving around the kitchen again. "I got to have a cigaret."

Frank held out his pack. Jessie took one, his hand trembling, and lit it with a rough gesture, the flame flaring up in front of his face.

129

"I know about that," Frank countered. "I know about all of it just like you do. In high school I even had a course about being a Negro and we wrote about how we should be proud of it because of things like that, because we overcame it. Yes, I know. So I found this picture in a book, and I have to do something."

"But you all ain't going to do nothing."

"Jessie," Frank tried to speak quietly. "I don't know what I'm going to do, but once I saw this I had to do something — once I saw this I wasn't the same Frank Lewis. You understand that? My mother grew up at the same time you did and she says the same thing, 'Don't think about it, let it go.' But you know I can't do that. Look at that white boy's face," and he jabbed his finger down on the grinning face in the foreground of the picture. "Look at him grinning like that. Sometime I'm going to find out where he is and I'm going to do something."

His uncle picked up the photo and held it close to his eyes, turning so the light from the window was on it. "That's the Walker boy. You won't do nothing with him. He was in the war and did all those things and got a medal just before he got killed."

For a moment Frank was too surprised to respond. "You know who that is?"

"Like I say, that's the Walker boy. He was another Frank, like you. Frank Walker. He wasn't much more than twenty-one or twenty-two when he got killed in the war."

"You know any of the others?" Frank's voice was thin and strained.

The other man shrugged. "It's a little place out here. I know them all."

"Is anybody still here?"

Jessie went from face to face, his finger wavering when he came close to his brother's contorted features, but moving surely from one to another of the faces glistening in the torch light. "Some of them's gone. The war took them away from here and they never did come back. I don't know if they'd even remember doing something like this. That one there," he pointed to the face of an older man, unshaven, with a torch in his hand, close to the tree where the body dangled. "That was old Robinson. He had the jewelry store in that brick building just before you come to the square, but he died a couple of years ago. That one," he put his finger on the face of a man who was holding on to one end of the rope, "he put a lot of land in rice for a while. I worked for him myself. Bailey was his name."

The finger moved across the photo. "That fellow there, Hankins, he still got a feed store just off the highway before you come into town, but he's sick. He went off to the hospital last I heard. That one there with the shotgun, Harry Shields, he used to have a furniture store, but he sold out. That boy next to him, he was just visiting for a couple of months and I suppose they took him along so he could see what it was like to string up a nigger."

Frank was trying to follow what the other man was telling him, but he felt as though his feet had been swept out from under him and he was struggling to get his balance. He hadn't understood that the people in the mob had been as much a part of the ordinary life around town as his father was. He was becoming so agitated he started to get up, to walk around the small room.

"There's a boy — an old man now — who's living out this way." Jessie was pointing to a white shape almost lost in the crowd of men behind the tree. It was the face of a boy who looked like he was in his late teens. He had a soft, pleased smile that shone in the glare of the torchlight and the photographer's flash. In one hand was a stick, and in the other hand he was holding a dark rag that Frank finally realized was his father's shirt. "That's Floyd Walker, Frank Walker's big brother. Frank was the one there . . ." and Jessie pointed to the grinning boy again, ". . . that got himself killed. Floyd went off too, got him a bunch of medals for being a hero like his brother. He never did come to much when he come back. Floyd was mean, I tell you. Even if you have them nice clothes and you not from down here, you still don't mess with Floyd Walker. But he's sick now. He got a shack not much bigger than this one on the road going east out of here. Just another turn from where you started to come to this place. It's six or seven miles further on. It's out in the woods and it's kind of hard to get to. Floyd's out

131

there. You can go see him if you want, but I don't know as how he'd even talk to you. He could take a gun to you as quick as you tell him what you'd come out for."

Frank took the picture out of his hands and looked down at it. "You know them all — you know everybody there." His voice was confused and wondering.

"It isn't so much out here. Just farm country. At least it was then. So we all knew the names. I don't know if them honky boys ever knew our names, but we knew who they were."

"Did you know they were out there that night?" Frank's voice was still tinny with surprise, but a harder, metallic, accusing tone had crept in.

His uncle shrugged. "It didn't do no good to ask around."

"You knew who did it."

"You got to know." And his uncle was angry in turn. "You all don't see yet what I'm trying to tell you. If you know you have somebody after you, watching you every minute you alive, you get to know his name and you never forget it."

"And you want to see if anything's going to happen to them for what they did," Frank persisted.

"Alright. That's the truth. You want to know if something's going to happen to them on this earth or if it's all waiting for them when they get over. But you don't ever forget about them. Look, Frank Lewis, maybe you think I'm as slow as one of them old swamp turtles, but you all are even slower. You still don't understand a damn thing I'm saying."

15

Frank drove his uncle to the grocery store at the crossroads so they could buy some whiskey and a little beer to wash it down. The store was in a battered frame building that had been put up about the same time as his uncle's cabin, but unlike Jessie the owner was tired and discouraged. His lined face bore the marks of a surprised disappointment and he was braced behind his disorderly counter as if he were expecting a summons that would order him to leave the place behind at any moment. The bottle of whiskey they bought was covered with dust, and the beer in the cooler was luke warm. But they opened it all up back in Jessie's kitchen, spread it out on the scrubbed table and began to drink.

"Now you have to tell me what happened." Frank's voice was a little unsteady.

"What you mean?"

"You must know what happened before those people took my father Frank out into the swamp."

"Just a whole lot of stories. You don't know what to believe . . ."

"Jessie, you're just trying to put me off." Frank slapped the table, breaking into his uncle's faltering explanation. "I know that's all you're doing. You sure as hell know what happened."

Jessie was on the other side of the room again, pretending to look out the window into the deepening light. "Goddamn it. You don't understand. It doesn't do nobody no good to go back to them times. You start worrying at things, you don't know what you going to stir up."

"You listen." Frank's voice was insistent. "Somebody's going to tell me what happened sooner or later. Why shouldn't you be the one? You can say what you want about stirring something up, but it's already happened — it's been stirred up. Isn't that right? You can't go back and tell me nothing happened." Frank was having trouble keeping the surge of anger he felt from coloring his voice, but he was also too impatient to care. "What happened, Jessie?"

Jessie had moved from the window to the sink and was rattling a pan. Finally, he stopped what he was doing and slid into a chair. "I mean what I say. You hear me. I'm telling you that if you go back to them times you just going to start things all over again." His voice softened, as if he were hearing someone whispering something to him from beyond the door. "But you Frank's boy, and if anybody got a right to know about all this, then you the one. But I don't want to hear about you carrying whatever I tell you outside of this house so as people come calling me down about it. You hear me?"

"I hear you, Jessie." Frank drank again from the bottle.

"That man your father got in trouble with was always mean to get along with. You best to stay out of his way. If he caught you laughing when he was around, he'd have that smile off your face faster than a snake gets down off a log when a dog comes 'round. He didn't want to see nothing from his niggers except the tops of their heads when they was bent over doing their work. And he'd hit you. They wasn't none of them any good, them fellows that had the big farms around here, but the rest of them got to you another way. They'd take money off what you had coming to you or they'd want you to pay up on your credit at their little store. But he'd just hit you. His name was Harry Rawley. He died just a few years back and give everything over to his son."

"Wait. Oh God." Frank took a breath. "I have to think about this. The man wasn't killed? My father didn't kill anybody?"

"Jesus, no. Frank wouldn't ever kill anybody."

"But they killed him!"

"When they all gets mad, them white people, you don't know what they're going to do. I don't think they know half the time themselves."

"Why did they kill my father?" Frank was staring across the room, shaking his head back and forth in his anger.

"It's for damn sure you didn't grow up around here. They'd go out after a nigger for less than what your father done. You don't ever talk about what I'm saying to anybody, but it's time you knew about these things."

Frank took another drink and pushed the bottle across the table.

"You be the one to tell me."

"What did happen?" Frank insisted when they'd finished the last of the whiskey.

His uncle stood up again and walked unsteadily to the sink. "I wouldn't tell you none of this, except you're Frank's son and he was my brother and I used to pick you up when you wasn't nothing but a baby. You better understand that now.

"It was one of those hot days. You don't get nothing like it up where you living now. It gets hot and you feel your clothes sticking to you and everybody gets kind of crazy. Your daddy had been having trouble with Mr. Harry, who was bossing him pretty strong, but everybody had trouble with that man. There wasn't nothing you could do with him. He thought your daddy was getting too smart. Not looking down quick enough when Mr. Harry spoke to him and things like that, so Mr. Harry took to giving him the meanest jobs. He knowed you was just born, so he wasn't afraid your daddy would quit on him. I was working over on another place all that time, so I only heard about what happened from some of the boys who was working with Frank. Mr. Harry give him the job to clean

135

out the shed where they brought in the mules, and then he come in and started calling down his name and pointing out this place and that he wasn't getting it clean. There was another boy there and he could see Frank was getting hot.

"Now sometimes people'll say Frank was easy to get worked up, but the truth of it was you had to be a little bit like Jesus Christ to hold on to yourself. If Frank seemed like he didn't have himself all quieted down, it was because he was fixing to get out. That's what you did if you couldn't keep yourself all bowed down like they wanted. Some boys couldn't do it, so they stayed drunk all the time and the people like Mr. Harry they'd say, 'You see, them niggers ain't nothing but shiftless and no-account. They ain't no better than the goddamn mules.' Then, if they'd see a boy who was tending to his business and getting ahead a little they'd say, 'You see, them niggers gettin' too big for themselves. They getting out of their place.' So there wasn't nothing you could do, and Frank was going to get out of it as soon as you got a little bigger.

" 'Course people like Mr. Harry knew the boys were running off from them, and they'd tell you that you owed them some money, or your daddy had owed them some money and you better stay where you was at 'til you had that money paid. But of course, you never owed nothing in the first place so there wasn't no way you could ever pay it back, so there wasn't nothing you could do except run off. If everybody went away then they'd have to do the work themselves, or get some of that honky trash to do it, but they wouldn't work for nigger pay, they'd have to get better than that. Then the people that was growing the crops would stand around in town, crying to each other like they just found out they got weevils in their cotton, and telling each other they got to do something about the niggers.

"So Mr. Harry was thinking about all these things and here was Frank working in the shed. Mr. Harry went away for a little, after he'd been calling down Frank's name, then he come back with a switch and come up behind Frank and hit him with it and said, 'Nigger, I told you to get this place clean.' Now Frank knew it was Mr. Harry and he jumped around and he had a pitchfork in his hand and even a mean son of a bitch like Mr. Harry should have knowed better than to come up behind a man who had a pitchfork in his hand. Without thinking what he was doing — the other boy said he didn't think Frank knew he was doing it, it all went so fast — but Frank swung that pitchfork and he got that white man in his stomach, just above the belt, and he fell over with that pitchfork still hanging out of him and blood coming down his pants and he started screaming for somebody to come. He tried to get this other boy to pull the pitchfork out, but he just got out of there as fast as he could. So that left Frank, and he was standing there shaking, too scared of what he'd done to get out of the shed, and Mr. Harry was screaming, and there's always somebody around a place like that, and Mr. Harry's son come runnin' and first he thought it was an accident, and he got the pitchfork out and he got his daddy lying back and he was trying to get the blood stopped and Mr. Harry started screaming for him to get Frank before he got out of there, that he'd tried to kill him.

"By this time Frank had started moving, and he was out the door, but the white boy was after him and he was shouting and everybody come running to get Frank. One of the boys working out in the yard said they run him down just as he was coming clear of the sheds. It looked like he was trying to get to that little path that went through the woods to where you and your mother was in the cabin. Three of the white boys working on the farm threw him down, and Mr. Harry's son was sitting on him and hitting him, and they all was shouting, and when they picked him up he was already too hurt to walk, and they dragged him back into the shed and then one of the boys went off and called the sheriff and the sheriff said he'd come out with the doctor and they come up in a cloud of dust a half hour later. Every nigger on the place was trying to slip off, but the boys kept watching them so they couldn't go, and they still was there when the sheriff came out of the shed with Frank. They had to lift Mr. Harry out on a stretcher, but the pitchfork hadn't gone in so deep and it didn't hit anything serious so he was in pretty good shape. Frank couldn't walk either, but they just dragged him and they threw him in the back of the sheriff's car. And when that happened everybody

137

on the place lit out. Nobody was going to stay around after that. I heard somebody run off to tell your momma, Ada. Nobody figured Ada could do anything, but maybe she could get herself ready to go if they come out after her. I don't know what she was thinking."

"She thought they were coming for her too." Frank shifted in his chair, his head down. His voice was flat and toneless.

"They did come for her," Jessie went on. "They come out at night. People out there said that her cousin, Willie Thomas, he come and got her in his car and they wasn't gone more than a half hour and people from town come out bustin' around and shouting. Just about everybody living there was out in the dark, hiding with their suitcases, ready to keep on going if something happened. They thought they'd be burned out. But them fellows in the cars, they just wanted her — they was out after you, too. They'd have killed you if they found you, just like they was going to kill her. But nobody was in the place, and they could see she'd taken some of her things with her and all your things was gone, so they just smashed up what was left inside. Somebody tried to set a fire going, but they all was pretty drunk, and he just managed to get a little fire going that didn't really catch. When they was out of there the people come in from the woods and they put it out."

"Did anybody know what happened then?"

"Like I said, there wasn't a nigger within five miles of that place they took Frank, but you could see the lights from the cars and you could hear all the shouting. I saw some of them going by on their way out there. We knowed Frank was dead, but we didn't nobody know more than just that."

"But they took his picture." Frank held up a bottle of beer, his tone bitter and mocking. "They took his picture. What do you think of that?"

Jessie came to the table and sat down again. "I don't know. I just don't know."

The picture lay on the table between them, empty bottles and glasses pushed to one side. From time to time Jessie picked it up and studied it, his thin face screwed up in his concentration.

As the light beyond the window thickened and darkened there was a noise on the porch, the screen door opened, and a teenager came into the room. He was tall and awkwardly thin, wearing baggy blue jeans and a purple tee-shirt with the sleeves rolled up. He stopped when he saw Frank.

"I saw there was a car outside, but I didn't know who was here."

Jessie nodded across the table to the other man. "This is Frank. He's another one of the family." To Frank he explained, "This is the grandson I told you about."

"Somebody was talking about a new person in town," The boy was looking at him curiously. "You all come from New York — at least that's what they said."

"I do."

"You look at a lot of basketball up there?"

Frank shrugged. "You can't go anywhere in Harlem without seeing somebody playing basketball."

"That's just the same as it is here." The boy was thinking about what he was saying. "No, what I mean is professional basketball. All the teams you have up there playing in Madison Square Garden. You look at a lot of it.?"

"Not much now. I used to go down to the games sometimes."

"I try to catch them on the TV. They have a game on every now and then. A lot of times it's Houston that's playing. I usually stay and watch it if it's a good game. But I don't go much. You have it on TV up there?"

The boy had a teenager's awkward seriousness. Frank began to explain that he had moved out of New York so he didn't get in so much, and while he was talking the boy came to the table and picked up the picture. Jessie tried to take it out of his hand.

"That's nothing for you."

The boy stared at it a moment longer. "That's one dead nigger." He put the photo back on the table and lifted two or three of the bottles to see if there was a sip left.

Jessie looked annoyed. Before Frank could stop him he picked up the photo again and held it up so the boy could see it.

"You all seen it, but you didn't see what you looking at."
Jessie thrust it at him, making him take it. "You see what it
is?"

The boy looked uncomfortably around the room. He
pushed up a sleeve of the purple tee-shirt with his free hand. "I
know what it is. Everybody knows about things like this
happening. We had a picture like it in the history book we used
in school."

"But you see who it is?"

The boy held it up to the light. "Louisiana. 1937," he read.
"It doesn't say anything except that, and I can't tell from
looking at him who he is. His face is all twisted up so bad."

He took a step back. It was obvious they'd been drinking,
and he wasn't sure of their mood. Frank had stopped watching
them. He was staring into the cluttered shelves across the
room, but he wasn't conscious of seeing anything. He felt for a
moment that he was drowning in what his uncle had told him.

"That's my brother there."

"In the picture?" The boy's eyes widened. "Somebody told
me something happened to him. Was his name Frank?"

"That's right."

The boy suddenly turned to Frank, his expression confused.
"You both called Frank and I heard some story about my
grandad's brother getting killed like this and he was supposed
to have a wife and a little baby." He pointed to the photo, his
voice pinched with surprise, "Is this your daddy?"

Frank managed to nod. The boy carefully put the photo
back down on the table. "You bring the picture down with
you?"

Frank nodded again.

"What you going to do?" The boy was still trying to grasp
the reality of the photo. "You going to go to the police?"

Jessie began to laugh. "You think the police going to do
something after all this time gone by? When it wasn't nothing
but a nigger in the first place?"

"It isn't like that now," the boy protested. "You going to
do something?"

"He'd still be living today if they hadn't done that to him."
Jessie had taken the photo back and was staring at it again. "He

140

would be your uncle now. He'd be kin to you. You know who these others are?" He pointed to two or three of the white faces around the dangling figure.

"No."

"You wouldn't, I don't suppose, but they all from around here."

Frank suddenly leaned across the table and jammed his finger on the face of the man who was holding his father's shirt. "I want that one."

"Who's that?" the boy asked.

"That's the old man living the other direction from the crossing. Floyd Walker," Jessie answered.

The boy was silent, then he looked across at Frank. "What you going to do with him?"

Frank realized he was drunk and angry and tired. He didn't know what to answer. "I just want him. I'll know what to do." He stopped and cleared his throat. "I just want him."

16

It was hours later before he got back to the motel. He felt as
though his skin had been rubbed raw, as though giant hands
had been pressing against his head. He had talked too much
and drunk too much, and his headache was a swollen
throbbing and his voice was so dry he had to keep clearing his
throat. He was trying to make some coherent whole out of the
things he knew now, but he was past the point of tiredness
where his mind could hold anything clearly in focus for more
than a moment. He fumbled with his clothes, let them fall on
the floor and dropped into bed, letting sleep overwhelm him.
When he woke the next morning his mouth burned and his
head still felt too large for his body and a sour nausea had
settled in his stomach, but a little coffee helped steady him, and
after an hour he tried eggs and toast and stretched out on one of
the plastic couches beside the pool.

It was almost impossible to accept everything he'd been
told. He spent most of the morning trying to fit his mother's
story with Jessie's story. They were like pages that had been

torn down the middle, then crumpled and forgotten. As he smoothed them out he could see where the edges fit, and together they told the same story. He could piece out the whole day now, and the new dimension of it forced new dimensions on the pain and anger he felt again — with the same intensity he had felt when he had first listened to his mother tell him what she knew. He couldn't find any way to accept some of what he had been told — that the man his father had attacked was only slightly hurt — that the mob had gone out to the cabin looking for his mother, looking for him. He felt almost helpless. Even if he knew everything, it still was too confusing. Everything that had happened was so far from his ordinary experience that he couldn't find any clear direction telling him how to move next. He lay quite still on the plastic mattress, listening to the preoccupied lap of the water against the pool sides, smelling the sting of the chlorine that kept it clean.

As the hours passed his anger began to take on a new shape, a new focus. It was no longer the vague flood of rage that had overcome him when he had found out from his mother what had happened. Now his anger had a name to work with, and it gnawed at the name with relentless concentration. The name finally crowded out everything else. Who was this Floyd Walker? He still had only a confused impression of his face, but it was no longer an anonymous face in a photograph — just as his father had become real, the others had become real. Could they be as ordinary as any of the people he had seen in the little town? Didn't evil like this take people who were more than ordinary? Who were clearly evil? How could all of them in this tragedy — his father, his mother, himself, the mob — how could they be ordinary people? What kind of man was Floyd Walker?

As soon as he had some dinner he drove back to the bar. It was the only place he knew where he might find out something. He couldn't go back to Jessie's, he was still struggling with everything the old man had already told him. Once he was inside the familiar door he felt more like himself. It looked just the same. The same dimly lit tables, the colored lights from the advertisements on the walls. He even recognized three or four of the younger men from the crowd that had been near the door. There was an empty stool and he ordered a scotch and soda. He let an hour pass, the drink sitting untouched in front of him, watching the door and waiting for someone to come in who looked old enough to have known Walker. The room was filled with its murmur of voices, the jukebox interjecting its louder tones at irregular intervals. Finally a man came through the door, thin and dark-skinned, in a suit and tie. As he came slowly toward the bar, Frank could see that his face was lined and that his hair was graying. He said something to someone further along the bar and Frank heard the same accent as the other voices around him. When the man sat down Frank went to stand beside him, putting his drink on the bar in front of him.

"You know most of the people around here. Isn't that so?"

"What you mean?" The man looked ready to move away.

"I didn't mean to come up on you like that," Frank apologized. "I heard you talking the same way as the other people who live in town here."

The other man's expression cleared. "You all that fellow down from New York who's been asking questions around."

"Can I buy you a drink?"

The man drew his head back, thinking about it. "If you buy me a drink then I'm going to buy you a drink, so you don't get the idea you have to buy somebody a drink to talk. We're all friendly down here."

They bought drinks for each other and Frank slid the new plastic cup next to the one he'd carried over with him.

"I know you all looking for somebody." The man's tone was friendlier.

"I was looking for somebody who lives around here. Jessie Lewis. And I found him. It's somebody else I want to know about now. It's a white man living outside of town somewhere. His name's Floyd Walker."

Perhaps the man would also know that Walker was evil, that he'd done this evil thing, but he simply nodded his head. "That's Frank Walker's brother. Frank got himself killed in the war after he got all them medals. Floyd's still out there in his little place, I suppose. I don't get out that way too much."

"But you don't think anything about him?"

The man thought a moment. "He's just ordinary. Getting old now." The man held up his drink and shook his head. "Floyd's not the only one that's happening to."

Frank tried to think of a place to begin. "What's he been doing all these years?"

"What you want with Floyd Walker?"

"I just want to know about him."

"I hear Floyd's been sick. He don't come round in town much. He has a boy out there with him who sees to most everything."

"What did he do around here after . . ." Frank caught himself, ". . . after the war."

"You'd have to ask somebody else about those times. I just got out of the army and I was too busy getting myself going again to pay much attention." He waved to the bartender. "You know anything about Floyd Walker?" The bartender, a stocky man in a pale blue, belted jump suit, tried to remember. "The only Floyd Walker I can think of around here is that old white man who lives outside of town."

"That's the one. The man from New York here wants to know what sort of business Floyd was into after the war."

"Little bit of everything. Had him a tire shop for six or seven years, but he couldn't make it pay nothin' so he went to work for one of his cousins. They got a lot of Walkers in this town. What you want with him?"

"I don't want anything . . . nothing. I wondered what kind of person he was back then."

The bartender shrugged. Despite the youthful flair of his clothes Frank saw that his hair was grizzled and thinning. He was thinking, trying to remember back thirty years. "Average. Floyd was just average. I don't remember nothing out of the way. What would you say about Floyd now?" he asked the man sitting beside Frank.

"I don't know nothing special about him. Nobody's said nothing I know about."

Frank hesitated, sipped his drink. It was inconceivable to him that they could talk so easily about someone who had

145

been part of that mob. Maybe they didn't know — had they even tried to find out?

"What I was thinking about, how was he when it came down to . . . when you had anything to do with him, how was he toward black people?" He could hear that his question was phrased clumsily, but he didn't know any other way to ask it.

The two men looked at each other and began to laugh. The bartender noisily slapped the space in front of him with a bar rag, and his gesture answered Frank's question. Neither of them had even thought about it. "Now I know you not from here. Floyd Walker was no different from any of them son of a bitches 'round here. They was all the same, everyone of them. They was all bad," he finally answered.

The man beside Frank bent his head, his shoulders shaking with his laughter. "That's right. They was all just like the dummies you see lined up in a store window. They wasn't one of them different from another. They had a way of staring at you if they didn't think you was keeping in your place. Like it was some kind of ray gun they had pointing at you. I think they used to stand in front of a mirror to practise up on it. When Floyd stared at you it wasn't any worse than when anybody else stared at you, and he paid okay when he had his own business. Now you didn't like it when they was after you over something, any of them, but Floyd — I never heard nothing special about him one way or another."

The bartender nodded in agreement. "When they got to acting like that I couldn't tell one of them from another. I heard stories Floyd was mean when he was young — both of them, Floyd and his brother, but it didn't mean nothing special. They was mean to everybody. You didn't take it personal because the Walkers was calling you down. They did it all around town. They had a gang of them like that. They was all just about as bad."

The man beside him emptied his glass. "Now they all running their own little businesses and they on the Board of Education and they got jobs for the town — just like everybody else. Now they got a new gang running around town, just kids, but I still wouldn't want to mess with them.

Only difference between now and then is that they got black and white running together, but I don't see as that makes it no better. But in a few years they going to settle like all the others. That's what happens in a place like this."

The bartender wiped off the space in front of them and turned to go off to some girls in summer dresses who were gesturing to him from the other end of the bar. "Don't you worry none about Floyd Walker. He's old now. It never was nothing but the young ones you had to watch out for."

He bought himself another drink. The man he'd been talking to joined a woman he knew at one of the tables. There was an electric advertising sign just above their heads, a simulated waterfall rushing out of a garish blue sky, with a bottle of beer hovering over the shimmering horizon. From across the room, where Frank was sitting, it looked like the water was cascading down over their heads. He turned back to the bar, staring down at his drink. He was sitting there with the face in the photo, trying to fit what the other two had told him, when the door opened and a new couple came in. He hadn't seen the man before, but the girl was Doris. She was in a dark sheath dress, her hair swept up in an elaborate hairdo, a scarf carefully knotted at her throat. They went to a table and her companion sat down. She hesitated, looked around her, then she saw Frank sitting at the bar. She leaned over and said something to the man she'd come in with, then she came across the room. Frank again could see the casual grace of her body, and when she came up to him she gave him one of her mocking half-smiles.

"You don't have to buy me a drink, since I got one of the boys from around here trying to see if he can get something tonight." She swept onto the empty stool beside him and turned so that her strong thigh was pressed against his. She picked up the plastic cup. "What you got in there?"

"Scotch and soda."

"I'll just give you a little help with this one, then you can get yourself a fresh drink." She emptied the cup and leaned closer to him. "You did find out some things, didn't you?" Her voice was low, and she glanced around at the other people at the bar.

147

He could see that the man she'd left sitting at the table was watching them stiffly.

"What you mean?" he answered cautiously.

"I heard you found out something about what happened to your daddy and you know who did it to him." She was stroking his arm with her fingers as she talked.

Obviously Jessie had been too excited to keep anything to himself. "You know Jessie Lewis?"

"He's some kind of cousin to my mother. We all cousins here. He's been talking about you all coming out to see him. He didn't say what it was all about, just that you found out something."

It was the first time since he'd left Jessie's that he could feel himself beginning to think about something else, but he still tried to put her off. He didn't want to talk. "I don't know who I got in my family down here. You're probably my cousin too."

She nudged him and laughed. "Not close enough so it would matter. But you been asking around, and now you found out what you been asking about."

He nodded toward the bartender, who was watching them from a stool set up beside the beer cooler. "You sure you don't want a drink?"

"I got my friend over there who's going to give me anything I ask for." She pressed close to him again, her lips brushing his ear. "You hold on to your money."

He knew she was teasing him, but for a moment he let himself go. He pushed away the names and the faces and let himself laugh at her — at her preening self-satisfaction, at her frank physicality. She put her hand on his shoulder and stood up, still close to him so she could talk in a low voice. "I'm giving you your chance tomorrow night. I just decided. This one here, he's been trying for a year and he's no closer than the day he started, but I like to let him take me around sometimes. That way I keep the others guessing.

"Now you get to try tomorrow. You hear? I'm going to come in here about nine, after I get back from work and get myself looking all pretty for you and we'll have a little supper. You don't even have to buy me supper. How about that? I earn

148

my own money so I don't have to let nobody buy me nothing. I just let them do it when I know it's going to make them feel good. Men got to think they're doing something for you every now and then or they get all upset. You get all upset when somebody treats you like that?"

He looked at her and shook his head. "How do you know I'm going to sit here waiting for you tomorrow night?"

She leaned close again. "Oh, I know it. I just know it. You be on time, you hear? I get up early for my job and I got to get my sleep or I won't look so pretty for all of you."

"I can help you get that little sleep," he said in an insinuating tone.

She squeezed his shoulder. "You beginning to sound like the local trash." Her voice sounded satisfied. "A girl likes to know when she's appreciated. Now you be here at nine o'clock," and she slid off the stool and went to the table. She didn't look back, but he noticed that she was swaying her hips for him, letting him see the movements of her body under the tight dress. When she slid into the chair beside the man who was waiting for her, she leaned over to give him a kiss on the cheek and Frank had to turn around, to keep from laughing. He shook his head at the bartender, who had also watched her progress across the room, then he pushed his cup aside and stared emptily up at the bar mirror. As she was turning away from him he had already sensed his mood change, and it was the name again that began to crowd his thoughts.

It still was warm outside, despite the darkness. The air was heavy and coarse, the sluggish movement of the wind heady with the scent of leaves and new flowers. The streets were empty as he drove slowly past the closed store fronts and into the town square. A restaurant was still open on the corner, and he could see the last few customers through the window. Two or three waitresses waiting to close up were idly folding napkins and moving up and down the counter flurrying a damp rag. He found that somehow he had managed to sort through the new emotions of the last two days so that what was happening now seemed to have its own reality. He still didn't know what he was going to do, but he had found some

149

kind of footing in the flood of feelings he'd been struggling with.

He could make out the trees only as irregular dangling masses of leaves and branches in the yellowish street lights. Out of reach of the soft gleam they were a heavy canopy that stretched over the streets above him as he drove away from the business district. He wasn't used to them. There were trees lining the streets close to his apartment in Bridgeport, but he'd grown up without them in Harlem and their presence sometimes intimidated him as he drove under their dark mass. The motel was the usual conglomeration of colored lights and strident advertising signs that he could see from half a mile away when he turned onto the highway. He parked close to his room, walking by the swimming pool to see if anybody was using it. It was empty, the water rocking in an unhurried rhythm against the lights set into the pool's bright tile sides.

He had no thought of anything happening when he unlocked his door. He needed to use the bathroom, so he didn't stop to turn on the air conditioner. Was there someone outside? He thought he heard footsteps, and stopped to look around as he closed his door. He didn't see anything. He wasn't expecting anything. He went past the bed, starting to unbutton his shirt, then just as he stepped into the bathroom, behind its projecting wall panel, there was a deafening roar. He felt a heavy push as something crashed against the front of his room. There was a vicious cracking, and he felt himself falling on the hard tiles of the bathroom floor. The carpet of the room behind him suddenly glittered with flashes of light as thousands of shards of glass spun through the room and rattled against the wall. The mirror over the sink collapsed with a sliding crash, and a sudden, coughing cloud of dust filled the room.

17

"Somebody in there?" A frightened voice was trying to reach him through the billows of dust. He was slumped against the bathroom door, half deafened by the explosion. He didn't seem to be hurt. He tried to get to his knees, but he was trembling too much to hold himself up. The light in the bedroom had been blown out with the explosion that had destroyed the room, but the light over his head had been protected by the same projection of the bathroom wall that had shielded him. In its yellowing glare he could see the wavering dust, the glistening bits of glass strewn over the carpet. He could feel his heart pounding and couldn't control the shaking of his hands.

"Is somebody in there?" The voice called out again.

Frank tried to speak, but his throat was constricted. He managed to get out a faint response. "Here." He cleared his throat and tried again. "I'm back here." He could hear footsteps coming cautiously into the room. He could hear bits of glass grating under soles of shoes. "The light's gone out and there's a million pieces of glass on the floor." The footsteps stopped. "You alright in there?" someone asked hesitantly.

"I don't know . . . I can't hear . . . I think I'm going to be alright," Frank called back in a shaking voice. He managed to get to his knees. He could hear other voices outside his room, other footsteps hurrying across the pavement. "Look at this," someone shouted in a voice so high-pitched it was almost a whine, "You all come and take a look at this." The crunch of shoes on broken glass resumed its grinding close to him and a tall, thin white man in an undershirt and rumpled khaki trousers looked down at him from around the edge of the wall that had shielded him.

"You must have been hid by this little bit of wall. Do you know what happened?"

Frank stayed on his knees and took a deep breath. "All I know is I started in here and there was a noise, the light in the other room went out and all this glass came flying back here."

"Anybody in there?" Another voice from the other room, a sound again of scraping glass under shoe soles, like heavy cloth being roughly torn.

"Fellow here says he's alright," the man looking down at him called back. "I was just lying stretched out in the room next to you," he continued to Frank, "and I heard this crashing noise and I got up and heard somebody running away, and when I come to the door whoever it was running had already gone on around the corner of the building so I didn't get to see who it was. Can you get up?"

Frank breathed heavily again and scrambled to his feet. He could feel a layer of grit on his fingers from the pall of dust that hung in the air. He stared at the littered floor. "What happened?"

The man shrugged and began uncomfortably tucking his undershirt into his pants. "I just heard a crash, like something going off." He backed away. "Looks like somebody wanted to get you." Other faces were staring around the partition at them, and there was a push at the door to the room. Frank heard a strained voice. "I'm the night manager. The police will be here in a minute so you all can go back to your rooms. It's going to be alright, you hear." He pushed through the group staring at Frank. "You alright?" He was very young and very nervous. He had on the usual shirt and tie, but the tie had obviously been loosened, and when he'd pulled it up again he'd jerked it to one side in his haste. One of the points of his collar was riding up, making him look as though he were leaning to one side as he talked. He was wearing glasses, but he was perspiring and he had to take the glasses off and wipe his face with one of Frank's towels. He looked back at the others in the room again. "You all can go back to your rooms," he insisted in a hurried tone. "I got the police on the way and they'll know how to take care of all this."

Frank followed them outside, stepping awkwardly on the shards of glass that were strewn over the carpet like a kind of glistening gravel. He could see that where the glass-paneled wall had been there was now a jagged opening. The flowered curtain hung in shreds from the twisted pole. His bed was gouged away on one side, as if something had run into it head on, then changed its mind and blundered away. What had happened? He was too confused to make any sense out of it. His suitcases, against the wall, didn't seem to be damaged, but the leeching dust had begun its slow, sifting descent, and the drift was slowly whitening their dark sides.

Despite the manager's ineffectual efforts to move people out of the way, there was a small crowd on the sidewalk trying to look through the blasted hole in the window. Some of them were in undershirts, a woman was in a bathrobe and curlers. They stopped talking as he came out through the door, and he could feel their eyes turning toward him. Most of the faces gathered in front of the room were white, but a few, like his own, were black.

With a spiral of spinning lights and a guttering choke of dying sirens, two police cars slid to a stop in the parking lot. The officers who got out of the cars were young and gangling, but their faces, as they came in a bunch across the motel grass, were carefully serious. One of them was black, and he knew some people standing in the shadows. He stopped to ask them if they knew what had happened. The night manager had left Frank and went toward a wiry, dark-haired officer who was a few steps ahead of the others. There was a glint of lieutenant's

153

bars on his collar, and the policemen hurrying after him seemed to be waiting for him to go over to the expectant group. They went past him to look at the damage.

"I'm the person who called in. I'm the night manager and I heard this noise and I looked out and called you."

The officer looked around.

"You have some kind of explosion?"

"That must have been what it was," the manager answered immediately, in an effort to be helpful.

The other officers were standing beside the shattered remains of the window. "It don't look like it was an explosion," one of them interjected.

"But it must have been something like that," the manager protested, becoming more and more nervous as he realized he was going to have to explain what happened to the people who had hired him. "Like I said, there was this noise. It was just like something going off, and when I come out there wasn't anything left of the window there. You all can see it's been blown in."

One of the officers had climbed in through the ragged opening and was shining a flashlight around the floor and the walls. "You damned sure heard something. The glass is gone and most of the window frame's gone with it. But it doesn't look to me like it was an explosion. You just come see the walls, and the bed there, the way it's all bunched up, like somebody had put their fist into it. I think somebody just pulled both triggers on a shotgun and blew in the window."

People in the crowd were straggling closer to look at the damaged window.

"Anybody inside when it happened?" the first officer asked the manager. He had taken out a small notebook and was starting to write in it. Frank realized that the manager was still a boy, probably in his late teens, a student making a little extra money. He pointed toward where Frank was standing. "This gentleman here is our guest for the night and he was in the room."

"You alright?" The officer turned to look at him.

Frank nodded, touching one ear with unsteady fingers. "I'm still having a little trouble hearing."

154

The officer turned and went over to the others who were standing around the window. One of them detached himself from the group and walked toward the police cars. He opened a car door and began speaking in low tones into a radio microphone.

"I think it was a shotgun," the first officer said when he came back to them. He took off his uniform cap and wiped his forehead with his sleeve. He glanced up at Frank as he wrote something in his notebook. "And your name is?"

"My name is Frank Lewis." The officer was silent a moment, studying his face; then he held out his hand. "My name is Fontenot. Lieutenant Arnold Fontenot. Do you know who it might have been that come after you with a shot gun?"

"I don't know anybody in town. I don't think anybody was looking for me, whatever they were doing."

"You know anybody from out of town? It could be dangerous for you, Mr. Lewis. Whoever done that could come back and try again."

Frank shook his head. "It couldn't have anything to do with me. I don't know anybody at all who would do that."

Fontenot shrugged. "If that's really true, Mr. Lewis, then we going to have us a time trying to find out who did it."

The people who had come out of their rooms when they'd heard the noise had slowly dispersed. One of the police cars still was sitting in the parking lot, its whirling light attracting a confused swarm of night insects. Frank had been moved into a new room upstairs. The manager had found a night watchman, and they'd carried his things up the stairs. He tried to slap the dust out of a jacket that had been hanging in the room downstairs, but as he held it up to look unhappily at the handprints the slapping had left on the back of it, he saw that his hands were still shaking, and as he turned to hang it up again felt his whole body beginning to shake. He was trembling with a slow and steady rhythm, as though he had become chilled.

He realized that his first shock had worn off. He stumbled across a room that suddenly had a slanting floor, and reaching out to steady himself he sat down in an armchair that was

155

beside the small table at the front of the room. As he was leaning back in the chair, he realized it was also in front of the window. He flinched back from the opening involuntarily and dragged the chair closer to the wall. He had left the curtain open and below him he could see police talking to the people in the other rooms. There were lights everywhere, blinding in their flat glare. No one could come after him again through that barrier of lights, but he pressed against the back of the chair, his hands clenched between his thighs, withdrawing into himself as he had done that night in his mother's shabby room when he had first begun to learn about what had happened so long before.

He hadn't changed his position when Lieutenant Fontenot returned fifteen minutes later. The officer stood in the center of the room looking through the pages of his notebook. He took off his uniform hat again and wiped his forehead. Frank had forgotten to turn on the air conditioner. "You say you don't know anybody in town. Is that right?" Fontenot asked.

Frank wouldn't look at him. His head was down and he was rubbing one shoe back and forth over the carpet. "I have an uncle. I didn't know that until I met him just two days ago."

Fontenot was speaking in a deferential tone. Frank decided that if he weren't a southern white policeman it would sound like he was trying to be respectful. "Could you tell me his name, Mr. Lewis?"

"Jessie."

"Is that Jessie Lewis?"

"You know him?" Frank was surprised.

"Jessie did a lot of work around city hall before he started getting his pension. We all knew his name."

Frank shrugged. "Then you know about Jessie. I talked to some people at a bar, I danced with a girl. I could find out their names, but I don't think they'd have anything to do with this." He was purposely speaking with a distinct northern accent, for some reason not wanting the other man to hear the traces of the local country in his speech. "I know that none of them would blow in somebody's window," he insisted. "If you really want them I can get the names, but it wasn't them."

"I don't need names unless it's somebody you had some

trouble with." Fontenot's tone was reassuring. "But you can't tell, Mr. Lewis, that girl you danced with — she might have a husband somewhere around and maybe he doesn't like it when she does that."

"I don't think this has anything to do with me." Frank was becoming impatient. "I don't think whoever it was blew in the window even knew who was in the room. One room looks like any other, and the light's so bad out there you can't read the numbers."

"I don't mean to upset you, but you said the shot came just after you went inside; so whoever it was, as you say, must have gotten a look at you. We talked to the other guests and they heard somebody running away right after the gun went off. So they were out there, and they certainly saw you."

"Then they were mistaken," Frank said doggedly. "I still say they just had the wrong room."

The policeman shrugged and wiped his forehead again. "Would you mind if I put on the air conditioner?"

Frank shook his head and Fontenot bent down to look at the dials. He turned a knob and a stream of cool air eddied across the carpet. "You certainly could be right." He straightened up and put his notebook back in his shirt pocket. He obviously wasn't satisfied, but he just as obviously hadn't decided what he wanted to do next. "I can't say much because of all the procedures we have to go through when we do stop somebody, but we have three teenagers who were speeding in a vehicle that was stopped a little ways from here. They had a shotgun in the trunk of the car and it still was warm from being fired. They said they was out after rabbits. A lot of people go out like that and shine their headlights until a rabbit comes up to them and then they shoot it. It's just their word against the officer's, but we're going to do what we can with them. They're all pretty drunk."

"Were they white?"

"I don't know as how that makes any difference."

"Were they white?" Frank persisted.

"All three were white," the officer admitted, "but I don't think this has anything to do with color. I'm going to have to wait for you to tell me, or I can find it out from one of them."

"How could I know anything about it? It could have been the wrong room." Frank felt like the policeman was leading him through some kind of a meaningless lesson, forcing him to repeat the same inconsequential answers over and over again.

"It certainly could have been the wrong room, Mr. Lewis." Fontenot was as patient as he was persistent. "But somebody who's going to blow in a window like that usually doesn't get the room mixed up. I think they had the right room, but I still don't know what they were trying to do."

Frank wasn't afraid of him. He was almost like a small boy trying over and over again to make a puzzle come out right. If he were just patient enough he would find the way to make it go together. Frank still was shaking from the effects of the noise and the shock. He wanted the officer to leave. There was a scattering of lights flashing across the stretch of grass below them, a strained sound of voices shouting over the noises of the highway.

"Tomorrow morning we're going to put the boys up in an identification line-up. You'll have to come and tell us if you know any of them."

"I don't know anybody here," Frank insisted.

Fontenot seemed to be thinking about his answer, then he turned to go. "I guess, like I said, it's going to take us a little longer to straighten this all out."

18

For a moment he didn't know what had wakened him, then slowly he realized that he was lying stiffly in a different motel bed. His hands were balled under him, and his head was nudged tensely against the pillow. It was fear that had wakened him, like a clock that was ticking somewhere inside his body. Its bell had been nothing more than a swelling in his pulse, a tremor in his chest, but he had heard it more clearly, more distinctly, than he had ever heard the exasperated rattling of an alarm clock beside his bed.

He moved his eyes cautiously from object to object in the room. The chair, the door, the garish art print on the wall, the low bench with his suitcase opened on it. Everything was bathed in the same vague light he remembered from the morning he had wakened on the couch in his mother's apartment, a directionless illumination that came from below a curtain that hung the length of one wall. The suitcase he could see was his, but it was lighter in color than he remembered, and it looked smudged. Then he saw that his suitcase was covered with dust, and he remembered why, and he was immediately, tensely awake. He slid from the bed and went cautiously to the window, pulling back the curtain as if he were slowly tearing the covering off a package.

Outside, on the lawn of the motel, it was quiet. Nothing was moving. Everything looked the way it had the day before. He could hear the voices of the maids, and they were saying the same things they had said yesterday morning, and probably said every morning. Then, suddenly, he noticed a figure by the side of the pool. A policeman was sitting in one of the pool chairs in the shade, idly turning his head as he looked around him, his uniform a splash of color against the pool's tile apron. Frank felt a rush of blood to his head. He had been trying to tell himself that nothing had happened to him, that what he remembered had been part of a dream. He let go of the curtain with the abruptness of someone who has found himself touching another person's skin.

As he fumbled with clothes and went through the mechanical gestures of shaving, he tried to sift through the confusion of his thoughts. In one part of his being he realized that what was happening was out of his control, that it was as though he had stepped onto a slide and it was carrying him down its gleaming course — but he couldn't accept that. He needed, desperately, to feel that he could stop what was happening to him. But what *was* happening to him? He looked down at his hands as they fumbled with the razor, trying to clean it, and his fingers, beyond his ability to do anything about them, were helplessly trembling.

As he put on his shoes, conscious of a struggle for breath as he bent over in the chair, he tried not to think of what Jessie had said — that if he went back to what had passed he would only make it happen again. He pronounced the word "mistake" silently to himself as he looked in the mirror, running his hand carefully over his hair and smoothing his mustache. As he left his room and went down the motel steps, he tried not to see that the policeman had left the side of the pool and was waiting for him.

"Mr. Lewis." His voice was polite. Frank nodded warily,

160

trying to anticipate what the man might want from him. "Lieutenant Fontenot would like you to come down to the courthouse before you do anything else. I don't mean you all have to rush down there right away, but he wanted you as soon as you had some breakfast."

"What does he want?"

"I believe he has somebody there he'd like you to identify." The officer was trying to make it sound like a casual request, but it was obvious that Frank was expected to go to the courthouse, whether he wanted to or not.

He protested ineffectually, trying to still his nervousness. "There's no way I could identify somebody I didn't see. I didn't see anything and I didn't hear anything, just the noise when the window was blown in."

"I expect Lieutenant Fontenot will explain what it is he would like you to do. If you all would like I can drive you down there now." The officer waited for him to answer, the only interruption in his watchful silence a flick of wind that stirred his necktie.

"No," Frank answered hurriedly, "If you tell me where the courthouse is I can find it myself." He had to get away from the other man's scrutiny. "I can find it," he repeated before the man could interrupt him.

The courthouse had been built on the usual grass square that functions as the center of most southern towns. The square was lined with one- and two-storey buildings, some wood framed and square backed, the others were made of discolored brick or painted and repainted cement blocks. Half-visible advertisements lingered on some of the walls, whispering messages that no longer had any meaning for anyone. Sodden piles of papers and street trash had accumulated in some of the doorways. The trees around the courthouse were thick and old and heavy, with a sweeping reach of branch and leaf. In the dark they would have given the square an air of splendor, but in the flat morning light it was easy to see the broken stretches of paving, the dirty street signs, the hardened earth where there had been grass, but where grass no longer grew. Seeing all of it, and at the same time not seeing any of it, he walked

161

slowly toward the courthouse. The heat had begun to make its way into the streets, and he absently wiped his forehead with one of his new work handkerchiefs.

He had to go almost all the way around the building before he found the small door that was marked "Police." He followed the indecisive line of the concrete sidewalk that crossed the stretch of grass, shifting back and forth through the straggling clumps of bushes that had been planted between the trees. He was about to open the door when he hesitated. He still couldn't bring himself to face Fontenot. He retreated down the cracked squares of the sidewalk and circled the building again. It was finally the heat that forced him back toward the door that led to Fontenot's office. As he walked along a bare corridor, going toward a brightly lit opening just beyond a hanging neon light, he told himself again that there couldn't be any connection between what he was doing in town and the shotgun blast. And since the two things were unconnected, his first thought was to get the meeting over with as quickly as possible. If it weren't for the residue of his fear, he could have pretended that whatever had happened, it hadn't happened to him.

"You don't look like you got much sleep." Fontenot had shaved, but he looked drawn and sallow, with the tight stretch of skin across the bones of the face that marks someone who hasn't gotten enough rest.

"I think I kept waking up and listening to hear if somebody else was coming around." Frank wiped his face again and stared bleakly at walls that were as bare as a naked bulb.

"We had somebody keeping a watch on you for the rest of the night." Fontenot had a loose sheaf of papers in his hand, and he bent down to put them away in a drawer. "I picked up some of the buckshot that was in the wall of your room, and we looked around at the ground outside. Nobody dropped anything, and with all that crab grass they got growing around the motel, there wasn't any kind of footprints for us to check on." He hunched his shoulders in tired discouragement.

"After I came back here we spent a lot of time talking to those boys. They wouldn't change their story. It was still all about going out in the bayous to jack a few rabbits. What happened was that when we picked them up the officer that had them in the van had to leave them by themselves for a couple of minutes while he checked their car. That's always a bad thing to do, but there wasn't no way he could help it and that gave them enough time to work up a story together. So it didn't make any difference if we worked on them one by one or all together. I shouldn't have brought them in, and I'm going to get a little noise back on it, but I've been wanting a chance to bring in those three. I know sometime they're going to do something, and I want them to know I'm thinking about them."

Fontenot's voice was strained and tired. He sat in the chair behind his desk and leaned against the wall. "If it had been a smaller shotgun, or if they'd aimed it down at the ground I wouldn't have held them, but if it was them, they pulled both triggers on a twelve gauge shotgun from close up, and if there had been anybody behind the window they would have died. I'm not saying things are all that quiet in this part of the country, but I mean to tell you it isn't all that often somebody drives up to a motel and tries to kill whoever is staying in one of the rooms there."

Frank was half-sitting on the edge of the wooden table across the room. He was fanning himself with a folder he'd found on the table, despite the drift of cold air from the air conditioner. The silence finally became uncomfortable. He shrugged. "I was telling myself just outside the door that you were going to say nothing really happened."

Fontenot opened a manila envelope that was in front of him on the desk and spread a handful of misshapen shotgun pellets out on the blotter. "I picked these out of the wall. The ones in the mattress didn't get flattened. There was a hole in the side of the mattress that went in eight or nine inches. I don't like to say anything that's going to frighten anyone, but these would have done the same thing to you if you'd been between the window and the bed. You can't tell much about one shotgun or another, but the one the boys had in the back of the car was a twelve gauge, and this shot came out of one of those." Fontenot stifled a yawn. "I'm sorry to be a little sleepy. If

163

somebody was going to blow in your window I wish they hadn't gone and done it in the middle of the night."

Frank was still fanning himself, staring past Fontenot at the bare wall. The noises around him gave him the feeling that the room was slowly moving, bearing both of them along with it. The steady hum of the air conditioner, the buzz of the neon light, had become the vibrations of a distant motor, the faint sound of voices further along the corridor was the murmur of other passengers. Fontenot brushed the small metal lumps back in the envelope, his abrupt gesture stopping the room's motion. Frank looked at the crumpled envelope, he hadn't seen shotgun pellets since he was a boy and he wouldn't have recognized them if the other man hadn't told him what they were. Despite his efforts to stay calm Frank could feel himself slowly becoming frightened again.

"When you read those detective stories nobody ever gets tired." Fontenot was rubbing his face, trying to wake himself up. "If they do get tired enough to go to bed, it's only because they got hold of some girl who wants to go to bed with them. When I got back to the house I only had an hour to sleep before my wife had to get our little girl up for school. Like I said, Mr. Lewis, I have to figure that whoever blew in that window thought he knew what he was doing. I went out to talk to Jessie Lewis this morning, and he didn't have much to say, but he did tell me something about a picture you all brought down with you."

Frank looked away. He didn't want the police officer to see the picture. He didn't want anyone to see it. It only concerned him now.

"I know that picture didn't have anything to do with what happened. I know that as well as I know my name," he insisted.

"I'll still have to see it." Fontenot's tone was apologetic, but Frank realized he had no choice. The photo was in his pocket. He slid it across the desk.

Fontenot studied it without expression, then he grimaced. "You hear about all these kinds of things that used to happen, but it doesn't make it any better when you see a picture like this." He looked up at Frank's face in the poorly placed light.

164

"I can't see you well enough to see if you look like that man there, but I can see it's Jessie's brother. The two of them have the same face, even if Jessie's a good bit older." He pushed the photo back. "It don't make it any easier to look at when you know some of the people doing it."

"You know them too?"

"Jessie must have known everybody there."

"That's right."

Fontenot pulled it back toward him and glanced at the faces again. "That's Jessie's generation, so he'd know them all. I think some already had moved out of town when I was just growing up. I don't see any French people in the crowd. You didn't grow up around here so you probably don't know all that about what the English did to the French people that drove them to come to Louisiana. Down south of here, in the bayou country, you won't find nothing but French people. Now, I'm not going to pretend that the French people were perfect when it came to the way they treated black people, but they didn't do things like this. Hell, I used to think that if somebody spoke French those back bayou French people wouldn't care what color he was. Now you take that boy there," and Fontenot put his finger on the face Frank's uncle had identified. "Floyd Walker. He's old and sick now, but he was a bad one when he was young. People around here still talk about Floyd Walker. He was no damned good to anybody, including himself. That son of a bitch should have been hanging on the tree there for some of the things he done."

"But he's still around somewhere."

"I don't think he could have been the one who blew your window in."

"Whoever did it didn't even know who was in the room," Frank repeated stubbornly.

"I don't really know anything, Mr. Lewis," Fontenot gestured toward the photo, "except that I'm glad I didn't have to tangle with Floyd Walker when he was young like that."

Frank was becoming more and more impatient. He shifted his weight against the table, still fanning himself with the folder. "Somebody mixed up a room," he said again. "Did you check the people in the rooms around mine?"

165

Fontenot was leaning forward with his elbows on the desk, one hand rubbing the back of his neck. "I never like to use too much imagination — you know what I mean about trying to guess why somebody did something. You always look like a damn fool when you find out what really happened. But the bed was blown in. Most of the shot went into the side of the mattress, low down. Now you had just come in the room, which meant you weren't sleeping. I think they knew that much. I think if it was you they were waiting to take a shot at then they were there waiting for you to get back. Anybody could park close to the room without causing much notice.

"Now, the shot from one of those things scatters out as soon as you pull the trigger. It's like you're trying to throw a handful of sand into the neck of a little bottle. Some of it goes in, but most of it just scatters around. What it looks like to me is somebody who didn't have a hell of a lot of idea what they were doing was trying to shoot low. Down where it would get your legs. They must have been far back enough that they didn't think it would do that much harm. What they forgot was that glass window. It scattered the shot all over, and the glass would have done more damage than the pellets from the shotgun — all those little pieces flying around in there."

Fontenot stifled another yawn and went on, spreading his hands on the desk in front of him, "I'm sorry to go on like this when I'm sure you have things you want to do. I don't like to build anything up when I'm just guessing, but it could be that those boys tried to warn you about showing that picture around. So they let go with a shotgun when you just had come into the room, not trying to do much more than scare you, but if you hadn't kept going on into the bathroom you'd have been dead."

"But nobody . . ." Frank began, but Fontenot interrupted him. "I know what you think, and that's why I always feel like a damned fool when I'm just guessing about what might have happened. If we go along and look at those boys you can tell me if they give you any ideas, and I'll decide what to do with them." The policeman stood up and pressed his fingers against his head, in a futile attempt to do something about his headache.

166

Frank supposed he should have been more involved in the procedures Fontenot had set in motion, but like everyone else he had seen violence and police routine so often on television that all of it seemed predictably familiar. He also found it difficult to believe that any of the nondescript line of men led out on the lighted stage in front of him could have been interested enough in anything to fire a gun over it. He could recognize their efforts to seem casual about the whole idea of a line-up, but beneath the facade of disinterest they mostly seemed to be empty of the will to do anything. The police had managed to round up ten men, seven young whites and three blacks. Fontenot must have brought in every prisoner they had, whatever they were in for. He knew none of them could see him, but they didn't seem to be interested enough even to try to find out who was looking at them through the bright lights. They didn't look beaten or mistreated, only rumpled and sullen, standing back against the wall with their arms folded.

He had seen one of the white men before — men, boys — the glaring light altered everyone's appearance so much it was difficult to distinguish something as ordinary as age. The face was familiar. But he couldn't remember where he'd seen it before. His memory of the face was so slight that he could have seen the person on the street or working in a store. The men began to fidget, some of their attempt at self-control giving way as they felt themselves being stared at, and a whisper was like a sting, even though they couldn't make out what was being said. A policeman standing below them told them to turn sideways. In profile the face seemed even more familiar, but Frank still couldn't place it. He could see now that it was a teenager, in a sweat-ringed tee-shirt and jeans. The boy was nervous, but he wasn't any more agitated than the others. There was still a sense of total emptiness to the entire line-up, as if the most serious offense they could ever have considered was leaving their car too long in the church parking lot. Frank found himself wondering what it was they could have done. Maybe they had decided to take a nap on the street and they had been arrested for obstructing traffic. They were turned to face him again, their eyes still staring in every

167

direction except toward the darkened space where he was standing.

"Did you see any of them around when you were out last night?" Fontenot had leaned close to him and was talking in lowered tones. The men in the line-up for a moment seemed to stop breathing.

"I've seen one of them around somewhere, but it wasn't last night."

"Which one?"

"The boy in the tee-shirt. The third from the left."

Fontenot made a note. "Was he paying any special attention to you when you saw him?"

"If he had been I would have remembered more about him. Everybody's been giving me some attention because I'm a stranger, but I can't think of any reason for him being different from the others. Maybe he was just waiting around someplace when I was buying gas."

"You don't remember anything more than that?"

Frank shook his head. Fontenot gestured toward the policeman and the straggling line was ordered to turn and walk through a door at the end of the platform. With their dismissal a little sense of bravado returned, and one of the black prisoners turned and made a casual obscene gesture in their direction. Fontenot held up his hand, returning the compliment, but in the darkness his gesture was noticeable only to Frank, who was already walking away, impatient with the uselessness of the procedure.

He had to wait in Fontenot's office until the policeman came back after giving instructions to the officer still holding the boys they had picked up.

"If you had seen any of those boys following you around last night then I might have had something. At least they know we're around, and if it was them they might think twice about doing it again."

"I still can't believe it has something to do with me."

Fontenot shrugged. "At least we're trying to find out what it is about." He looked away, and with an effort to seem casual said, "It's not like the old days. You have to give us that much."

Frank was fanning himself again. Fontenot's trim waist made him feel heavy and clumsy. He smoothed his mustache and told himself he would begin cutting down on his weight as soon as he finished what he'd come down to do. "Fontenot . . ." He stopped, confused. "What should I call you? Is Fontenot alright?" The officer nodded. "Fontenot, I don't know what it was like in the old days, but I get an idea about it from the picture. No, what you're doing doesn't look like anything that might have been going on then — no one can say that anything that was going on down here then was any damn good."

"No, no, I agree. And I don't want you to misunderstand what I'm trying to say. I don't think you'll find anybody who knows what went on who would defend it. Of course, there's a lot of people who don't want to know. That's not the same thing. I think that's the way it works for most people. There's something lying back in the past there that they just want to let lie. Like a dog you see sleeping on a doorstep. You just step over him and let him sleep."

"I've been doing the same thing, Fontenot. There was something in the past, but I've just been stepping over it. I think that's what made it possible for me to go on with my life. If I let myself get involved with what happened to people like me, to Negroes, blacks, whatever — then everything else would get pushed out of my life." A sudden touch of exasperation colored his tone.

"You've got yourself involved now."

"That's right." Frank stopped fanning himself and the two of them stared at each other across the room.

"What I mean to say," Fontenot continued after a clumsy pause, "and I think you know what I'm coming to . . ." He sat up in his chair and looked down at his hands. "It is a long way from those old days, and things have changed and you have policemen now that wouldn't let a thing like that happen. There never will be another lynching around here. They'd have to get past me first. I don't mean to sound like anybody's hero, but we do things a different way now. What I'm saying,

169

Mr. Lewis, is that you shouldn't go ahead and try to do something yourself because of what's in that picture."

Frank went on staring at him, his expression tightly guarded. "Why would I try to do something about that picture?" His tone was sarcastic. "Why do you think I'd try to do something like that?"

Fontenot slowly shook his head, and for a moment seemed to hold his breath. "Because I would," he finally answered, his mouth set in a tired smile.

The colorless, hard light outside the door made Frank blink. He started across the bare stretch of stringy clay with his head down, but something made him glance up. He had already begun looking around him with sharper attention. Something was different. Something had changed since he'd gone inside Fontenot's office. He had noticed a few people sitting in the uneven shadows as he crossed the courthouse's scrabby stretch of lawn. Two or three old black men with lined faces were talking to each other with a slow rhythm as their eyes followed everything that passed around them. A drunk who had been sitting on the end of a bench unsteadily tried to get a can of beer into a paper bag. A man and a woman walked along one of the pathways. They were in office clothes so they probably worked nearby.

Frank began walking more slowly, looking around him. Then he saw what it was he had noticed. A gawky white teenager in the usual tee-shirt and chino trousers was standing in the shade under one of the trees. He looked away as soon as he saw Frank glance toward him, but Frank had the sensation that the boy had been watching for him to come outside. He was thin and wiry, with the strongly-muscled arms and shoulders most of the boys who worked out on the local farms developed when they were young. His hair was long and light-colored, and he wore it brushed loosely back from his ears. He had turned his face away, but he was holding his body so tensely that he was leaning forward in the shadows.

Frank was so surprised he turned his head to see if there was anybody else waiting, then, when he looked back, the boy was drawing away toward the bushes. Frank stopped, trying to decide whether he should go up to him and say something, but already the boy had slipped out of the shadows and was walking rapidly in the other direction. He was pretending not to notice anything, but his head was half turned, his shoulders hunched, as if he were expecting the man behind him to call out. Before Frank could take more than two or three steps, the boy broke into a run and disappeared around the side of the building.

19

Years ago, when he was in school, one of his teachers had said that most of the time when you think people are looking at you, you're just imagining it. You think there's some reason they should look at you, so you're certain you see them doing it. The teacher was Japanese, and all through the war years he was sure people were looking at him when he walked along a street in New York. He had Chinese friends who were just as sure nobody was looking at them, and the truth was people couldn't always tell the difference between a Japanese and a Chinese face.

Frank was sitting at the bar, waiting to meet Doris, and he was certain everybody was observing him, even though when he glanced around, their faces were turned away and they pretended to be deep in conversation with somebody else. He stared down into the plastic cup the bar served whiskey in. There was so little light along the bar he realized it would be hard for anybody to see him, but he still had the feeling he was being watched. Would the feeling ever leave him? He had the irrational conviction that where he was sitting was the only brightly-lit place in the room. But who would watch him here?

He bought a bag of nuts and split the package open on the bar in front of him. If there had been more light the combination of red, yellow, purple, and blue bulbs strung along the top of the mirror behind the bar would have seemed garish, but since it was so dark he only thought of them as gaudily decorative, a misplaced reminder of Christmas. Below the lights, taped to the mirror, was a hand-printed notice with large, clumsy letters that read,

If any fighting here all will be put out.

No exceptions.

He was trying not to think. He knew that he would have to decide something, but he wanted to put it off until he knew what was happening. Who was the boy? What was he doing? If he let his mind stay too long on the things that had already happened, his hand would begin to shake again, and he'd be back on the bathroom floor, staring uncomprehendingly at the glass on the carpet. Instead, he picked at the nuts on the bar, he listened to the songs on the jukebox, and he made himself stop going back over the last two days.

He was starting a third drink when Doris came into the bar. He had heard the same soul numbers a half dozen times on the jukebox, he had told two other girls that he didn't want to buy them a drink, and he had finished the bag of nuts. He looked at his watch and was surprised that she was only twenty minutes late. He had expected her to be later than that, and he was ready to sit there until she turned up, because he had been just as certain that she finally would come. She slipped through the noise and the array of colored lights with the sleek assurance of an ocean yacht drifting up to a dock. He half expected people to move out of her way. She was wearing another dark dress. This one, he could see when she got closer, was in two shades of blue. A light sky blue crossed the bodice, and the skirt and sleeves were in a shade of blue so dark it was almost lost in the

173

room's dimness. She put her hand on his arm, then picked up his drink.

"Scotch and soda?"

"You got it."

"I'll just help you with this one, then you can take me out of this place." She sipped at the straw in the drink. "I come around here so often I think sometimes I ought to pay rent for one of these stools." She emptied the cup and put it down. "Now I know you already had a drink or two, since I kept you waiting, so you won't mind going someplace else. You can have another drink there, and I got to get me something to eat." She shrugged. "When you got a job you can't get away when you want sometimes." She stepped closer to the bar, sliding against him and leaning her face close to his. "You don't mind?"

"Oh, I mind very much." He stood up and tried to match her tone of easy banter. "But since my drink's all finished and nobody else has come along with a better offer I'll go along with you."

As they left the bar and moved through the crowd toward the door, he was sure that for the first time what he had felt was real, for a moment everyone in the room was watching him.

Once they'd gotten out the door she insisted that they drive in her car, and she took them to a restaurant at the edge of town. She drove quickly and efficiently, and when they'd come to a stop in the restaurant's parking lot, she put her hand on his thigh and slapped it lightly.

"When it's my car nobody can take me someplace I don't want to go, or give me any of that line about get out and walk. You understand?"

He was amused by her. She helped him push the things that were obsessing him back to a manageable distance, and at the same time he was so conscious of the touch of her hand on his thigh that he had trouble thinking of something to say.

"I know I did say you wouldn't have to buy me dinner. Right now I'm too hungry to think of doing anything more than just look you in the eye until I've gotten something in me,

174

so you're going to have to sit there and wait for me. But you don't have to pay unless you want a little something too. I'll even buy you a drink. If I do the paying now then you won't get to thinking I should pay you back for something later."

And she opened the door and was standing outside the car waiting for him before he could think of anything to say. He followed her toward a strip of neon lighting that framed the doorway of the restaurant like a distended mouth. He watched her body move under the dress, enjoying her physical presence too much to care where they went or what they did. He was wearing new slacks that made his waist look smaller, but they were too tight for him. He ran a thumb along the waistband, trying without success to give himself a little more room. He realized he was feeling again like the clumsy, ill-at-ease Frank Lewis he thought he'd left behind him in Bridgeport. As they came into the restaurant he looked uncomfortably around for a mirror while they waited for a waitress. When Doris was looking the other way he quickly bent toward a small square of mirror he'd found set into the wall and carefully smoothed his mustache.

She had a salad and insisted that he try some Louisiana food. After he explained that he really didn't like food with a lot of spices, the dish she ordered for him turned out to be a mildly-flavored shellfish stew. She wouldn't talk until she'd finished the salad. "When I don't eat I'm not fit to talk to." The waitress brought them coffee and she leaned back in her chair. She studied his face at the same time. "You know, I never did get a look at you in that other place. It's too dark in there to see what anybody looks like."

"You sure you sitting here with the right man?"

"Well," she leaned her head to one side, "You look alright. But I'm going to have to see a little more before I can make up my mind. Now you haven't told me how I look."

"What are you asking me a thing like that for? Don't tell me you are one of these girls who has to have her men telling her she looks pretty all the time?"

"New dress. You never know how a new dress is going to go over."

She was quiet until they'd finished their coffee, then she began talking again.

"I don't want you to get the idea that I change my mind all the time. When I say I'm going to be somewhere then I'm there — but I couldn't get away from my job and I didn't have time to eat, so dinner it had to be. Like I said, you're not paying for it. A salad is what I wanted and a salad is what I got."

He sensed a defensiveness in her tone. She obviously had wanted to give him the impression that she was free to do what she wanted with her life, and she was uncomfortable letting him glimpse the ordinary realities of a job and responsibilities that would make her late for a date she had set up herself.

"What do you do?"

She fiddled with her fork. "Nothing so very romantic. I work in a hospital. I'm the one who makes sure people get their exercise." She said it with a kind of flourish, but he realized she was embarrassed at doing a job that had so little relationship to the air of nonchalant casualness she tried to present.

"Somebody's got to do it," he said, without any inflection in his voice.

He understood her embarrassment, but they would stay at this level of teasing banter unless they could come a little closer to each other, and before they could be easier together they had to know a little more about who this other person was. She could have said something else, she could have avoided saying anything at all. Instead, she had left herself exposed for a moment, and he knew she would decide about him by what he said next. She was like a slight, nervous bird that had settled on a bush, and it was waiting for the thing that had surprised it to move, and it would decide what to do then. He wondered what she wanted him to say. If he sounded patronizing, if he pretended to be too serious with her, he would lose her, and even though he still wasn't sure who she was, or what she was — what kind of bird it was that had let him come so close — he could not face losing her. He could hear other voices, a sound of dishes clattering in a distant kitchen. She was still smiling, waiting to hear whatever he would say. She had told him so

176

little about what she was doing, but he guessed that if it involved some kind of therapeutic care she would have had to get some training. She wasn't doing some kind of menial job.

"Where did you get your training?" he asked, hoping it was the right question.

"You know about the schools you go to for your training?" She was satisfied. She touched the hair on her forehead with the tips of her fingers, smoothing its curl into place, preening herself for him. "I went to Baton Rouge. Some of my mother's family is there and they kept their eye on me. Wouldn't do to let a girl like me run wild in one of those big cities." She had slipped back into her usual role. She stretched back against the chair again, easing her shoulders against it with a sudden, pleased smile. Then she studied him again, her expression changing.

"You alright?" she asked suddenly.

"What do you mean, 'Am I alright?' If you mean am I alright down here in Louisiana, I have to say the place is too hot. But if you mean right now, sitting here, of course I'm alright."

"I mean about the window of your room getting blown in."

"How did you hear about that?" He was surprised.

"I don't suppose they're going to put much about it in the newspaper. Something like that isn't supposed to happen to a tourist, and that's what you look like, a tourist. It would look bad for people around here. But the police come into the hospital all the time and one of them said something about it. So you have to tell me the rest."

"What did he say happened?"

"The policeman?"

He nodded.

"He didn't say much more than that. Just said somebody took a shotgun and blew in a window in one of the motels out on the highway. He said it was the room where that new nigger was staying and he asked me if I had met him and I told him he never needs to ask me that question because if there was any new talent in town I had him covered." She laughed at herself, and stretched her arms in a gesture of relaxed pleasure. "Of course I asked him if anything had happened to that fine

177

figure of yours, but he said they missed you. If you had gotten hit he thought there wouldn't be much use taking you to us, they'd just have taken you right down to the cold room they got there in the bottom of the courtroom."

"Did he say what it was about?"

"Just something about some boys, some white boys who always run together. That's the part I was waiting for you to tell me about."

"I told the policeman who came around afterwards, Fontenot, I told him I didn't think it had anything to do with me. Somebody must have gotten the wrong room."

"So you just think it was a mistake?" It was her turn to be surprised.

"Now why would anybody want to take a shot at me?" His tone was casual, but she could see he was serious. She reached across the table and squeezed his arm.

"Why honey, they think you trying to steal off with the one lady with some class in this town."

She drove them out of town, through the flat dark fields and shadowed stretches of straggling brush and trees, until they came to a brightly-lit bar with a scattering of cars parked alongside it. Once inside he found it wasn't as noisy as his usual place and there were fewer people standing around the door.

"I wanted to get you off by myself where nobody's going to come up and interrupt us. Now I'm going to tell you one time, and I'm not going to tell you again. I'm going to go home tonight to sleep by myself, and I'm not going to put up with no discussion. If you don't want to accept what I'm telling you, then you can call yourself a cab and the boy will get you back to your motel."

At the same time she was saying this she had moved closer to him, and she was touching his cheek with her fingers. She watched his eyes, then she began to laugh, her voice low in her throat. "You supposed to say something now."

"You the one who's doing all the talking."

Trying to make him say something she leaned her shoulder against his chest. He could feel the strength in her body, the muscular line of her hip and thigh. Beginning to laugh himself

178

he pressed back against her. She took a step away from him.

"You don't mind taking your chances, do you?"

He still didn't answer, making her finish what she had started to say. She touched his face again. "I don't hear you agreeing with what I said, but you still standing here so you know what you're doing."

He shrugged, still laughing. "I know what I'm getting into."

"No." She pushed his face away. "No. You know what you're not getting into. I don't know one thing about you."

"What you see is what you get."

She snorted. "If that's the best you can do we not going to get nowhere at all. You buy me a drink, you hear."

"The last time we were drinking you couldn't keep your hands off my scotch and soda. You going to stay with that or will you drink anything the man puts in front of you?" He couldn't be serious with her, and he sensed she was having even more trouble with him. Despite her manner she still didn't seem to be sure she was handling him the right way.

"A scotch and soda will be fine," she said in a lower tone.

When they'd gotten the drinks he nodded toward a small table off to the side of the room and led her to it. He suddenly was impatient with their perfunctory bantering. It had been a way for them to first get to know each other, but now it had become an increasingly labored game that neither of them seemed to know how to end. When he began talking again the teasing tone was gone and he was speaking in his usual New York accent.

"Doris, sweetheart, I heard every word you said. If you come right down to it I didn't get much sleep last night, and you had to put in a long day at the hospital, which means neither of us is up to much. So why don't we just talk without all this messing around? We'll have a couple of drinks and you can tell me who you are and I can tell you who I am, then we'll go off to our own beds and get some sleep."

Despite her effort to seem as casual and unconcerned, he could sense her surprise at his sudden emotional shift. It was his turn now to find out about her. Did she have anything to her besides the figure and some easy talk? As if to answer him her expression had become as serious as his.

"Are you sure you weren't hurt when your window was blown in?" Even the tone of her voice had changed as much as his.

"I had trouble hearing for an hour or so, and I got some dust on my clothes, but if it was me they were aiming at, they didn't hit me."

"You don't think it was you they were after?"

"I don't know why they would be."

"But you must have some idea."

Frank hesitated. Something kept him from telling her about the picture.

"It could be something to do with my talking to people like Jessie about what happened back in 1937. Fontenot thinks it is. But I don't see how it could be. I haven't talked to anybody but Jessie about it. Do you know anybody who would get worked up if somebody began talking about those things?"

"Fontenot's the fellow in the police, that right? I know what he's thinking. There's always some white boys out there who get a little wild if they think some nigger boy's going to start something. Now, it could be that some of the black fellows around town might get it in their minds to do something about the things that happened then. If they really got started, and the rest of us began thinking about what had gone on, there wouldn't be a lot of white men left living in this part of Louisiana."

"But I haven't come across anybody who's going to do that," he insisted.

"No," she admitted. "I haven't either. But I don't know if I understand those white boys either, even the ones in a family living down the street from me. I think if they got worried enough they'd shoot into somebody's window."

"You have any trouble?" His voice was low.

She looked down at her hands. "Long time back. Not to me, but to my daddy. I suppose everybody had some trouble some time or another."

"Bad hurt?"

"No. They just beat him and burned out what was in the feed barn. I think they were drunk. He never did know what it was about."

"You think about it much?"

"Would it do me any good?" Her tone was challenging.

"No." He finished his drink and smoothed his mustache. "No, it wouldn't do you any good at all."

"I told you I was just going to drop you back here."

It was two hours later, and she had stopped the car beside his, back at their old bar. Once they had started talking it had been just as hard for them to stop. They had learned, almost to their surprise, that they liked each other. So much about them was different, but his mother had grown up in the same countryside, and he had picked up so many of her attitudes that he and Doris found themselves starting to say the same kinds of things to each other. It was as though he had opened a new door inside himself and found someone else there. Or had he left some other person behind there in Connecticut? Even with his moment of clumsiness when they'd gone into the restaurant — had he turned into someone else?

Her head was back against the car seat, and he could see her smiling in the darkness. "You see now that I meant it when I said I was going to go home alone." A light, brushing tone to her voice, as if she had softly touched him.

"You the one that keeps talking about it," his voice feigning petulance.

She spread her fingers on his thigh. "Maybe I'm thinking about what I'm missing."

"You had your chance." He was laughing. "You had your chance, but it's too late now."

Her laughter chimed with his. "Sometimes that's the way it goes."

They had begun to slide closer to each other as they talked, and they slowly and carefully let their mouths touch. It was a hesitant, questioning kiss, but it was a kiss. They stopped, then kissed again with less hesitancy, and he could feel the tentative brush of her body against his. When he lifted his hand to touch her breast one of her hands took his, but held it against her for a moment before she put his hand back in his lap.

"I have been known to drop into the bar here on other nights."

"You just might be here tomorrow night?" he asked lightly.

"Wouldn't surprise me."

"Then I won't be surprised." And they kissed again.

He still was thinking about her as he drove slowly back through the deserted streets to his motel, but she began to fade from his thoughts as he got closer. Instead, he was suddenly filled with images of what had happened the night before. Telling himself again that it hadn't been meant for him, he still knew that he had to decide something. He couldn't put off his meeting with the man in the photograph. The face once again began to crowd everything else out of his mind. As he slid out of the seat and closed the car door he looked sharply around him. Everything looked just the same. It was dark and nothing was moving close to the motel — the only bright light the row of flood lamps above the looming outlines of the parked trucks. Beside him was the darker patch of grass, the dim line of pathway. The fronts of the buildings were lit with yellow mosquito lamps, but he had to walk across one of the shadowy stretches of grass to get to the stairway leading to his room.

He had taken a few steps over the rough crab grass when he stopped short, his breath caught in his throat. A car was pulled up beside the building, and he could see someone sitting inside it. The face was turned away, but there was enough light for him to recognize that it was the same thin teenager who had been waiting for him outside the door of the police station. He stepped back, but the boy had already seen him glance in his direction and he started the car. Despite his fear Frank wanted to stop him, to find out what he was doing. He started toward the car in a loping run. Without turning on his lights the boy began backing away. In the first burst of speed the car thudded against a wooden fence behind it. The crash didn't seem to do any real damage, but Frank could hear a scrape of metal as the car turned and spun toward the highway. When he had reached the motel office the car was already out of sight in the stream of highway traffic. Frank stopped on the ribbed stretch of pavement, staring into the blur of lights, his chest pounding, and his hands bunched in a trembling grasp on his shirt.

III

20

He began driving as soon as he finished breakfast. When he was in a car he always looked around at what he was passing, but now he wasn't seeing anything. Only the concrete line of the highway held his eye, as if the painted center stripe were a confusing gesture whose direction he was struggling to understand. He was driving badly, veering in and out of the line of traffic with sudden yawing swings. He was as little aware of the noise of the motor or the thump of the tires against the pavements as he was of the clusters of farm buildings sliding past him.

The little sleep he'd gotten the night before had been fitful and uneasy. He had wakened again and again, straining to hear footsteps, thinking he'd heard someone outside his door, certain, in a moment of half-wakefulness, that he'd heard voices whispering. His first emotion had been a new awareness of the fear that had never left him. It had become almost physically painful. But as the hours of the night slid past, the fear had yielded to a new sense of anger that had

185

swept over him with the immutability of a wave. In his sleepless imagination the two faces had merged, the face of the leering white man in the photograph and the face of the teenager who had been lurking at the motel. Each had become an aspect of the other, and as their features had changed and shifted to become like each other's, something had given way inside him. Whatever had been restraining him was gone. He was on his way to Mississippi to buy a pistol. At least he'd have something to fight back with.

What would he do with the pistol? He had been so disturbed he hadn't properly looked at himself in a mirror in days. It seemed now that he had changed so much — would he even see the same face reflected back to him? The things that had given his life its shape and definition had been wrenched from him and he'd been compelled to find a new way to pattern everything he'd ever thought about himself. It would show in his eyes now — in his expression. He could feel the change within him. His body was harder, his face would have a tighter line to the mouth and the shape of his jaw. He was holding the wheel stiffly as he drove. It was his anger that had changed him, and he knew that the anger had left its stamp on every part of his body.

For the first two or three hours he drove on a divided highway that took him east. He was in a continuous stream of traffic. Trucks swayed past him. Clumsy cargo carriers crowded him against the shoulder of the road with their intimidating weight, even if they came no closer than the small cars that sometimes pushed by. As much traffic was scattered along the other side of the highway — trucks, trailers, cars, all the rush of people over the cleared earth that would have taken weeks to cross if there had still been the land's first growth of trees and brush. Noone in any of the cars noticed anyone else. He knew that the car windows were rolled up and everyone was enclosed in a veil of air conditioning and sounds from their radios. A station from a nearby small city was broadcasting an endless succession of over-familiar songs and aggressively amateurish commercial messages, and most of the cars were probably tuned to it, as he was. The people around him were traveling together on the same road, listening together to the same voices, but this didn't mean that they had any feeling of sharing anything with each other.

It wasn't until the road began its sweeping turn toward the bridge over the Mississippi that he realized he'd never seen the river before. It had been close to him for several miles, but only as a wall of earth against the edge of the horizon. The countryside he was driving across had been flooded over so many times that it had a harried flatness to it, and the markings of fences and dirt roads that divided it into fields and farmsteads seemed arbitrary and inconsequential. If the river were to swell over the earth wall containing it again, the markings, in a moment, would be swept away.

The shape of the bridge was the spindly, lean gray metal structure he had expected, but he wasn't prepared for the long circle up to it, the long rise on clumsy stilts that carried the roadway above the ground beside the river. Then below him was the river itself. It wasn't what he had imagined it to be. He had been taught as a child about the majestic sweep of the Mississippi. What stretched under the bridge was a thick, stocky, mud-filled stream that was confined on one side by the twisting, sinuous line of the levée, and across from him by the bunched gathering of bluff where Natchez had been built. Perhaps at another time he would come back and look properly at the river, now it was only an obstacle he had to get across.

He followed highway signs that took him around Natchez. He wanted to stay out in the country, where there would be fewer people to notice him. The land was different on the river's east bank. Instead of the miles of flat fields, he found himself driving through an area of low wooded hills. Small farms had opened clearings in the forest, but there was still a feeling of what the land must have been like before it was settled. He hadn't ever been concerned about this countryside, or the fields and the streams he had driven across all morning, but he was seeing it now as the land his mother and father, and their families and their mothers and fathers, had crossed, had cleared, had worked with their hands, and he was seeing it with a new intensity.

He knew that if he kept driving east and north he would come to Jackson, and then beyond it to the cotton country of the Delta, but he had driven as far as he wanted to go. He would find what he was looking for in the next few miles. He turned off onto the smaller roads and at a railroad crossing in a string of buildings at the edge of a freshly-tilled field, he saw the first shop sign for guns and ammunition. He slowed down as he approached it, but the place looked too isolated. He would be noticed just as much in a place this empty as he would in a place like Natchez, where there would be many more people. The sign was on a square clapboard building painted a dull gray. It had probably once been a gasoline station, and a roof hung out over what once could have been the service area. Only unpainted wooden supports still held the roof up over the chipped concrete island where the pumps had stood. An ornamental iron railing had been placed on the roof to dress up the building's sorry appearance, and nailed close to the eaves were the usual advertisements for soft drinks and beer and fertilizer. In a space left clear between the swollen soft drink bottle caps someone had painted the words GUNS AND AMMUNITION in square letters. The incongruity of the iron fence and the fertilizer signs and the advertisement for weapons was as disconcerting to him as the building's isolation and its shabbiness. He accelerated again and left the gathering of buildings behind him.

He wasn't following his map, and without noticing which direction the road was leading him he found himself coming close to the river again. He slowed down to drive through a small town, then just beyond it he reached a rambling wooden building at the edge of a muddy stream. Three or four cars and a truck loaded with logs were parked in front of it. Stretched above the cars was a large white sign with the words,

> Minnows 50 for $1
> Discount Tackle
> Mississippi Fishing Licenses

Closer to the road was a smaller metal sign, with neon tubing outlining the letters.

Henderson's Bait Shop
PISTOLS
AMMUNITION

He parked his car at the side of the building, pulled open a torn screen door with an old advertisement for laxatives dangling from the wooden frame, and went inside. It was dimly lit after the harsh afternoon sun. He stayed close to the door, waiting for his eyes to adjust. The store was a clutter of fishing poles and reels, racks of hunting clothes and piles of metal buckets. There were several men inside, but they were in a side room, gathered around a table, drinking beer and talking loudly. One or two of them looked up when he opened the door, but they paid no attention to him. Suddenly nervous, he crossed the jumbled store to a display case that was filled with pistols. He had seen them sometimes when he was a teenager in Harlem — he'd even held a pistol in his hand once — but he'd never fired one, and he never had considered owning one. They looked so solid in the glass case. Even the smallest models had a concentrated weight and bulk to them. He could see most of the pistols on display were second-hand, and the metal had taken on a dull gleam that gave even more emphasis to their weight. He was leaning over to look at them more closely when he heard someone coming toward him. The man was slight and so white-skinned the freckles stood out like dark spots on his thin arms. His hair was combed straight back from a knobbly forehead and he was wearing a cotton shirt that had been washed many times and only occasionally ironed. His khaki trousers looked like he had worn them to clean fish.

"What can I do for you all, boy?" The man's voice was rough and dark with a marked southern accent. Frank still was bent over the case, but he straightened up with a jerk. The man had used the word "boy." Frank had never been called "boy" before. He looked at the man's face, so surprised that he was more curious than frightened. The man stared back at him, his face hard-edged and completely without expression. After a moment Frank pointed at the case. Just as he was about to speak, he remembered that it would be better if he tried to use his mother's accent.

"I was thinking about buying me a pistol," he said slowly, with a Louisiana softness to his voice.

"I got all kinds," the man answered flatly.

Frank looked at the case again. He didn't know one from another. He only knew it should be something small enough to go into his pocket, but with a big enough bullet to be a real threat. He pointed vaguely toward a well-handled silver pistol in the middle of the case. The man lifted the glass and took out the pistol. He snapped the barrel open, spun the cylinder to make sure the gun was empty, and offered it to Frank with the barrel still open.

"It's done a lot of shooting, but the grooves are good in the barrel, and it's got a new firing pin." Frank didn't know how to hold it, but he took it by the butt and held it up to the light so he could look into the barrel, since the man seemed to expect it. He could see there were some twisting grooves that must be the rifling, and the barrel seemed to be clean.

"What you all going to use it for, boy?" The hard, unfriendly voice again. When Frank couldn't think of anything to say the man continued to talk. "Target practise, most likely. Isn't that right? That's what most people use a pistol like this for. It's not one of your little .22s. With something like this you can see what you all doing to the target."

It was obvious the man knew everything about the pistols in his case, but Frank was certain he wouldn't give him much help. "I like the size of it," he said tentatively, "but is this the best one you got like it?"

Without hesitation the man snapped the pistol shut, put it back in the display case and lifted out a dark blue-metaled pistol beside it.

"Hasn't been so much wear on this one, and the trigger's set a little lighter."

He handled it as he had done the first one — reaching it across to Frank with the barrel opened. Frank peered down the barrel, and imitating the other man's movement he snapped the barrel in place and took the pistol by the grip. It felt as though it had been made for his hand. He had been surprised by the way a pistol felt when he had first touched one. Years of

190

refining the design had fashioned the grip to become more and more an extension of palm and fingers. He fumbled with the catch until he was able to get the barrel open again and clumsily spun the cylinder a half circle. He was torn between a sick, nervous certainty that he should put it down and get out of the store and his confused resolve to buy it and go back to the car with it in his pocket.

"How much is it?"

"Seventy-five dollars. But if you get your shells here I'll give it to you for seventy."

Frank stared down at his hand. It was finally the feeling of weight, of the smoothness of the metal that decided him. He put the pistol down and took out his wallet. The man crouched down behind the display case and fumbled with boxes and small cartons. He put a box of shells beside the pistol. He lifted the pistol again and pointed to a small lever behind the cylinder.

"Safety catch is there. But you know all about that." Frank could hear the tone of derision in his voice, but he was only impatient to get the purchase over with and get out of the crowded store. He was suddenly conscious of the presence of the men in the other room. The man took the money from him and crouched down behind the display case again, this time putting a slip of paper on the glass top.

"Registration slip for it. You fill it out." Frank stared at the lines on the paper. He had expected something like it, and he had already decided on a false name. He filled in the blanks as his cousin, Willie Thomas, and gave an address in Jackson. He didn't know if there was any such street and number, but he didn't think the other man did either. The man picked up the paper and glanced at it casually. He ran his fingers through his straggling hair.

"I have to check this with you all's driving license."

Frank shrugged uncomfortably, trying to think of something to say. "I didn't remember to bring it with me."

"You all remember the number?"

Frank tried to think of how many digits might be in a Mississippi license. Finally he said six random numbers in a low tone. The man wrote them down on the bottom of the paper. "You all bring it in with you next time you come by, you hear boy?"

Frank started up again at the man's tone, but the other man's eyes were expressionless. His mouth dry and stiff, Frank took his change, slipped the pistol into his pocket, picked up the box of shells and went out into the heavy glare of the afternoon.

With the pistol locked into his glove compartment he stopped in Natchez before he crossed the bridge. There were submissive groups of tourists around some of the older mansions, but in the business district the stores were half empty. He bought postcards, and the woman at the cash register told him where to find the post office. He was so dismayed by what he'd done that he needed to have some contact with people he knew. At a writing cubicle in the post office he addressed cards to his son, to Jimmy, to Inez — and then he tried to think of something to say.

What could he tell them? That he'd just missed being killed when someone shot up his room? That he'd just driven a hundred miles to buy a pistol that was hidden in his car, and that he was taking it around with him for whatever would happen next? That he knew about a man in the picture named Floyd Walker who was living in a little shack outside of town? That he felt he was suddenly changing into someone else — not the person he had been when he had seen them last? He stood for an annoyed moment in the cool, disinfectant scented dimness of the post office, trying to think of what he could say to them. Finally he wrote on the card to his son,

Dear Lester,
    It sure is hot down here. Lots of old buildings in Natchez. Hope everything is fine in school.
                                                    Your father.

To Inez he wrote,

Dear Inez,
    I just drove across the Mississippi River and it wasn't so much. It's certainly hot.
                                                    As ever,
                                                    Frank.

His last card, to Jimmy, read,

Dear Jimmy,
   Lots of brothers down here and none of them talks like you.

                                             Frank.

21

He turned off his car lights as soon as he came off the highway into the motel parking lot. Was anyone waiting for him? He circled the rows of darkened rooms, down one driveway and back along another. He had taken the pistol out of the glove compartment and it was on the seat beside him. He slowed down behind the cars parked in the shadows, leaning forward to see if he could see a face inside. He didn't see anybody, but when he got to his entrance he left the car in a secluded area and walked quickly, keeping to the shadows. The pistol was in his coat, pulling it down in sagging creases with its metallic weight.

He was tired and sweating and impatient when he got to the room. With the gun, now, he could find Floyd Walker, but he couldn't do anything in the darkness. When he'd taken a shower and made himself a drink he thought about going to bed, but he was too nervous to sleep, and he found himself staring at the curtained window. He couldn't make himself stop thinking it might blow in on him again. The room was too small, too confining, its cheap prints and the flowered curtains hiding too many places on the walls and the glass front. Without thinking about what he was doing he slipped the pistol into a trouser pocket, went back into the darkness and walked to his car. He locked the pistol in the glove compartment and drove to the bar.

Doris wasn't there. He walked along the line of parked cars looking for hers, but it wasn't with the others, and she wasn't on her usual bar stool. He felt a tired disappointment, but he couldn't face the room he'd just left. When the night was over and he'd finished what he had to do tomorrow, then he could go back to it, but not now. At the door he stood looking over the strips of light and darkness that alternated in a night quilt over the dirt parking lot. He didn't have any place else to go. Annoyed and petulant he swung back toward the bar and pushed his way close enough for the bartender to see him. It was the man he knew. Frank made a show of pointing to the bottle of scotch behind the bar and the bottle of soda down near the sink. The man made him the drink in the usual plastic cup, then left the cup on the back counter and went to the end of the bar. Irritated, Frank started to call after him. All the man had to do was give him his drink. When he came back and put the cup down on the bar in front of him, Frank started to say something, then he saw that the bartender had also put a piece of paper down beside it. He had gone down to the end of the bar to get it from the shelf below the cash register where he'd put it away. Frank put some change down in front of him and picked up the paper. It was a note, written on the back of a bar receipt and folded over.

> I need my sleep and all, but you probably would like to have somebody to say hello to. If you get this before 11 o'clock call me up and we can have a good night talk before I go to bed.
>
> Doris

Under her name she'd written her telephone number. It was a few minutes before 11. Frank put a dollar on the bar and pushed it over to the other man, who put it in his shirt pocket, and gave him a knowing grin as he turned to get somebody else a drink.

"That better be who I think it is."

Her voice was brightly impatient. She obviously hadn't gone to bed yet.

"Who do you think it is?"

"I know that voice. I'd know it anywhere. It's come half-way up from Louisiana, and worked its way half-way back down from New York, and it doesn't have any place at all to call home."

"It could be somebody else calling you and letting on so you wouldn't be able to guess," he answered mildly.

"I don't let any of those others call me up. If I let that trash worry me late at night I never would get my sleep. But I left you my number, and I told you to call me up, so that's alright. If I didn't know who it was I'd let the telephone just go on ringing."

"How did you know to leave a note there for me? I was all the way over in Mississippi." He couldn't help the tone of suspicion in his voice.

"I just had a feeling. Once I start in doing my work on somebody he doesn't wiggle loose so easy."

He tried to joke with her, finding it difficult to be casual. "When does it come my turn to start in doing my work on you?"

"Now you do talk pretty, I'll give you that, but you have enough to do just taking care of your own business." He could hear that she was choosing her words carefully. "I told you I have to get my rest, but you can come over and tell me about Mississippi. That's all, but you come on over." Without waiting for him to answer she gave him her address, made him read it back, then as abruptly put the phone down, leaving him in the dimly lit telephone booth, shaking his head over her unpredictability.

She lived in a new two-storey apartment building close to the center of town. The street was lined with small, wood frame houses, set behind deep, plant-filled gardens and a scattering of trees that cast a heavy shadow over the recently-patched stretch of sidewalk. The apartment building was built of brick, with bright wooden paneling by the doors. It was obviously newer than the other houses, and the fact that she was living there explained some of her casual self-assurance. Her apartment was on the lower floor toward the back of the building. She opened the door before he had a chance to ring the bell.

"No need to make any noise at this hour of the night." She was wearing a dress again, one he hadn't seen before. She had taken off her shoes and was barefoot. She had turned off the overhead light in her living room, but there was a soft light from small lamps on the wall and the table. She stepped aside to let him look around. The room was an incongruous collection of colors and styles, but he could see that everything was new and expensive, and the newness in itself helped hold everything together. The lamps were painted black, designed in simple lines, but the couch and chair were covered in a vivid splash of reds and blues. The table was a severe square of chromium and glass on which she had spread collections of shells and small metal colored vases. One wall was dominated by a large reproduction of a modernistic street scene of Paris, across from it was an embroidered piece of cloth covered with flying birds in shades of blue and orange. It was clumsily done, and in one corner he could make out her name in large, haphazard letters. It must have been something she had done when she was a girl, but she didn't seem to feel it was incongruous to hang it up with the new furnishings of the apartment. The effect of the room, richly imagined, gaudy and satisfied, was as strong and self-indulgent as she was herself. As distracted as he was, he still felt himself responding to its personality. He liked it. She could see his expression as he looked from one side of the room to the other, and she closed the door with a smile.

"You keep your place looking a lot better than I keep mine," he said finally.

"I always keep things looking the way they should. I never know when somebody's going to come knocking on the door."

"You don't have to let them come in." He couldn't keep up the bantering tone. He stayed in the center of the room, watching her. She confused him, and for the first time he was

197

impatient with her. On the one hand she was playing at a kind of vivid performance she'd learned to do with a certain flair, but at the same time part of her was standing to one side watching everything with a cynical shrug. She had stayed close to the door, and the muted light from the small lamps outlined her body against the pale wall behind her. He was conscious of the outline of her hips, the dark weight of her breasts and thighs. She was standing with her arms crossed, her feet spread. He watched her, not sure what he needed of her pretenses now. She was smiling as if she were mocking him for the effect she thought she was having on him, but she could sense his restlessness. It was obvious that something had been decided.

He tried to respond to her tone, but he could hear the forced quality in his voice. "You got to be careful about letting those boys come in. You can't always tell what you're getting just by looking at it."

Still not sure of his mood, she went on with her studied casualness. "I only let them come in if I think they might do me some good," she answered lightly, her eyes not leaving his face, her lips still parted in a half-smile. He changed his mind. She was beautiful. It wasn't important what he'd thought about her before. She was beautiful just at this moment, and that was reason enough to be there.

She took a step toward him. "A girl knows. At least she better know." She reached up and touched his cheek, then turned away to look at herself in the mirror beside the door. "It's a long drive to Mississippi." She was running her fingers through her carefully teased curls. After a moment he realized she had said it as a question.

"Wasn't any way to avoid it."

"Something you had to get that you couldn't find in town here?"

He waved the question away. "I suppose that was it."

She was thoughtful. Slowly, her eyes on his face again, she walked a few steps around him, as if she wanted to measure some new dimension about him.

"It's a hot drive going over to Mississippi," she continued after a moment. "You get all thirsty on a drive like that."

"You not offering to do anything about it."

Each of them had lowered their voices, and they were speaking slowly as though it had become difficult for them to remember what they were saying. She took a few steps further, completing her circle around him.

"I suppose there's something around in the kitchen. Those boys leave things behind, especially when they find out they have to go home sooner than they expected. But I'm not going to get you anything to drink."

They were both silent. With a tentative gesture, as if still uncertain what to do, she reached up and slowly touched his face again. He had turned to face her, but he kept his arms tight against his sides. He stood without moving as the tip of her finger rubbed back and forth on his cheek.

"Frank Lewis's son," she said finally, her voice a tight whisper, "that's what everybody calls you. Frank Lewis's son. Now Frank Lewis's son, it's late at night for people who have to get up early in the morning, so I'm not going to get you a drink and I'm not going to ask you about what you did in Mississippi, and I'm not going to tell you about the things I did today at my work." She hesitated again, her eyes looking into his, steadily, narrowly. "That would just waste our time. Isn't that right? That isn't what you have on your mind." She ran the tip of her finger lightly over his mouth. "I know that you're thinking about something else, Frank Lewis's son." Her whisper had become a soft crooning. "I know that, I know that, and I know that we don't have much time."

She stepped away from him and opened the door into the other room. She stood waiting for him, one hand reaching out to take his.

At first the room seemed dark and he caught only glimpses of her body as she undressed. He straightened up, holding his own clothes, not sure where he could put them. There was some light coming through the half open door to the living room. She hadn't bothered to turn off the lamps. He saw the outline of a chair against the wall, let his clothes drop on it and went toward the bed. She had drawn off her own clothes a moment before and was already stretched out in the shadows,

199

her body a lean dark shape against the pale cloud of the bedspread.

For now he could forget everything else. His mood was a confused blending of tenderness and nervous excitement, but when he stretched out beside her and reached out to touch her arm she twisted free and sat up, leaning back on her elbows.

"What you want to do with me?" Her tone was soft and teasing, her eyes gleaming in the shadows.

"I'm going to lay you down on your back and I'm going to make love to you," he finally managed to answer.

She thought about it for a moment. "That sounds nice, but I don't know if you're going to find it all that easy."

Sitting up, he bent toward her, still not sure what to make of her. She was as exasperating in bed as she had been on the dance floor the first night he'd met her. At least she was always the same person. She let him kiss her, softly, tentatively, then with a sudden movement her mouth fastened on his and her teeth bit into his lower lip. He cried out, and tried to seize her mouth, but she had already pulled loose and her body had drawn away to the other side of the bed. With a sudden flood of irritation that swept away the last of his nervousness he rolled toward her, but she was now slipping over him, and he felt her arms clasp tightly around his body, holding him helpless as she pressed herself against his back. Her skin was smooth and cool, and he sensed the easy strength of her arms and thighs. Just as suddenly she pressed her lips against his neck and let him pull her arms apart and twist free until his body was against hers. Her breasts, thrust against his chest, were as hard as her thighs. There was the same smooth strength in her waist as he had felt in her arms. She turned her face away from his mouth, but her arms went loosely around his neck as his mouth went down to the heavy curve of her breasts and their tight, hardened nub. Their legs had clumsily tangled and in the tossing darkness he could hear her begin to laugh. Finally she sprawled back.

"You got this far. What you going to do now?" She was breathing so hard it was difficult for her to say anything, but he could see her mouth opened in her mocking smile. He was so conscious of her body he could feel himself shaking. He was

200

breathing as hard as she was and their skin, that had been cool and smooth, was slick with perspiration. He didn't answer her. He shook his head and lightly laid his fingers on her lips. When she started to say something again he covered her mouth with his hand and as she twisted her head, trying to free herself, he pulled her body to him. She was still for a moment as he entered her, as if he had surprised her. Her mouth was open, but she had stopped moving her head as if she had forgotten what she was going to say. She lay without moving, but he could feel a stiffening within her. When he started to move more deeply inside her, she lifted her legs and clasped them around his thighs. Her head had begun to twist from side to side on the pillow below him, her legs holding him so tightly he couldn't move.

The sweat was streaming off his face. He could hear the heavy rasp of their breathing. She began to laugh again, a low, tight laughter deep in her throat, and the sound was a sudden goad against his ear. He pushed at her with a new insistence, he pressed her thighs back and he won his way into her body with the strength of his impatience and his hunger. She slowly gave way to him, grudging each slight advance, but he could feel her breasts heaving, her arms beginning to tremble. Just as he felt her giving herself to him her legs began to twist, her fingers dug into his neck, and with a strangled cry they lost themselves in each other.

When he found his way back to himself again they still were lying tangled together. Her eyes were closed, her arms thrown back over her head, but as if she sensed him looking at her, she lifted her mouth to be kissed. In the dim light from the lamp in the other room he could see that her lips were puffed and bruised. He kissed her gently, feeling the sting of the cut in his own mouth where she had fastened her teeth onto his lip.

"Don't you do that to me again," he whispered.

"I'll do whatever I want with you." Her voice was subdued, but her tone was still defiant.

"Then I'll do what I want with you."

"That wouldn't be so bad." She breathed with a deep sigh, then gently moved away from him. They still knew each other so little they had to find out how each of them wanted the other to lie. It was a moment before they were stretched against each other. Her head was on his chest and one hand carefully cupped his slack penis. He was quiet, his eyes closed, his fingers slowly stroking her neck. He hadn't been with a black woman for two or three years, he hadn't been with a woman so young for many years. Her smell was different from Inez's, stronger, more insistently physical. He touched her again. The clustered, tight pubic hair was different from Inez's softer whorl. Even more different was the strength of their bodies. Inez was so much older than this other woman, her body had yielded more, to time and to other people. From the sleek resiliency of Doris's breasts and stomach he knew she had never had children. He knew that someday she would, but her body was still too exultant in its supple strength to give itself over to another being. In a few years her body would be ready, but it wasn't now. He kissed her softly again, his lip still throbbing from her bite.

"You bit me, you know that?" he whispered against her cheek.

"I didn't know it if I did. You bit me."

"Where?"

"It feels like you bit me all over." She laughed again, but this time the sound was affectionate and relaxed.

"I got carried away a little."

"Just because you got carried away, you didn't need to drag me along with you."

They held each other silently for a moment, then she stretched her arms, thrust herself away from him with a push of her thighs. "You know you don't have to pay much mind to that little game I play."

"All that talk?"

"All that talk." Her voice was flat and resigned. "I have those boys coming after me all the time, and the only way I can get them to leave me alone is to act like there's nothing I don't know and nothing I wouldn't do. Mostly they get all nervous then and start looking for somebody who won't expect so much from them. And that works for a time, then they start getting all excited again and they come back and begin worrying me all over."

202

"You do this with somebody and you can't expect them to go off somewhere and never think of you again. You know better than that."

She curled back against his shoulder. "I don't do this with any of those boys. I've got enough trouble with them as it is."

"You can't tell me you just stop with all that talk." His tone was skeptical and amused.

She was still, holding her face against him, then she turned on her back.

"That's the only game I can play. You'll just have to accept what I tell you. If I didn't keep them away from me this way I'd never be free of them. Now I got them all wondering and worrying, and I don't get all that stuff about 'Sugar, I can show you how to be a woman.'"

"What are you going to do with all of them?"

"Wait, I suppose, for something to come along that looks a little better. You wouldn't think it would be this way, but what can somebody like me do? I went to school and got my training and I'm well qualified at my job. I didn't want to frighten you off that night when I had to stay at the hospital, but I supervise the therapy work and sometimes I have to stay with a patient to be sure the therapist I put on the job knows what she's doing. But I can't let those boys at the bar know about that. They'd get so confused about a woman, a black woman like me, doing that kind of job, I'd never see them again.

"I have three or four white girls on the job with me, two of them are supervisors, the same as I am, and you know what they got their eye on? They got their eye on a doctor — that's what they want for themselves. And there's enough white doctors around — all those young ones doing their hospital year — so I know they're going to get them one. But what's a black girl do? We have one black doctor at the hospital, just one, and he's got so many of those black girls there chasing after him that he comes in every morning looking like he's been run over by a steer, and after the steer ran him down he stopped and licked him all over. So what am I supposed to do with that? And what am I supposed to do with the trash that hangs around the bar there? Nothing. So like the song says, I'm going to sit on it until I'm ready to give it away."

She laughed again and her fingers began gently working on his penis, tracing its slickness against his thigh. "You think you might be interested if I gave away a little of it now?" Her other hand reached for him and with a shudder of impatience she drew him onto her. She held him away for a moment. "After this, you go home or you let me go to sleep. I have to be at work tomorrow." Then, as he pressed into her quickening body, her mouth opened in a tight, hungry smile.

He woke an hour later. Tense and uneasy, he lay on his back with his head on the rumpled pillow, staring up into the shadows of the ceiling. He could remember waking the same way — when was it? — how long had it been since he was with Inez? He had lain in the darkness then, staring up with eyes that didn't see anything, and he had been as tormented with his confusions and his indecisions. The two women had drifted close just as a current was sweeping him out beyond his depth. He had clung to them like they were some kind of vessel that would bear him to a shallow eddy that would save him. Now he could feel the weight of the woman beside him drawing him against her in the hollow of the bed.

In the living room the light was still turned on, and he could see the outline of her face and hands, her breasts and the curve of her stomach. Her hands were clenched against her, as if she were determined to show, even in sleep, that she needed no-one. He knew she was helpless to decide how she would look when she slept, but there in the half darkness he saw her more clearly than she had ever let him see her before, even when their bodies held each other. He was aware that he wouldn't sleep again. Each moment he lay there in the silence he could feel himself drifting further from her. There was no reason to delay any more. It was time for him to finish what he'd come to do. He bent down to kiss her again, his fingers stroking her thigh as though they were tracing the contours of the mist. He slid off the bed, quietly pulled on his clothes and let himself out the door.

22

One road led to another road. One dirt track merged with
another dirt track, but the two didn't become larger, didn't
swell in size as each one joined the next. Instead, each seemed
half-heartedly to lose itself in the other as they continued their
meagre way toward the flat horizon. He drove slowly. In
places the surface was ribbed with sticky patches of clay that
clung to the wheels as he slid through, hunched forward to see
where he was going. He was afraid of getting stuck. He would
have to find somebody to help him out, and he didn't want
anyone to see him. He couldn't see any buildings, but he was
aware that there were small hunting cabins and boat launching
platforms at the ends of some of the smaller roads he was
passing. On either side of him were newly planted crops —
sugar, soy beans — for one muddy stretch of road he drove
between diked fields sown with rice. A light wind rippled the
gray-green water, but the reflection of color and shapes of
clouds on the surface made it seem as though the car was
drifting slowly through a section of the sky.

There was another road he could have taken. He could have driven out of town to a crossroads with a country store like the one where he and his uncle had bought beer and whiskey. From the crossroads Floyd Walker's place was only three miles back in a cut-over growth of trees and brush. But the road to get out there was narrow and open. He would be seen driving toward the house. So he had looked at a map of the area and found a string of farm roads that would take him to the house by another route. No one would notice a car coming from that direction. He had made a crude copy of the map on motel stationery, and it was on the seat beside him. When he came to a fork in the road, he went even slower to study the drawing, then, when he had found the way, he picked up speed again.

The sun was almost directly overhead, hazy and unblinking, and after an hour he realized, with a tightening knot in his stomach, that he couldn't tell if he was driving in the right direction. In the flat, featureless countryside there was no way for him to tell if he had lost his way. For a sudden, almost frightening, moment he had the sensation that the whole earth was reeling around him, and as he drove, the car remained where it was, in one spot. He had to keep driving just to stay in this place he'd gotten to — in these monotonous passageways between the twisted strands of wire that hemmed him in. He made himself stop thinking about it. He mustn't think of anything except why he'd come.

For the first few miles he was paying too much attention to his rough map to notice the sides of the roads, but now he began to notice the signs of slaughter along the patched surface. The dirt lanes had a heavy traffic of farm vehicles, and alongside the ruts and the grayish covering of crushed shells that had been dumped on the surface, the overgrown margins of the road were strewn with dead animals. Most of the bodies were opposums, with naked, white bellies swollen into grotesque balls in the heat, the skin gray and discolored under the straggling fringe of hair, but when he looked closely at the pitted earth, he could make out the bodies of mice and lizards almost flattened into the dust. He swerved around the dried

206

shapes of muskrats that had been thrown up onto the center of the road. Occasionally he had to slow down to avoid a shape like a dirty, cracked bowl — armadillos that had been struck and left to die helplessly in their crushed shells. Once he drove over the elongated, elaborately patterned shape of a dead snake. When he'd driven further into the empty countryside he found he could anticipate the small, broken forms by the sudden flapping of dark wings ahead of him. Crows always found the bodies first.

Despite his efforts to concentrate on the map he couldn't shake off the feeling that he had come to a place where death was a continual presence. The bodies along the road were a pervasive symbol of the death that had brought him there, like pieces of a frieze, or lines of a design that formed an inextricable part of a larger pattern. He shifted uncomfortably in the seat of the car as he planed across a shallow ditch and felt a surge of muddy water against the floor of the car. Other signs of death were continually around him. On most of the telephone poles following the twists of the road he could see the hunched, staring shapes of large birds. He knew so little about the countryside, but he realized they must be hawks. A flurry of black specks wheeled into the hazy sky ahead of him. He could see that a flock of crows had driven a hawk off its perch and were pursuing it across a sky that was as featureless as the fields he was crossing. As he passed under them he could hear the shrill cawing, and for a moment it seemed to turn into his own name. Frank. Frank. Frank. Frank. As if he had become part of the sky with them.

After another hour it was obvious that he'd lost his way. The last turn he'd taken led to a dead end at a clearing beside a dark, slow moving stream. He could see from the pattern of old tracks on the bank that it was used as a place to put boats in the water. The opposite bank was thick with weeds, and behind the weeds was a dense palisade of trees. He got out of the car to make himself think more calmly, to give himself a chance to shake off some of the tension that was gripping him now, but the air was heavy and thick with smells of the decaying plants at the water's edge. He heard a noise behind him and spun

207

around to see what it was. There was a circle of ripples undulating across the stream, and he realized it must have been a turtle. He could see the humped shell of another turtle on a log further out along the bank. He wiped his face, looking around. Without thinking of what he was doing he began to breathe heavily, his mouth open, as if the coarse growth were stifling him. Even the water was choked with drifting clumps of weed, and high in the air were circling forms of birds that never seemed to drop down toward the earth below them.

He got back in the car. He couldn't stop wondering what he was doing there — in the confusion of his anger, his almost strangling sense of anticipation, he didn't know if he wanted to stop thinking about it. He carefully backed in a tight circle, keeping away from the darker patches of muddy earth, and after two or three wrong turns he found his way back to the place where he had been mistaken at a crossroads. The drawing finally led him back through the farmland to a two-lane secondary highway, a dark line moving between the fences, with its humped ditches brightened with motel advertisements, stretches of barbed wire with tufts of cotton impaled on the barbs, and a new scattering of dead animals. He turned in the direction he thought would lead him further out, away from town, but with the sun high over his head it was difficult to tell which way he was going. He could only watch the sides of the road, waiting for an advertisement to tell him something besides which beer to drink and which pesticide to spread on his crops.

He finally found a weathered grocery store with a gas pump outside it. There was the usual hopeful sign paid for by one of the soft drink companies in exchange for a metal banner advertising their beverage, the usual worn patch of earth that was supposed to be a parking lot. He slowed down, trying to see if the customers were black or white. The few dusty cars in front of the building were pointed in different directions, as if everyone intended to scatter as soon as they came out the door. He couldn't decide what to do. The place didn't need to advertise which race used it, since everybody who lived close by already knew. He tried to see through the large window in the front of the building, but it was covered from the inside.

208

Still hesitating, but too impatient to go on, he finally pulled off the road. Whatever kind of place it was, at least he could ask directions.

He had just opened the door of the car and started to get out when the screen door of the grocery slammed shut with a flat, slapping sound. A man was walking slowly across the dusty space to one of the parked cars. Something about the body, thin and edgy, seemed familiar, and he stiffened, drawing back behind the car door. The man was Fontenot. Before he could close the door Fontenot saw him, waved casually, and came across the bare earth toward his car. He was in a checked, short-sleeved shirt, jeans and dark western boots, but even out of uniform there was still the same suggestion of tight watchfulness to his movements. It was this that had caught Frank's attention.

As he waited tensely for the other man to get closer, Frank could feel himself becoming more and more nervous. What would Fontenot think about meeting him here? At the same time, he felt a new rush of emotion that momentarily eroded his nervousness. He realized he was angry. Somehow he had slipped past an unnamed border within himself. Something had given way. He wasn't angry with Fontenot only because he was a police officer, he was angry with him because he was white.

He already had invented a story to explain what he was doing in that area if anyone stopped him in the bayous, but he still waited warily for the obvious questions.

"How you all doing, Mr. Lewis?" Fontenot stopped beside the car door, smiling casually. Frank could see his eyes already noticing splashes of drying mud along the fenders. Frank nodded. He knew that if they talked for more than a moment Fontenot would sense his nervousness, and he felt himself struggling to keep his face expressionless. Fontenot nodded toward the massed green tangle of leaves and limbs behind the bar.

"I was thinking of doing some hunting around here. If anybody knows where to look it's the fellow that runs the bar here." He was still smiling, his young face clear and unlined in the half light that filtered through the covering above them, then he abruptly changed his tone. Frank couldn't tell when the other man slipped back and forth between his identity as a policeman and as an ordinary person who was thinking about things like hunting, and he was sure that Fontenot couldn't tell either.

"Has everything been alright, Mr. Lewis? You know, you haven't seen anybody else hanging around?"

Everything had gone past the point where Fontenot could stop anything. Frank couldn't tell him about the boy he'd seen waiting for him. "No. I haven't seen anybody." His own voice was carefully casual.

"You know, I had to let those boys go," Fontenot went on after a pause. "Like I knew would happen, I caught all kinds of hell for keeping them as long as I did. I had to listen to one of those lectures about what kind of money it could cost the city if somebody decided to sue us. But I know they were the ones that shot up your room, and they know I know it, so I figure it did everybody a lot of good. All them boys run together, so the word will get around to the ones that matter."

A truck rattled by, trailing the debris of the previous season's sugar crop. They watched it pass, unable to hear each other over the clatter.

"One of the boys in the crowd is a grandson of that fellow Walker who's in that picture you had with you."

At the mention of Walker's name Frank's head snapped back involuntarily, but Fontenot was still looking at the truck, and he missed the reaction to what he'd said. Frank's anger was tightly reined in, but he felt a kind of trapped bewilderment, as if their conversation were a maze, and he'd lost the way out of it. He had to find a way out before he stumbled further in. As the rattling died away Fontenot went on talking.

"I didn't say anything about it when you showed the picture to me, but it came into my mind. Most summers he stays with his grandfather at his place on the outside of town. It isn't too far from the road your uncle Jessie lives on. You go on a little further, then you take the other fork of the road and go on four or five miles to a turn that goes off there into the woods. But what you doing around here?"

210

Frank had been ready for the question, but now he felt that he had somehow lost the thread of what they were saying.

"I already went out to look at the place where my mother was living when I was born. I told you that," he managed after a moment, looking at Fontenot's face momentarily, then glancing away. "That was out in that place called Wardell. But she told me that before she was married she lived out here in these parts."

Fontenot shrugged. "I didn't know anybody lived out here then." He took a step back. Frank, feeling the policeman's attention beginning to wander, slid back onto the seat of his car.

"She must have been just young then." Fontenot smiled.

"Not much more than a girl," Frank answered and slowly pulled the door toward him. As he closed it he saw, with a sudden dismay, that Fontenot hadn't finished. He leaned against the sill of the window that Frank had rolled down when he was trying to look in the store window.

"I didn't know so many people were living in this part of the country, but there's been lots of changes. I see it the way it is now, just crops and pastureland, but I saw an old map when I first came into the office here, and there used to be people everywhere around. Most of them moved off somewhere before my time. I drive past one of those places where they used to live, one of those houses that's falling down, or a row of cabins, and it makes you wonder what kind of life they had around here then. One thing for damn certain, they were all pretty poor, every one of them."

With an abrupt gesture, as if there were something he'd just remembered he had to do, Frank turned the key and started the car. With his head down he thought ironically that now there was something he did have to do. He could feel his anger taking over again, and this time there would be no way he could conceal it. He said in a constricted voice, "I think most of them are living the same way now."

He had to get away from this man. He slowly began to pull the car out of the place where he'd stopped. Fontenot stepped back and shrugged in agreement. He said loudly, over the noise of the car motor, "If you see any of them boys again,

211

now you tell me and I'll get on them."

Frank nodded, and with a glance over his shoulder to see the road was clear, he edged back onto the highway. There wasn't any need for him to ask questions. Fontenot had told him everything he needed to know.

23

He stayed on the main road until he had come close to his uncle's cabin, then he turned off again onto the small dirt tracks. The land was higher here, with a dense overgrowth of stripling pine and weeds. It was uneven, crowded ground, the occasional fences finally losing their way as they tried to push through the brush. Some of the leaf trees were blossoming, and there was a shading of lighter green at the tips of the pine branches. He had pushed the map he'd drawn onto the floor of the car. He knew now where Floyd Walker's cabin was. He was almost at the end of his journey. He fingered the photograph. He'd folded it up and pushed it into his shirt pocket. Finally he could force this man to see himself as he was on that night. Despite the car's air conditioning system he was wet with perspiration, but at the same time his mouth, as he ran his tongue over his lips, was as dry as old skin.

He cautiously turned into a rutted opening through the trees and could see that he was coming to cleared ground. Beyond it was another dirt road. The cabin had to be somewhere at the end of that road. He drove the car toward some overhanging trees, to shield it from the worst of the sun, then backed around so he was facing back the way he'd come. He leaned over the steering wheel, staring narrowly around him, almost reluctant to turn off the motor. He held a hand up in front of his face and could see its trembling, but now he had to get out of the car. He had to go into the trees. He had to make himself do it even if he knew only so imperfectly what he was doing. He made his fingers turn the key, and in the abrupt silence he could hear the quickening sound of his own breathing, as if he were trying to catch up with some part of himself that was hurrying out of sight. He leaned across the seat, pressed the button that opened the glove compartment and fumbled inside it until he found the pistol. Its shape seemed to have changed: instead of smoothly fitting his hand it was large, nubby, angular. As he jammed it into his pocket he could feel the cloth yielding reluctantly, ready to tear if his clumsiness forced it too roughly.

He walked stiffly along the road, one hand brushing away the stray insects that flew too close to his face. He stopped at a line of trees near the cleared area. He could see the other road picking up as a gouged indentation beyond the trees, but he was reluctant to follow it. He wanted to come to the cabin through the woods, and he could see that to the left of the field was a depression in the earth that seemed to run parallel to the road. Perhaps it would shelter him as he came closer. He crossed the field and found he was standing on the bank of a muddy, sluggish creek that had worn a deep channel into the earth. The stream itself was no more than ten feet wide, but it had made a path for itself that was at least twenty-five or thirty feet across, and the surface of the water was ten feet below the level of the field. The water was dark, almost motionless. It seemed to be stagnant, backed up on itself, and despite the brightness of the sun the water gave back no reflection. He was looking down into an opening in the earth that seemed to be without life, but as he slid down the crumbling bank to the edge of the stream he realized that its stillness was deceptive. It had flooded in recent weeks and had only within a day or two shrunk back to its present depths. The banks were stripped of any plants or debris, and as he walked his feet broke through a half-dried layer of clay and mud that coated the stones and mounds of buried weeds.

He turned and began following the stream, awkwardly picking his way through the shrouded jetsam of the flood. Everything around him was covered with the same gray-brown film. He could follow the mark the water had reached by the line of mud deposited on the trees. The line was as even and sharply delineated as a piece of paper slashed with a knife. Above the line the trees were green, the branches thick with leaves, below it there was a colorless web of broken twigs and the gray, thickened shapes of tree trunks. He stumbled through the still, dead thicket, his city shoes slipping on concealed roots and knots of detritus that had swept against half-buried stones. It was a land that could have been inhabited by the dead creatures he had found along the first roads he had taken.

He was disturbed by the lifelessness of the sloping bank, and he tried to walk faster, despite the tangle underfoot. The rushing noise in his ear now was his own labored breathing. It was as though the emotional tumult that had driven him this far was threatening to overwhelm him. Behind the bushes he could hear his mother's voice whispering to him, through a screen of leaves he could see the resignation in his uncle's eyes. Words kept coming back to him — the things they had said to him hemmed him in like small clouds of insects. He shook off the words that were trying to tell him to stop, to go back to the car, to drive away. He knew this is what they would tell him, and to escape the hiss of their whispers he found himself running, swaying to avoid the tree branches, pushing the clinging leaves aside with outstretched arms. For once his body didn't feel heavy. He was coming close now — he was coming close.

He struggled up the bank, veering away from the stream, but when he passed the line of gray mud that marked the flood's crest he found himself in a coarse press of weeds that tangled against his legs. He couldn't see the ground and something tripped him. With his arms reaching out helplessly he fell headlong. For a moment he lay spreadeagled on the ground. He was gasping for breath, and perspiration was streaming down his forehead. He had torn his shirt.

He sat up and wiped the dirt from his arms with his handkerchief. He put it back in his pocket and got clumsily to his feet. He still couldn't catch his breath, but he realized it was as much because of his fear as it was the heat and the ragged terrain. He took a few steps and leaned against a tree. He had to decide what he was going to do now. He had avoided this moment, but he couldn't go on until he had decided something. Was he going to kill the man? As he had looked at the pistol in the motel room, he had felt such a fierce, pure rush of rage. His fingers had shaken with impatience as he had fumbled to load it. But now he was close to the cabin, the man was only a few hundred yards away from him. Was he going to kill him? He pressed back against the ridged bark of the tree, his chest heaving. He could feel the weight of the pistol dragging at his pocket. Was he going to kill this white man who had helped murder his father? He still didn't know, but he knew he had to make Floyd Walker think he would kill him. Then the expression on the face in the photograph would finally change.

He began walking again. He was moving more slowly, his eyes nervously searching the coarse growth around him. His breathing had become heavier, he could hear himself grunting as he moved. Trickles of sweat stung his eyes. He turned his head from side to side, staring around now, staring without focus, only half aware of what he was doing. He saw the slight figure of a boy bent down in a clump of bushes in front of him, but for a confused moment he didn't take it in.

"What you doing here?" It was the boy's voice, quavering with fear, that stopped him.

It was a moment before he made out the crouched figure in an opening through the trees fifty yards ahead of him. He stood breathing heavily, staring at him. Even at this distance he could see that it was the teenager who had been watching for him outside of the courthouse. The boy was thin, and his

216

hair was stripped down to his forehead with the heat, and as he took a step back Frank could see that he had a rifle that he was holding up close to his chest.

"What you doing here? You hear me?" His voice was thin and shrill, but it was steadier than it had been when he first called out.

Frank studied the pale face. What was the boy doing there? He took a step away, shielding himself behind a tree, but the boy's voice followed him. "What you doing here? I don't know what you all looking for, but you not going to find nothing here."

Frank could feel himself beginning to be afraid. What did the boy want? He crouched and ran a few steps to his left, to the shelter of another tree. He bent down, his chest heaving, and saw that the boy had also moved, still facing him. "They ain't nothing here you want." The boy's voice was frightened again. "You ain't going to find nothing here."

Abruptly Frank decided to run. He had to get away from him. He began circling through the trees, the slick soles of his dress shoes slipping on the surface of fallen pine needles and decaying undergrowth. He was vaguely conscious of his torn shirt flapping against his stomach. The heat was building up to an oppressive weight. He wiped his face with his handkerchief as he ran, then stuffed the handkerchief back in his pocket as he slid against a tree and looked nervously behind him. The boy was still there. He had kept up with him.

Frank forced himself to begin running again. He slid down into a hollow filled with brush and came up against a rusted length of wire fence. He straddled it and lunged ahead into the bushes beyond it. He thought he must still be moving in the direction of the house and began moving faster, swinging his arms as he ran in an effort to sweep the raw green bank of weeds out of his way. He dodged behind a cluster of the thin, young pines, his feet sliding on the needles, then he pushed through a tangle of vines and came to a narrow path. He started to follow it, but it seemed to be going the wrong way. He plunged back into the forest. He could feel his chest pounding, his shirt had caught on a branch and torn in another place, his sweating arms were streaked with perspiration, and crisscrossing the dark skin were marks where he had been scratched.

He must have gotten away from the boy now. He slid to a stop behind a clump of thick plants and hurriedly looked back the way he had come. He could see the broken line of branches where he had pushed his way forward, and in the soft earth there was a wavering line of tracks his feet had left. The boy wasn't behind him. He straightened up, feeling a thin trickle of exultation. At the same time he could feel his heart pounding and his breath was a coarse band of pain in his throat. He turned to look ahead of him to see where he would go next. And there was the boy. He was fifty yards ahead of him, just as he had been when Frank had first seen him. He didn't seem to be breathing hard and the rifle still was held stiffly against his chest.

"Oh, Jesus Christ, oh, Jesus. What is he doing? How did he get there?" Frank was whispering to himself. Without thinking he began running again. He still was going toward where he thought the house lay, but he was dodging now to confuse the boy. He must have been running to where the boy was waiting, that was why the boy had found him again. He slewed to the side of a heavy clump of bushes, changed direction again and labored over a small rise. His chest was burning, his face and body soaked with sweat, but this time he would get past the boy. His steps were slower and he was dimly aware that he couldn't lift his arms when he wanted to pull a branch out of the way.

The branch rasped across his face and he could feel the pain as the cut opened and the perspiration mingled with the thin trace of blood. He wiped at the blood with his handkerchief, running with a limp now, half doubled over from a pain in his side. With a last stumbling step he fell against the trunk of a dead tree, the bark stripping away and the upper branches torn and scarred by woodpeckers. He thought he could see a break in the trees. The house must be close by. His breath an unsteady gasping, he slid to his knees and began crawling toward the lighter opening in the leafy wall surrounding him. After twenty or thirty yards he slowly lifted his head to look around.

218

The boy was still there. He was standing half-shielded by a tree, clearly frightened now, holding the rifle out in front of him. He also was breathing hard. Frank could see his skinny chest heaving, but he dimly understood it was only because of his fear. The boy could go on running, but his own legs were so heavy he didn't know if he could stand up.

"I'm not letting you get past me, you hear." The boy's voice was trembling, but there still was a shrill intensity to his tone. Frank sank back again against the ground. He slid forward a few yards so he wouldn't be in the same place the boy had seen him last, and he pulled himself to his feet, holding on to the low branches above him. He knew now that he couldn't get past the boy. The boy was fifteen, maybe sixteen, he had grown up in this patch of forest. He was thin and hard, he had hunted since he was a child, he knew how to use the rifle. In a despairing moment of clarity Frank could see himself as the boy saw him, an overweight black man, clumsy and out of condition, his face streaming with sweat, his shirt hanging in torn shreds, the pain in his side almost doubling him over. How could he hope to find a way past the boy and get to the man in the house? He felt himself shaking with his helplessness, his frustration, his sudden flood of rage.

Still hanging on to a branch, his legs awkwardly spread to keep himself balanced on the bed of pine needles that covered the ground under his feet, he knew, finally, that nothing had changed about him. His lips began moving in a monotonous whisper. "You thought you going to be all changed. You weren't that same man who was riding that airplane. You didn't look like him, you didn't feel like him. Look at you now. Look at you." He stopped a moment to try to catch his breath, then the whispering began again. "You just the same. Just the same. You can say anything you want, but you know that now. You just the same man you were when you come down here. Everything about you is ordinary, just like you always knew it was. You wear ordinary clothes and you work an ordinary job and you live an ordinary life. What did you think? You so soft and out of shape you couldn't walk two blocks without running out of breath, and you got yourself out here in the woods. You just the same. The same. You just going to go on being what you are. Ordinary Frank Lewis. That's all."

He rubbed his forehead with an unsteady arm, trying to wipe the perspiration out of his eyes. His whispering stopped, it was too hard for him to breathe. Dully he forced himself to accept the fact that he wouldn't get to Floyd Walker. He knew now that if he had found him, if he had seen something in his face that was like the face in the picture, he would have tried to kill him. But he couldn't now, despite the rage he felt consuming him. Someone else could do it. Somebody should do it, but he couldn't.

In the turmoil of his thoughts, as he struggled to suck air into his heaving chest, he momentarily forgot where he was. He felt himself clutching at the limb of a tree. The air was thick with smells of torn leaves and half-dried mud. He lifted his head and looked around in confusion. What was he doing in this clump of trees? How had he torn his shirt? How had he gotten here? He could feel the weight of the pistol in his pocket. Why did he have a pistol if he wasn't going to use it? Did he even know how to use it? Did he know how to aim it, how to hold it, how to make it fire? In a sudden wave of self-disgust at his uselessness, he decided he shouldn't have a pistol, but what could he do with it? He should throw it away. Anywhere. In the bushes close to him. He stared around, his eyes seeing only the dangling shapes of leaves in the shadows, as he fumbled with the pistol in his pocket. He pulled it loose, held it up and was just about to throw it into a tangle of weeds when the boy desperately jerked up his rifle and fired.

Frank knew that one moment he had been standing, the next he was lying on his back. He tried to sit up, but something was holding him down. Something had thrown him out of the way there and wouldn't let him move. His chest was numb, but somehow the pain was gone in his throat. He was no longer out of breath. He tried to get up again. His left arm didn't seem to work, but with his right arm he pulled at branches and managed to get to his feet. As he stood swaying in the leafy shadows he tried to remember what had happened. There had been a sudden cracking noise just as he had been

220

flung backwards. The boy had shot him. He looked dumbly down at his chest and could see the blood soaking through the left side of his shirt. He felt himself starting to fall again, but his fingers clutched at the branch and held him up. He took a tentative step. He could walk.

He felt suddenly clear-headed. The boy would come back and shoot him again when he saw that he was still alive. He had to run. He had to get to his car. He turned and started back the way he had come. It was all silent around him. There were no sounds in the forest, not even the sounds of his feet as he stumbled along his own tracks. He was listening so hard for the sounds from inside his body that he heard nothing else.

It seemed easier to run now. With his left hand he was clutching the place the blood was coming from. He could feel the beginnings of a dull ache, somewhere where the skin was torn open, but he didn't pay any attention to it. He seemed to be breathing without any trouble, he still was running, but he noticed he had begun to stumble more often. He didn't understand why he was stumbling. He fell, but he was able to pull himself up again. He could see his left side glistening with its slick of blood. The pain in his side was gone, but he didn't seem to be able to straighten up. How far had he come?

After a time he realized he couldn't see his tracks any more, but he couldn't let himself stop. He had to keep running, even though he seemed to be staying in one place as his legs moved. Somehow he was running, but his face was pressed against a bank of grass and he felt himself sliding forward. It was quiet. He lifted his head, then decided not to get up for a moment. It was quiet with only a low buzzing somewhere in the trees, and he knew he must have been running for a long time because it was getting dark. He could see the shadows thickening in the wavering clump of weeds where he had fallen.

24

He didn't understand why it was still light. It had been dark
before, but now it wasn't dark. The sun was somewhere high
above him. Just beyond his outstretched hand the grass was
pale and yellow. It had been darkened by a shadow then.
Could the sun have moved? He wanted to touch the grass, but
he found he couldn't move his fingers. No, now he could
move them. Slowly. Slowly. If he concentrated very hard he
could move his head. Just a little. It was so still around him. A
few inches in front of his face was a small bird. The bird must
be making some sound. But it only dipped and wavered
nervously as it moved out of his reach. He moved his fingers
again and the bird fluttered to a bush a few feet away. The
grass around him was higher than his head. Unless he looked
straight up he could see only a little way. He tried to lift his
head, but it moved so slowly he gave up. A darting shadow
over his face. The bird had flown to a branch somewhere
beyond him. He was thirsty and with slow care he licked his
lips. Beyond the insubstantial stuff of the grass the sun was a
thick haze of gold.

222

He remembered he was supposed to be running away from the place where he was lying, but he didn't feel like moving. He didn't want to run anywhere. His legs were too weak now to hold him. He couldn't feel any weight to his body, but somehow he had become trapped inside it and it wouldn't move any longer. He wouldn't run. He didn't have to run.

He wasn't aware that he had closed his eyes. He opened them. He could see that the sun had moved again. If he turned his head a little he could look at it. It had become a large yellow ball. Around him, on the grass and on the branches, the color had deepened to a rich orange yellow. The spot of light that had been close to his fingers had moved away from him. He tried to stretch his fingers out to it again, but it was too far to reach. The grass around him was darker now. A ragged fringe above his head. No, it wasn't a fringe. It was the edge of the earth. Beyond the grass, in the bushes, darkness was beginning. He knew about the darkness.

Something was hurting him somewhere. Not the hand he could see outstretched, not the fingers. It wasn't there. It was somewhere close to his other hand. But he was lying on his other hand. He thought about moving the fingers of his other hand, but something heavy was holding them fast. And something was hurting somewhere.

When had he closed his eyes this time? He tried to remember. Now he couldn't see beyond the grass. It had become an unkempt barrier hemming him in. Slowly moving his fingers, he tried to pick at the stem of grass closest to his hand. He didn't know which fingers he was moving. He closed his eyes to think about it.

He heard something. What was it? He tried to concentrate. It was the sound of a foot scuffing close to his head. He could see the foot. He could see the worn leather of a boot. Sounds. Now he couldn't see the foot. He could see ants on his fingers. Not so many ants. Three. Four. He thought of moving his fingers so they would go away. Not so many ants. They circled in the shadows just beyond his hand.

The sun was setting now. He knew about the setting sun.

Yellow and red and flaming. Consuming itself in gasping mouthfuls of breath that came so slowly. His fingers couldn't move. He could see into the distance beyond the trees above him. He could see into the distance beyond the sun.

Something. Sounds. Eyes half open he could make out feet, shoes. A hand took his. His shoulder was turned. He was being drawn up from the earth, drawn up out of the raw shadows. A sound close to him. A sound without ending. Like the mewing of a cat. A voice speaking. "The nigger had a gun . . . the nigger had a gun . . . the nigger had a gun . . . the nigger had a gun . . . the nigger had a gun." Fainter. He was being drawn up from the coarse stain on the grass beneath him, and in a dumb, faint incoherence he tried to say it to himself. "The nigger had a gun . . . the nigger had a gun . . ."

25

If he opened his eyes he could see his fingers. He told himself
to move the fingers and they lifted clumsily. They were spread
on something stiff and white. His skin looked very dark
against it. He tried to think where the weeds had gone. His
eyes closed.

When he opened his eyes again he could see his hand more
clearly. It was lying on a sheet. He lay without moving; then
slowly tried to turn his head. His head was on a pillow and the
creases of the pillow case made a pattern of ridges close to his
eyes. They led in crumpled folds to the dimness of a sheet. He
was on a sheet. He found he could spread his fingers. He
carefully touched the sheet with his fingers. It was cool. The
air was cool. He wasn't perspiring. What had happened to the
sun? His eyes closed. He tried to remember something. He
tried to think what it was.

He opened his eyes. Someone was sitting in a chair close to
the bed. He looked like he had been waiting for some time. He
was wearing some kind of uniform. Frank pushed through

shifting paths of uncertainty, trying to remember who he was. When the man saw that Frank's eyes were open he leaned forward and lightly squeezed his arm.

"When they called me and told me you were beginning to show some signs of noticing where you were, I left everything sit at the office and drove on over."

Frank tried to make his mouth form a word. The other man leaned closer to hear what he was saying. Frank turned his head away and tried again to form the word. Finally he managed to make a sound. The man didn't understand him and he had to try again.

"Where?" His voice was thin and unsteady.

"You haven't talked with anybody at all?"

Frank slowly shook his head.

"You're in the hospital. We brought you here right when we found you."

This time it wasn't as difficult for him to talk. "When?"

"It was four days ago."

Frank stared up at the ceiling again. He was trying to think what had happened to the four days. He was slowly becoming conscious of a wad of bandages against his left side.

"I don't know . . ." he began, then he became confused and stopped. He heard a movement and the man in the chair seemed to be talking to someone. When he leaned forward again Frank thought he had seen him before. He composed his voice and managed to say in a low whisper, "I don't know who you are."

There were more hurried sounds of someone talking, then the man pulled the chair close to the bed.

"Fontenot, Mr. Lewis. I'm Lieutenant Fontenot with the police in town here."

"I couldn't remember your name." It was becoming easier for him to talk, but his voice was so low the policeman had to strain to hear him.

"I know you shouldn't talk too much, but I have to ask you a few things because I have to decide what to do with the boy I'm holding."

"What boy?" A hoarse whisper.

"You were shot. Do you remember that?"

Frank considered it, trying to make his memory focus, then he shook his head.

The room was silent. Beyond the wall there seemed to be a large window and the light was glaringly bright beyond it. Finally Fontenot spoke again. "I wouldn't worry you at all now, but I've got to try to talk to the boy and if you could tell me anything it would make it easier."

"What . . .?" Frank started and stopped again.

There was another urgent sound of low voices, then Fontenot leaned closer to him. "I'm going to tell you how much I know, then you can tell me if you remember anything else. I've got to do something with this boy I'm holding. I won't keep it up too long, and then you can answer me and you can get some rest."

Frank stared up at the ceiling again. It had become more distant from him. He tried to listen to what the policeman was saying, beginning vaguely to remember his face.

"I saw you about an hour before it happened, and I think I put you on the way to the old man's place. I said something to you about how to find his cabin from the turnoff. I don't know what happened after that, except you went off there. I don't know how close you got, or what you thought you were going to do, but the boy said you were trying to slip up on him through the patch of woods behind the cabin, and he'd been waiting for you to do something, so he had a rifle with him.

"Now he says you kept trying to find some way to come around him through the trees to get at his grandfather, and when you saw you couldn't shake loose from him, you pulled out a pistol, and that's when he shot you. There's no question about the boy doing it. He says he wasn't trying to kill you, but he wanted to get that pistol before you could use it. And I don't think there's any question about what you were doing out there in the woods. But according to him you never got to fire a shot and he put a bullet in you, so he's the one I got in jail. He was so scared he didn't even go over to look at you. He just ran back to his grandfather's place and told him what had happened. This is only his story, but it all seems to fit with what I could see. Of course, the old man had already heard the shot and was coming with a gun of his own. While they stood talking about it you must have been running, because they couldn't find you for a while. The boy hadn't been paying attention to where he was standing so they had to walk around until they found your footprints."

Fontenot broke off for a moment. "You remember any of this?"

Frank seemed to know what he was talking about, but it was unreal. With a questioning movement he pressed his arm against the wad of bandages and there was a reply of pain, a deep, insistent pain. He lay motionless, trying to think about what the man had told him.

"Mr. Lewis," Fontenot persisted, "what I need to know is what you were thinking of doing when you got to that cabin. The boy shot you. He says he did it. The only thing I wondered about, maybe he was covering up for his grandfather, but we checked their hands and he was the only one who fired a rifle. I can do what I want with him now. For all I know, he caught up with you when you were standing out in front of his grandfather's place, he walked you into the woods with the rifle on you, and then he shot you and left you lying there. If you didn't have a pistol then he's in jail for attempted murder, and he can go away for a long time. But if you did come through the woods the way he says, and if you did have a pistol and he saw it in your hand, then what happened could be claimed as self-defense. I need to know what went on out there."

Fontenot was leaning forward in the chair. Despite his effort to hide it, there was an anxious expression on his face. Frank shifted his head so he could look up at the ceiling, and in a moment forgot that the other man was there. It was a long way to the ceiling, and the space to it was filled with light. He thought about the light. It looked like it was made of particles suspended in a haze. He tried to make out the ceiling through it, and as he stared he seemed to be drifting slowly upward, and then he was asleep.

When he woke again he found this time that the pain he was feeling was hunger. He was eating when Fontenot returned to talk to him.

228

"You looking better." Fontenot waved over to him and sat down in the chair opposite the bed to wait for him to finish. He was in uniform again, which now included two-toned cowboy boots.

Frank went on eating. He still didn't know what to say. He took a long time over everything, tasting the food for the first time. He finally finished and leaned back against the pillow. A nurse came in to take the tray away.

"How close did I come?" His voice still was weak, but Fontenot could hear his question.

"Another hour. Maybe two. If the two of them had waited around any longer it would have been too dark for us to find you, and that would have been it. You wouldn't have made it through the night out there. You lost too much blood when you were running."

"They would have left me where I was?" Frank's voice was confused.

"I can't say that, Mr. Lewis. It wouldn't be fair for me to say. When they did find you lying there they thought it was already too late and I think they got frightened then. The boy — Odell's his name — was still crying and carrying on when I got there."

"The nigger had a gun."

Fontenot looked up in surprise. "I didn't think you were hearing anything then."

Frank tried to concentrate on what the policeman was saying.

"Then you're beginning to remember a little."

To Frank it was clear, despite the uncertainty of his memory, that the moment had come when he had to decide how everything would end. And it was just as clear that there was nothing to decide. There was only one way it could end.

"I did remember something else," he said finally. It was still difficult for him to breathe, and he spoke in a low, uneven monotone. "Was the picture still in my pocket?"

"It's with the rest of your things. You were shot lower down so it didn't get too messed up. Just some creases."

"Jessie has a kid who drops by sometimes. I think he's some kind of cousin of mine, like everybody else out there."

"That's right. He goes to school in town."

229

"The boys all hang out together now, don't they? Black and white don't stay apart like they did when my mother was living here."

Fontenot didn't answer. Frank was running one hand back and forth over the sheet, not looking at the other man as he talked.

"I saw a bunch of them together in a little coffee shop in town. Late one night. One of them was the boy you had in the line-up. I couldn't remember where I'd seen him, but that was it. When they were hanging out in the coffee shop a black boy about the same age came in and sat down with them. They must all know each other."

"What's that mean, Mr. Lewis?"

Frank had remembered the boy who had come into Jessie's kitchen. "The boy who's staying with Jessie Lewis, Jessie's grandson, he saw the picture and he heard me say something about what I wanted to do with the man in the picture who was smiling and holding on to my daddy's shirt. I even said his name. Floyd Walker."

Fontenot straightened and rubbed his hands on his pants legs. "It must have been before you got your window blown in."

"It was the day before."

"So we know what that was all about."

Frank didn't answer. He lay back, trying to catch his breath.

"Odell won't say a thing to us. He doesn't want to involve anyone he knows, I imagine. The only thing he told us was that he was out in the woods, going to do a little practise shooting, when he saw you trying to slip up on him. Odell keeps saying he wasn't trying to kill you. He said he was aiming for the arm with the pistol, only there was some bushes in the way so he couldn't get off a clean shot. Odell's good with a rifle, and if he'd been trying to kill you he'd have done it."

Frank lifted the hand he was able to move. "I couldn't run in the woods because I had on those damn shoes. What do you think about that, Fontenot? Every time I tried to run I slipped and I fell down. I came all this way, I asked all those questions until I found out who the man was I wanted, I went out there

230

looking for him, and I wore a pair of city shoes out in the woods. I'm out of shape, I'm carrying around too much stomach, and I think I could use some glasses. I haven't been out in the woods since I went out on a Boy Scout trip when I was thirteen, and there I was, trying to crawl through the bushes. What was I thinking about, Fontenot? I know I thought I could do something about that picture. I thought I could . . ." He fumbled for a word. "Do you hear that? I can't even make myself say it. If my mouth won't say it, how could I make my hand do it? I thought I could kill him."

He tried to laugh at himself, hopelessly, derisively, but it was too difficult for him to breathe. He went on in a lower voice.

"I have to say it. If I'd gotten to him, Fontenot, I'd have tried to kill him. You can do what you want with that, but I know I would have tried to do something. I found that out about myself out there."

Fontenot ran a finger over the stitching of his boots, considering his response. "You going to try it again? If you say 'yes' I'm going to have to do something about it."

Frank shook his head. "Knowing I've got that inside me doesn't mean I'm going to do anything about it. What would it do to my life? I'd have to become a different person, and I know now that I can't do that. Someway, somehow, I thought I could take care of something that happened when I was a year old, but somebody else will have to take care of it, and they'll have to take care of it some other way. I'm just a bookkeeper, Fontenot, and part of me says the numbers would add up the same no matter what color I am. So what was I doing in the woods, trying to get past that boy so I could get at his grandfather? I don't do any of that. I sit in an office and I write numbers down in ledgers and I worry about invoices and freight bills. I can't do anything but that. But I tried. God, I tried."

He spoke in halting phrases, but Fontenot listened without interruption, still tracing the patterns of the stitching in his boots. Finally he said in a neutral voice, "If you had a gun on you and you took it out, then the boy isn't in too much trouble. But, like I said, if you didn't have a gun then I'll have to charge him with attempted murder." Fontenot smiled tentatively. "Of course, that would be one way to take care of the Walkers. You could let us put Odell away for you. It wouldn't be the same thing, but that way you'd get something out of it." As he was smiling his eyes were carefully watching the other man's. "I wouldn't tell you that, except I'm sure that's not what you're going to do."

Frank lay silent. He had turned his head so he could see out the window again. The distant trees were still and unmoving in the afternoon sun, as if they were also trying to think of what he should answer. After a moment he shrugged and turned back toward the room. No, he couldn't do it that way, though there was still a cloud of anger within him that would never be completely dispelled.

"I had a pistol in my pocket. I drove over the Mississippi and bought it in some place over there where they sell fishing licenses. One of those run-down places alongside the road. I don't think I could find it again unless I drove around there a little. But you know — I never shot a pistol in my life. I didn't even know how to get the safety catch off it. For all I know the damn thing didn't have a safety catch on it, and the only thing I would have shot would have been my foot. When you think of it, it's all too crazy. I had on those city shoes, and I got lost looking for the cabin, I couldn't outrun that boy, and the final thing is, I didn't even know how to shoot the pistol.

"When I finally did get in the woods there, as close to the cabin as I could come, I knew what I wanted to do. I wanted that old man to look at that picture, and I wanted him to see himself in it. Then I wanted him to see the pistol I had. You know, that might have been enough, but how could that boy know anything that I was thinking? I was just so sick of myself and how sorry I looked out there that I wanted to throw the pistol away. So I took it out of my pocket."

"But you didn't know how to use it?" Fontenot's tone was noncommittal.

"I didn't have the first idea."

"Would you say some of this in court, about the old picture and how you wanted Walker to look at it?"

"Whatever you say I should do."

They both looked away, each of them aware of the truth of the other's discomfort.

"I think I can talk things over with Odell and work something out," Fontenot said finally. "I told you before, Mr. Lewis, if it had been my father and I'd seen that picture — I don't know, I might have done just what you did."

"You'd have been a hell of a lot better at it than I was," said Frank weakly and began to laugh.

26

He lay awake after Fontenot had gone. He didn't want to sleep. He wanted to think his clumsy way through his feelings. It was true what he'd said to the policeman. He wouldn't try to kill the old man. He wouldn't even try to find him. The man would know why he'd come out there the first time — Fontenot must have told him that it had something to do with that old picture. Floyd Walker had felt whatever he was going to feel. But what about his own emotions? Where had his anger gone? It had forced him to turn his life upside down — it had driven him to try one of the most incomprehensible things he had ever done — but where was it now?

What he realized was that his anger hadn't dissipated. It hadn't been a mood or a sudden reaction that time would smooth away. The anger had entered him instead. It had taken over part of him, and he was conscious that it simply had flowed into a place within him where there had already been anger before. He had covered it over years ago and then forgotten about it — since nothing in his life had made him draw it back up. It had always been there, and with the shock of seeing the picture everything had come back to him. What would it mean to hunt down a sick old white man in a country cabin? That was what he understood now. It was a society, an entire world that had committed this crime against him, against every person like him. Why single out any one of them? That somehow would trivialize the history and the emotions that had raged through him. What had happened was so large and so terrifying that he could only try to meet it with an anger that was as large and as encompassing.

So this would be the last thing he would be left with — that he would never be free of this anger he was feeling now. Perhaps his son would never share it — if only that would be true — if only there were things that could just be discarded, like a bundle of old clothes you throw in the trash when you don't need them anymore. But it would be there within him, and at the same time he would never give in to it again. He knew what it was, and he also knew that there was a larger dignity in his mother's refusal to let something like it alter her life. Could he ever learn this? He would have to try, and then he could go on. That was the paradox he would have to accept now — that the larger awareness of his anger would make it possible for him to live with the emotional reality of anger that would never leave him.

Sometime later he could see by the darkening of the sun's color that it was late in the afternoon. The door opened with the sound of a sigh. Was it his voice? He could hear light footsteps crossing the floor. Someone scurrying toward him. He didn't try to turn. He expected a nurse to come to him. The light burned with the same deep orange gold color he had seen through the grass as he had lain under the trees. He could tell the moment of the day from the sun now. He wondered if he would ever forget it.

"I thought you had something like that in your mind, but I didn't think you'd go on and do it."

The half-mocking, light tone, with a new hint of worry behind the words? He moved gingerly and looked up to see Doris leaning over him. She was in uniform, a white cap

235

fastened to her hair with bobby pins. She was in low-heeled work shoes and her uniform was like that of the other nurses, but she still had the same luminosity about her, the same physical sheen. He knew her skin would taste as warm and sweet as a plum if he pressed his mouth to it.

He tried to turn on his back, struggling with the shapeless weight his body had become. He gave up with an abrupt grimace and reached out toward her. She took his hand, lifting it and looking at his fingers with a surprised expression.

He managed to smile, but he couldn't think of anything to say to her. The silence suddenly became heavy and uneasy. They didn't know each other well enough to know how to be silent together. She finally began talking. "I never did think I'd hear myself say something like this, but I was almost crazy when I first heard they'd brought you in. Then the nurse who was in the operating room with you told me you didn't have too good a chance and I felt even worse."

As though it were a motion he was learning for the first time, he slowly turned his head and looked up at her and saw that her eyes were on his face, and for a moment she was completely serious. She let him see that in some part of her she was as involved as he was, then she lifted her shoulders in an impatient shrug, turned her eyes away and tried to laugh. "When somebody new comes to town you hate to see something happen to him. You know how it is in a little place like this." He only listened to part of what she was saying, more conscious that she still was holding his hand.

"It looks like now I'm going to start giving you some exercises in a few days. And don't you give me a look like that, because this isn't the kind of exercise you and I had before. You got to get out of this bed sometime and you're going to start walking again."

He found that what he wanted most was to say something else to her.

"I think I would have killed him." He still found it difficult to say the words, and he had to repeat what he had said.

"I know, my dear, I know." Her voice was unconcerned, skipping toward him through the light, but her face showed her anxiety. "I heard about what you said to Fontenot. The nurse who was outside the door told me what you told him. I heard you also told him you wouldn't try anything like that again."

"Yes," he hesitated, "but I could have killed him."

"I know that."

"I didn't." And he slowly turned his head back and forth on the pillow, staring at the stream of light that flooded in the window.

It was a time when everyone who knew him had to find him and say something about what had happened. Jimmy reached him by telephone an hour later.

"Frank — is that you, bro'?" He could hear Jimmy's worried voice on the telephone. He had given Fontenot his number and asked him to call. A nurse was lifting his shoulders and putting a pillow behind him so it would be easier to talk.

"I can get a plane and come down. I could be there sometime tomorrow. Or if you want Inez to come down instead of me. She's still too upset to talk, but I can get her on a plane."

"I don't need anybody to come. I'm just going to lie in bed until they tell me I can leave."

"I couldn't believe what that policeman told me. I don't know what you been doing down there, and the man who called me, Fontenot, he wasn't giving anything away. All I could get out of him was that somebody shot you and you were in the hospital. They tried to kill you, didn't they? Just like I always told you."

"It was a fifteen year old boy, and from what Fontenot says, he's a good shot. If he'd been trying to kill me I'd be dead."

"It was just some kid? I know those honkies down there have those feelings from the time they're young, but that's just a kid. They must be born thinking that way."

"Jimmy . . ." Frank tried to think of something to calm him down. "I'm going to come through it. You don't have to worry."

"What do you mean, don't worry?" Jimmy's tone was

outraged. "I know what you must be going through. What's this Fontenot doing about it?"

"He's not doing anything about it," Frank answered shortly.

"That peckerwood's white, isn't he? I know he's white. One of those southern policemen with a big belly and a cigar. You tell him that if he doesn't do something I'm going to come down and do something about it myself. And if I come down there he's going to know it."

Frank listened to him talk, his head back against the pillow. "No, Jimmy," he broke in finally, "It's over, and when I get out of the hospital I'll be back and I'll explain it to you as best I can."

"Does this Fontenot know who did it?"

"I already said it was a fifteen year old boy who knows how to use a rifle."

"Does Fontenot even have him in jail?"

"No," Frank had to admit.

"I can't believe that. Now you know there's no way I can believe that. Do the newspapers know about this? Has anybody at the hospital called the news services? Or is the South gathering around to protect its own, just like always?"

"Everybody knows about it." Frank could feel himself growing weaker. He didn't know if he could talk much longer.

"And they know the boy's free? Out on the streets?" Again the outrage in Jimmy's voice.

"Now you listen," Frank said slowly, "Fontenot isn't bringing charges against the boy and he isn't bringing charges against me."

"I suppose he's going to put you in jail for loitering, the usual thing for those peckerwoods down there." Jimmy's tone had become harsh and jeering.

"No." It was becoming harder for Frank to talk, but he had to finish. "The charge against me would have been attempted murder. The charge against the boy would have been shooting in self-defense."

For a moment he didn't think the other man had heard him. "They trying to do something like that to you, picking you up for throwing a paper on the sidewalk, reckless driving, anything they want to accuse you of."

"What Fontenot is trying to do is get me off without any kind of charge," Frank insisted.

Jimmy began to sound confused, as if he still hadn't understood what Frank had told him. "But you didn't try to kill anyone?"

"It's in Fontenot's hands."

"But you can't let them do this to you. You lying there on your back and they talking about charges they going to bring against you. That's what those people are . . ."

"Jimmy." Something in his tone as he broke in finally silenced the voice on the other end of the line.

"Did you try to kill somebody?" Jimmy asked. "You know I won't believe you, no matter what you say."

"I didn't know until the moment came what I was going to do, but I had a pistol. It was in my hand, Jimmy. The boy couldn't know what was going on in my mind. All he had time to do was shoot."

"Jesus Christ," Jimmy murmured after a silence. "Jesus Christ. I thought I knew you, I really did. I thought I knew all about you."

"In town a lot of people go around calling me Frank Lewis's son. That's a different person from Frank Lewis, whoever he is." Frank's tone was flat and resigned. "I don't think I know who this new person is, either."

"But you still the same old Frank, and that man would never get himself into the kind of situation you telling me now." Still a bluster to Jimmy's voice, still he was trying to fend off what Frank was telling him.

"You just going to have to get to know me all over again," Frank said finally, with a burst of impatience. He was too tired to go on talking, to go on trying to explain something he didn't understand himself. "Jimmy, I can't talk any more. Give me a day and I'll feel like somebody again. Now I don't feel like anything. If you want to know anything more about what happened you can call Fontenot."

The truculence hadn't gone out of Jimmy's voice. "I don't know how to talk to those people."

"Jimmy — you the one with the vocabulary," Frank tried weakly to joke.

"No. No, brother, I don't have those kinds of words."

His uncle visited him the next day, his wiry arms stiff and uncomfortable in a faded dress shirt. He'd found a pair of slacks, but they were creased and ended above his ankles. They had obviously been bought for someone else and found their way to him by chance. He stood just inside the door, his eyes moving nervously from one side of the room to the other. Finally he slipped into the chair beside the bed, as uneasy in the new surroundings as he'd been in his own bare kitchen. Frank thought of him as the kind of man who wouldn't feel at ease unless he was in the middle of a field, and then only if he were alone.

Frank turned on his side and held out his hand. The older man bent forward to take it in his for a moment, then drew himself back into the chair.

"I told you what was going to happen," he began, then he had to stop and clear his throat. It was obvious that to create some sort of defense against the tide of his emotion, the only feeling he was going to allow the man in the bed to see was exasperation. "I told you that, didn't I?" he went on, his voice noisy and rushed. "When you kept after me about how you wanted to know, I told you then, you just let all that alone. But you had to go ahead, and see what you got for it. You going to be alright now?" he added hastily, trying to make some order out of his incoherence.

"I can get out of here in a day. Maybe two. But it's going to be alright." Frank didn't know how to answer him.

"You know I told you," Jessie persisted, his mouth set in a thin, disapproving line.

"Some things you have to find out yourself," Frank shrugged.

"But I told you. There's some things that once you start on them, then you know what's going to happen in the end like it was written up in some book. It's like you was going down some kind of slide, and there wasn't nothing you could do about what was happening until you come out at the bottom.

You didn't need me to tell you anything, you were going to go on, no matter what I said. But I told you."

Frank shook his head in faint protest. "I didn't know what was going to happen, but I can look back now and maybe what you say is right. Maybe I'm the only one who didn't know what was going to happen. You telling me you could have predicted I'd end up like this, in a hospital?"

"That's right." Jessie started to get out of the chair, but with an abrupt glance around he realized that the room was so unfamiliar there was nothing for him to busy himself with. He slid back in the seat again. "The whole thing, from beginning to end, was all laid out for anybody to see. You go back into the past like that and all you doing is making it happen again."

"But Jessie, you're not going to tell me there's nothing I could do. I'm not going to listen to what you're saying if you tell me I was just supposed to sit somewhere and be quiet after I found out what happened to that man I didn't even know about, that man who turned out to be my father." Frank was becoming angry.

"The only thing it got you was shot," Jessie answered defensively. "That's the only thing it got you."

"You know, I understand what you were doing out there," Jessie went on after a moment. "There's nobody wouldn't understand. But you got to think about what you going to stir up. You think I don't have feelings just like you? Every black person in this country has to figure out what they going to do with those kinds of feelings — because there isn't none of us doesn't have them sometime in our life. I don't mean to show no disrespect for my brother, and I don't mean to say you ought to forget about how he got killed, but it happened to so many people. All of us got some story like that. All you got to do is ask. No black man as old as me is going to tell you there wasn't some time when he thought something bad like that was going to happen to him, and when we talk about our black fathers we know every one of them could tell us the same thing. Not so bad as what happened to Frank, but when they start in to talking it all comes out like the same damn story. You understand that? Do you understand?"

Frank tried to interrupt, but Jessie wouldn't let him speak.

Two black men alone in an empty white room had finally come to one of the irreducible patterns by which their lives had been formed. "But that isn't what I'm talking about. You know all about those stories and I know about them. What I'm talking about is what you going to do about those things that happened, and I say you got to make yourself live with them. You can't make things come back and change any more than you can make the sun come backward and take a day away. If one of those peckerwoods comes and tells me I'm not the same as he is, I tell him that's the goddamn truth. What I don't tell him is that what makes me different from him is what he did to me. And that's something he's going to have to carry around with him — knowing that he did it.

"You know, way back in the 'sixties, when all those riots was going on over in Birmingham and up in the North, people was saying every black person in the country should get some cash money to try to make it even for everything that was done to them and taken away from them, and I said then that there wasn't no use in going back, even for money. And that's all I'm going to say to you. There's no use in going back." Jessie took a breath. "And you not going to tell me that you didn't already tell yourself something like that when you were just a little boy."

"You sound like my mother." Frank had turned to look out the window. "You sound like Ada," he repeated. "I'm not going to say you're right, either one of you, but you sound so much like her it's like she was in the room." With a clumsy heave of his shoulders he turned toward the older man again, and finally he found himself smiling. "I'm not going to tell her what happened, and you know how that makes me feel? Like I was ten years old and I didn't want her to know I'd lost my money on the way to school." He sank back into the pillow, and added, "Now I got the two of you telling me what I should do." Their sudden, relieved burst of laughter forced one of the nurses to close the door to the corridor, so they wouldn't disturb the other patients.

The next day, with Doris fussing beside him, he stood up for the first time. The thick lump of bandages on his side had been removed and he was left with a more manageable covering for the wound. As he pushed himself up he felt a first rush of confidence and tried to take a step without her support. He was so unsteady they both thought he would fall, but when she reached out to steady him he tried to push her hand away.

"I got to do this by myself."

Despite his efforts her strong fingers closed on his arms and he felt himself lifted as if he were a piece of paper the wind was carrying.

"No," she said in a teasing voice. "You only 'got' to do one thing, and that's whatever I tell you to do."

But because it was Doris he was still distressed at feeling so weak with her. "I have to do it sometime," he said awkwardly.

Sensing his feelings she lightened her clasp on his arms, but she didn't step back. Her expression changed, and she was suddenly serious. "If you fall down and tear your side open again it's going to be bad for you because we don't know how serious it could be, whatever kind of bleeding that gets started, and it's going to be just as bad for me for letting anything happen. I'm not going to get myself in trouble for your foolishness. You hear me?" Her bantering tone had returned. He let himself lean against her, with his head resting on her shoulder. "Don't I have anything to say about it?"

"No, you don't," and she slipped a supporting arm around his waist.

He stared down at his body in its flapping hospital gown. "I got thin, didn't I?" Between them they had managed a step.

"You don't feel as heavy as you did the last time you were leaning on me, I'll give you that much. If you didn't have that good dark skin you'd be as white as the sheet on your bed."

With some hesitant shuffling he got as far as the door and carefully disengaged himself from her. "I know I can make it back." And he slowly walked back to the bed, moving as carefully as if he were feeling his way in the dark, his arms hanging loosely at his sides. Then he lifted first the right arm and then the left, slowly and gingerly.

"Everything's back to work." His tone was satisfied. He sat down in the chair beside the bed and squirmed to find a comfortable position. "I can see why nobody wanted to sit in this chair for long. It feels like I'm backed up against an iron fence."

She had stayed by the door. "I don't think they're going to keep you more than another day or two, but you can't go flying off and start your job again."

They both were silent. Finally she went on. "What I'm saying is you could spend a few days at my apartment until you mend a bit."

"That way I could get all the proper attention I need." His tone was suddenly teasing, a teasing that for the first time had a relieved lightness to it.

She looked into his face. "If we can get you back on your feet again I might get a little proper attention too."

And they laughed at each other across the room.

27

Fontenot was with him when he left the hospital.

"You going to stay quiet now, Mr. Lewis?" He was carrying Frank's bags. He had picked up everything at the motel and kept it in a closet at the hospital for him.

Frank was walking slowly along the corridor behind him. "I have to think about getting back to work some time."

"You won't decide to go out there looking for Floyd Walker again?"

Frank tried to make a joke out of it, unwilling for a moment to think about what had happened. "I haven't got the right kind of shoes."

Fontenot held open the door to a car parked in the hospital driveway. Frank noticed that it wasn't a police car. Fontenot came around to the other side and slid behind the wheel. "Is this your own car?" Frank asked him.

"I didn't want to bring you around in a police car and frighten that woman's neighbors."

"You know where I'm going?"

245

The policeman nodded. "I still have to keep a watch on you and that boy." And he drove off along the drab, heat-striped street that Frank had seen for so many days from the window beside his bed.

Fontenot was in uniform so he didn't get out of the car when he turned the corner to Doris's apartment. She was waiting for them with her door open, and she lifted the suitcases out of the trunk with a casual swing, carrying them as easily as Fontenot had done. Frank found he couldn't move as quickly, but he managed to get out of the car. He leaned back to look at Fontenot. "What about you? Do I see you again?"

Fontenot nodded, looking in the rear view mirror and fiddling with the covering of the steering wheel. "I got to make up some kind of story so you can get out of here and the Walker boy doesn't get more punishment than he should. In one of these towns down here nobody forgets anything, even if they don't ever get the story straight. Nobody can make up their minds about you, so you and I have to talk a couple of more times before I can let you go away from here."

"I didn't think I was going to stir anybody up."

Fontenot shrugged, not looking at him.

"It's a small little place, Mr. Lewis."

For an hour he just sat in one of the overstuffed chairs in her living room. He wanted to smell the odors of furniture and dust and cooking, he wanted to breathe air that was free of the hospital taint of sickness and disinfectant. Instead of voices down a congested corridor, there was the murmuring sound of a radio turned on in an apartment over his head. It was Saturday. He could hear children playing, he could hear people calling to each other across the street. At first he didn't do anything; then he wanted to move around again, he was restless. He went out into the kitchen where she was working over pans and bowls. She nodded to glasses and ice and he made himself a drink. He wanted to stand close to her, but she was trying to cook something for him, and finally she made him leave the kitchen.

"Would you look at me?" she said wonderingly. "Just a few days ago I was hanging around your door at the hospital, hoping you'd come around enough so I could say something to you, and now I'm telling you to go away so I can keep my mind on my business."

He stopped in the other room, shaking the ice in his glass. "Nothing funny about that. That's the way life goes. It's just one ordinary thing after another. We do something out of the way and change things a little, but it only lasts for a minute. Then everything goes back to the way it was, and it's all ordinary again." She could hear a petulant tone in his voice, and she came to the doorway, a towel in her hands, to study him.

"You really say so?" She was surprised.

He shook his head. "Listen to me," he said with a short laugh, "I haven't been in your house more than an hour, and already I'm sounding like I've got something to complain about. And you know that's not the truth."

"I don't ever think about anything like that," she answered after a pause. "And after what you just been through you don't need to think about that either. You got people out there —," she nodded toward the street — "spending half their time talking about what you did, or what you were going to do — trying to decide what to think about it."

"What do they say?"

"You know how people can't decide between one thing or another. What makes it worse is that nobody really knows what happened out there by Floyd Walker's place, so everybody makes up their own story. Some of them want to put you up beside the people who came down here to do the voter registration, and some of the older ones say you not much better than the white folks around here. They talk like you could be the first black man to get initiated into the K.K.K."

"What do you tell them when they ask you what you think?"

She laughed, holding out her arms to him. "I tell them you been up North so long you nothing but a honky yourself."

When she called him to come and eat he found that she had set candles on the small table in her kitchen. It had been so long

247

since he lived with a woman, he found he was touched by the gesture. Then he saw that she had set a row of bottles and jars in front of his plate.

"What's all this?"

"I know better than to give you some of the food we cook down here, with all the spices we put in it. I put everything out so you can take what you want. There's everything from mustard powder to filé to salse piquant. You can learn about it all yourself."

"I'm not going to have enough time to learn everything." He looked up at her, her face softly shaded by the light of the candles.

She looked steadily back at him. "I know that."

"You can help me."

"What would you like to try, Mr. Lewis?" Her abrupt, pleased laughter filled the space around them, the sound as bright and unpredictable as the gleam from the candles. "If it's something hot you want to try, I can give you this speciality of the supermarket called ground Louisiana pepper, or if it's something sweet, I can give you a little of this dill."

"You give me whatever you think I should have. I think you know what it will be." And he leaned back in his chair to watch her quick movements, his face bright with his new pleasure.

28

Doris was going to drive him to the airport so they had to be up early. They fell asleep lying against each other in the shadows of her bedroom. Her strong hips were pressed back into his stomach, her back against his chest. His arms were crossed over her breasts, and he could feel her smoothness, the stretched, slick warmth of her skin.

"I notice you're not asking me to come up there with you." She still wasn't ready to sleep, but her voice was soft and drowsy.

"You wouldn't come," he answered, gently rubbing his mouth against the back of her neck.

"I still like to be asked."

"I notice you haven't asked me if I want to stay on with you down here."

"No," she admitted.

"You wouldn't want to miss out on all that's going on."

He felt her sigh. "They might get another black doctor at the hospital, and the next one that comes in the door is mine. I don't care what anybody else has in their minds, he's mine."

He pulled her back against him, feeling the strength of her body, the heavy curve of her hips, breathing the smell of her skin and hair. "I don't know what I'm going to do," he said softly against her ear, "but I know I'm going to be thinking about you."

She was silent, considering something. "What about that woman you have up there?"

"I haven't thought about her for a few days now."

She pressed herself against his stomach. "I did what I could to keep your mind on something else."

"You did more than that, my dear." His head was resting on her shoulder. "You did more than that."

It was quiet in the apartment. In the darkness the occasional passing cars made a sound like the gliding of birds' wings. As they drifted asleep he was conscious of her fingers spread loosely and warmly against his thigh.

It was raining in the morning, so they left early to avoid traffic; but once they were on the street they found they were alone and they reached the airport with half an hour to spare. She parked the car and they sat waiting for the plane to come in. It was the same small country airport where he had landed only a few weeks before, but he saw it — its red brick control tower, the soaked fields and muddy cattle along the fence — with new eyes. He had become part of it somehow — even though he would always be a few steps outside of everything it represented.

"Do you still have the picture?" Doris asked suddenly. She had slid across the seat to be close to him.

"No."

"You threw it away?"

"I didn't see any reason to keep it."

"I never saw it," she protested.

"You saw lots of others just like it. It was the same as all the other pictures of lynchings you grew up seeing in picture books."

"Did you feel the same way when you looked at it again?"

"I don't know. Some of what was going through me won't

250

go away. When you come close to the edge like that you don't forget what it was that pushed you out there. I didn't know I was that man's son. I didn't know I was anybody's son. When I looked at the picture the last time I didn't want to kill anybody over it. I just wanted to cry."

Her eyes were following the veiny patterns the rain was braiding down the windshield. "What are you going to tell your own son about it?"

"What do we tell our sons? I don't think they know anything about their fathers. I know they don't listen to us. I think sons of black fathers mostly wait to see what their fathers do, what they get angry about, what they're afraid of. What we say doesn't mean much. It doesn't do any good for a father to tell his son not to be afraid if he's afraid himself. He can't tell his son not to be angry over the things that have happened to black men like him if he's filled with anger himself. No matter what I say to my son, I know he's going to stand there watching me, waiting to see what I do, not what I say."

"You have to tell him something. He's going to find out about you, and about what happened," she insisted.

"I'll have to tell him something. All of us have to tell our sons something. I didn't used to think so — but if you don't say something then you're lying in a different way. Just keeping quiet isn't untrue, but it isn't the truth. To be a son of a black father you have to know the pain that's made the father the man he is, or you won't understand him, and if you don't understand him, you won't ever understand yourself. I didn't used to think about this, and I don't want to make myself out to be so smart, but now I've had to put some things together." He shook his head and held up his hands in exasperation.

"But what if I do tell him what I was doing out there in the woods? What comes next? Do I buy a pistol for him and show him how to shoot it so he'll do better than I did? Or do I try to tell him he has no business going off trying to do something like that? What would his life be like if I told him he should go shoot that boy because he shot me? I know I got to tell him something. He has to know about what happened to me. He has to know what happened to the other Frank Lewis — my father. But where do I stop? I want him to understand the anger I felt, he has to understand why I did what I did." He stopped, and suddenly laughed. "But he comes out of a different time, and I don't know if I understand him. For all I know, his feelings will be on the side of the boy who had the rifle. One of them's just about as old as the other."

He took her hand and twined his fingers in hers. "But it isn't the same when he thinks about these things — about the things that happened to people like Frank Lewis and Ada, my mother. He goes over to one of the white boys he goes to school with, and he shows him whatever it is that's got him worked up, and they get mad about it together."

He broke off abruptly, ashamed of his self-absorption. "What did your father tell you?" he asked in a bantering tone.

She tried to match his casualness. "He told me not to get myself messed up with no man from out of town."

"And you didn't listen to him."

She looked at her watch and shook her head. "Like you say, there's that difference between saying and doing." Then, serious again, she took his face in her hands and kissed him. "You think of me when you're up there, you hear?"

"If I see a black doctor I'll send him on down."

"If you don't see one you could come back yourself." She softly bit his lip.

"I suppose I could," he murmured, for a moment holding her against him. "I suppose I could." And he opened the car door and reached into the back seat to get his suitcase and catch his airplane and go back to his other life. It was raining and he tried to walk quickly, but he was struggling with the weight of the suitcase and his side hurt and he walked more and more slowly, the rain soaking his jacket. Suddenly he felt the bag lighten. She had hurried after him and was walking beside him, helping him with the suitcase, her fingers around his on the slippery handle. A half-awake porter was leaning against a baggage truck inside the door of the terminal and they lifted the bag on to it together. He fumbled with his ticket to tell the porter where to take the suitcase, then began walking slowly to the ticket counter. He started to say something to her, but she was no longer beside him. He turned abruptly to see her slip through the door, her tall, strong body moving quickly through the splattering rain. He watched her until she was out of sight in the gray mist.

When he had checked in for his flight, he went into the little cafeteria and bought a postcard to send to Lester. For a last time he tried to think of something to tell his son, something to give him some idea of what had happened, of what he had learned about himself, of what he had felt. But again, he couldn't think of any way to say it. Finally, lamely, he wrote,

Dear Lester,
　　Next time I see you I'll tell you all about my trip. You have a lot of cousins here. It's still hot.
Your father,
Frank

He dropped the card in the mailbox beside the counter, looking for a morning paper so he'd have something to read on the plane. He wondered if there would be anything about the weather in Connecticut. He was thinking about the work that would be waiting for him as the plane splashed down the runway. His side itched, and forgetting why it was sore he started to rub it. The sudden smart made him remember, and he turned in surprise to look down at the dark ground as it fell away beneath the small window beside him.